Fifth Son

An Inspector Green Mystery

Barbara Fradkin

RENDEZVOUS
PRESS

Cover art: Christopher Chuckry

LE CONSEIL DES ARTS DU CANADA DEPUIS 1957 | THE CANADA COUNCIL FOR THE ARTS SINCE 1957

We acknowledge the support of the Canada Council for the Arts for our publishing program.

Napoleon Publishing/RendezVous Press
Toronto, Ontario, Canada
www.rendezvouspress.com

Printed in Canada
Second printing 2005

08 07 06 05   5 4 3 2

Library and Archives Canada Cataloguing in Publication

Fradkin, Barbara Fraser, date-
        Fifth son / Barbara Fradkin.

(An Inspector Green mystery)
ISBN 1-894917-13-8

I. Title. II. Series: Fradkin, Barbara Fraser, date- . Inspector Green mystery.

PS8561.R233F53 2004   C813'.6   C2004-903178-3

To special children, including my own

ACKNOWLEDGEMENTS

As always, *Fifth Son* is a collaboration between my imagination and the sober second opinion of those who read the various drafts, and I'm grateful to the ongoing advice of my critiquing group, Madona Skaff, Jane Tun and Robin Harlick, as well as my agent Leona Trainer, my publisher Sylvia McConnell and my editor Allister Thompson.

I am also indebted to a number of experts who answered my call for help in getting the facts right. For their help with dead bodies and the like, I'd like to thank Dr. Jerome Cybulski, Curator of Physical Anthropology at the Canadian Museum of Civilization, who cheerfully answered my questions about the appearance and excavation of bones, and Dr. Douglas Lyle, who helped me understand the science of estimating time of death. For their help with police methodology and equipment, I'd like to thank Inspector Mike Shanford and Staff Sergeant Mel Robertson of the Ottawa Police, and Sergeant Tim Spence, ERT co-ordinator of the Eastern Region of the Ontario Provincial Police, as well as other OPP staff who gave of their time and expertise.

And a very special thanks to Constable Mark Cartwright of the Ottawa Police for his continuing advice and editorial input in matters of police procedure and realism. Any errors that occur in the story, whether accidental or deliberate, are mine alone.

Fifth Son is a work of fiction, and any resemblance to persons living or dead is unintentional. Although the rest of the locales in Ottawa and Eastern Ontario are real, the village of Ashford Landing is a fictional composite of several small river villages within the City of Ottawa's boundaries.

One

Kyle McMartin loved shiny things. The sunlight danced on them and prickled his eyes, making him look away and then pulling him back again. At home he had a whole bookshelf of them; bits of broken glass, bottle caps, fishing lures...stuff everyone else just threw out. His mother had given up taking them away, because then he'd have to start all over again, and she was probably afraid he'd cut himself going through everybody's garbage.

But this afternoon he wasn't even thinking about shiny things as he hid in his magic spot with the tall red trees all around and his Sens cap pulled down low against the sun. He was thinking about his new teacher. Hannah. Not really a teacher, Mrs. MacPhee said, just a helper, but even so she'd already taught him a lot. Like how to find his classrooms in the big new high school, how to copy from the board, even how to print her name. And each time he got it right, she'd give him that big, beautiful smile that crinkled her eyes.

Hannah had blue hair, sparkly gold eyelids and so many shiny things in her ears that he couldn't count that high. Mrs. MacPhee had made her take out the one in her nose, but Hannah had a secret one in her belly button that she'd shown him once. "Sh-h," she'd said, winking her sparkly eye and putting her finger to her lips. He had never told on her.

He thought about her all the time. She loved shiny things just like him, and she was more beautiful than anyone he'd seen on TV. Every night, he looked forward to going to school the next morning, just so he could see her. He hated the weekends, because there was nothing to do in Ashford Landing, and all his old friends were going to a different high school now, and they wouldn't let him play with them any more. Like right now, he could see them through the trees, playing roller hockey on the village square, yelling and using bad words. He didn't know how to roller blade, and he could never keep up with them anyway. By the time he saw the ball, it was already in the net, and they all got mad at him.

It was more fun to sit in his magic place and watch. He could see the whole world from here; the squirrels stuffing their cheeks with nuts, the geese honking by in the sky, the gravestones in the churchyard by the square. He wasn't supposed to come here, but if he ran right home when the bell on the white church rang, then Mom and Dad would never know.

The graveyard always gave him a scary feeling, like the dead bones were going to poke up through the ground, and he'd slide his eyes away as fast as he could. Usually, there was nobody there, and the grass grew so high you could hardly see the stones. But this time that bad man was there, peeking out through the stones, watching the kids in the square. Hiding, Kyle thought, just like me.

A little shiver ran through him, and he looked away. Right beside him was the biggest, reddest tree of all. Perfect red leaves floated all around, so bright they almost glowed. He slid down from the rock and swished his new sneakers through the deep leaves. They tumbled and crackled, almost like they were laughing. Then he saw the sun winking at him from a little nest of leaves near his foot. Curious, he bent down. Something lay on the ground, shining gold. He reached into the leaves and picked it up, held it by its chain up to the sunlight. Watched it spin and dance. His heart beat faster. This was more beautiful than the pennies or the shiniest fishing lure, more beautiful even than Mom's special ring. He put it in his pocket, excited and swelling with pride as he climbed back to his magic place for one last look at the man in the graveyard.

Hannah will love this.

Two

In the Criminal Investigations Division of the Ottawa Police, Inspector Michael Green's Monday mornings usually began with an update from his NCOs on the disasters the weekend had wrought. Normally he arrived at his office by eight o'clock, in order to have all the reports completed by noon, but this Monday, at eight o'clock, he had not even escaped his house. Five minutes before departure time, the morning had still been progressing typically enough. His two-year-old son was running through the halls, practising his newfound speed and his newly acquired vocabulary to protest his departure for the day care. Sharon was in hot pursuit, gulping coffee, juggling an overflowing diaper bag and shoving her feet into shoes as she ran. Glued to her side, bouncing and barking at the melee, was Modo, Humane Society refugee, who had neither grown in beauty nor diminished in size since she'd been thrust into their lives three months earlier.

Green's daughter Hannah, another recent addition to the household, was propped obliviously in the kitchen doorway with her cell phone wedged against her ear, arranging her social life as she added purple stripes to her black finger nails. As usual, metal glittered in every imaginable orifice, and probably in some he'd rather not imagine. Still, she was going to a school of sorts, she was coming home at an hour which

4

could still be construed as night rather than early morning, and she occasionally even let a smile sneak across her face. When she thought he wasn't looking.

All this chaos would have been routine, brought to a merciful halt when he climbed into the sanctity of his new Subaru and tuned the radio to his favourite rock station. But on this morning, before he could make good his escape, the phone rang. He ducked into the bathroom and covered his free ear so he could hear. To his regret.

"Uh...yeah. Bob here."

The elusive kitchen contractor. "Hi, Bob."

"Uh...yeah. There going to be anyone there today?"

"When?"

"Don't know. Uh...this morning?"

"What for?"

"To take the cabinets out, eh?"

"Oh, good. So the new ones are ready?"

"Well, almost."

"Almost?"

"Uh...yeah. We have to take the old ones out, eh? Before we can put the new ones in?"

"But I don't want to be sitting here with no kitchen cabinets for two weeks, Bob."

"Oh, it won't be two weeks."

Green bit back a snide retort, for they still needed Bob. They had moved into their home over a month ago, and the place was now in pieces. Sharon had relinquished their brand new suburban house under protest, so each new crisis that surfaced was Green's fault. He had wanted character and history. What they had acquired was a dignified brick antique with character in spades but not a single room that could be spared the contractor's hammer. Furniture was stacked in the halls while they waited for the hardwood floors to be installed. Fresh patches of plaster blotched the walls, and the stairs still listed dangerously, despite numerous calls to the carpenter.

Green glanced out into the hall long enough to glimpse Sharon's expression as she wrestled Tony into some clothes. Bob would be the last straw.

"Look, Bob, when the cabinets are all ready, we'll work out a time. But we need a few days' notice."

"Hard to do. Depends on the weather, eh? We should at least get the cabinets out."

Green sighed. Five years ago, he'd been a bachelor living in a tiny downtown apartment and accountable only to himself. His only obligations had been weekly visits to his father and monthly child support payments to an estranged daughter on the other side of the country. Now he had a wife, a toddler in full terrible twos, a traumatized mutt, an instant teenage daughter with a disposition as black as her nails and a decayed monstrosity of a house that was consuming every penny he earned.

He glanced at his watch. "How long will that take?"

Bob assured him at the most two hours. Green said he would wait if they could get there in the next fifteen minutes.

Bob's van, trailed by a dusty pick-up and an elderly Cavalier, pulled into the drive an hour later, and Green ensconced himself in his study on his computer while Bob's hammers banged beneath his feet. The noise was so loud, he didn't hear the doorbell and vaguely became aware of someone shouting his name over the din. A minute later, Sergeant Brian Sullivan clumped up the stairs and shoved his head in the doorway.

"Fuck, I told you you should have let me help you, Mike! Those guys are massacring the place."

Sullivan's massive bulk filled the doorway, and it took Green a minute to register the grin on his ruddy, farm-boy face. Green was surprised to see him. Although the two men had been friends since their rookie days on the streets together twenty years earlier, their friendship rarely spilled over into their homes. Green knew there had to be a reason for the call. He glanced at his watch, which said eleven o'clock. Had he forgotten some crucial meeting?

"What's up?"

Sullivan shrugged. "Nothing much. I'm on my way to Ashford Landing."

"Ash-what?"

"Nice little village down on the Rideau River about thirty kilometres south of here. Now part of our megacity."

"What's in Ashford Landing?"

"A body. Probably nothing, but Ray Belowsky, one of the NCOs out there, is a hockey buddy of mine, and he wants Major Crimes to take a look at it."

Green perked up. Anything to escape Bob and his hammering. "What's so special about it?"

"Well, the guy seems to have fallen out of a church tower in the middle of town. Has folks a bit upset."

Green's hopes deflated. People did fall off things on a fairly regular basis, even in the country, so it seemed hardly a reason to call in Major Crimes. "They're sure he fell? Didn't jump off to escape the minister's sermon?"

Sullivan chuckled. "Could have. But they said it looked like a chunk of the stone wall at the top gave way. They found a piece of his jacket caught on the edge."

"That doesn't mean much. How old is the church?"

"I don't know yet. My buddy didn't feel comfortable just leaving it to the General Assignment investigators. Besides, they've been trying really hard to make sure the folks out there have confidence in our policing."

The alienation of the rural wards was the popular *crise du jour* not only in Ottawa City Hall but also in the senior offices of the Ottawa Police, which had tried to address the problem by creating rural community police centres and fostering links with local leaders. However, specialized services like Criminal Investigations remained under the thumb of downtown headquarters on Elgin Street, with much of their efforts geared towards the inner city crime wars. But Sullivan was an experienced investigator used to running his own cases, no matter where they took him. It was quite unlike him to come to Green for permission on such a routine matter, but when Green said as much, Sullivan gave an easy shrug.

"I thought you might like a drive in the country. See the fall colours, smell the cows. Get to know the rural side of our new amalgamated police force."

Green chuckled. Sullivan knew damn well that he was a confirmed inner-city boy with a passion for exhaust fumes, noise and decaying corner stores. But just as he was about to beg off, he heard a renewed burst of hammering downstairs. If he could trust Bob not to destroy the house in his absence, perhaps even cows might be a welcome alternative. As he logged off his computer and prepared to go downstairs to check with Bob, he felt that old quiver of excitement that always accompanied the hunt.

*   *   *

The forty-five minute drive to Ashford Landing took them alongside the Rideau River, past the bedroom village of Manotick and out across farm fields strewn with stubble and straw. Halloween scarecrows decorated the homesteads, and clusters of pumpkins dotted the yards. Sullivan drove with one hand on the wheel and the other drumming an imaginary beat on the console beside him. Behind his mirrored sunglasses, he looked relaxed and cheerful, although Green suspected he was probably fending off his share of memories. Farm life was an alien world to Green, who rarely ventured beyond the city lights and bustle, but it was only too familiar to Sullivan, who had grown up in a family as harsh and unforgiving as the Ottawa Valley land on which they had settled.

But to Green's surprise, a mischievous smile played across Sullivan's face.

"What?" Green asked, wondering what secret surprise Sullivan had in store for him.

"I was just thinking about you. Jesus, if anybody would have told me... And you're still smiling! Living in a dump that's falling down around your ears, sharing a roof with a dog and two offspring as pig-headed and impossible as you are, but you're smiling!"

Green laughed. "I kind of like the dog, actually."

"Yeah, dogs don't give you grief at the end of a hard day." Sullivan sobered and cast Green a quick look. "How is our blue-haired girl, by the way? Still wanting to stay with you?"

"I don't know about 'wanting'. More like I'm the lesser of two evils, parents being evil by definition. I also think she loves driving her mother crazy. Ashley thought she'd be back on a plane to Vancouver before the month was out, and it's been almost four months."

"Is she still in school?"

"That's part of the deal. Thank God for Sharon, and for alternate school. Hannah picks her own credits, does her own course work at her own speed, puts in only half a day—"

"Half a day! What does she do with the other?"

"Cooperative education placement. She gets credits for it

plus valuable job experience, that's the theory. Hannah is working in a school, of all places, and enjoying it, so there may be method to their madness." He sighed and rested his back against the seat. Hannah still evoked a strange mix of emotions whenever his thoughts ventured near. "I don't want to fuck this up. Nothing Ashley's tried has worked for Hannah, and I just want to...connect. But damn, when you've got nothing to build on but resentment, it's tough."

"It's tough even if you have raised them all along. Especially girls. There are times Lizzie doesn't talk to me for days on end. Boy, you got to learn patience, and that was never your strong suit anyway." Sullivan steered around a tractor hauling a wagon of baled hay. "But believe in yourself, Mike. If you love the kid, that's going to show."

"If you love the kid..." Green thought. Not the pig-tailed imp of his imagination, but this sullen, spiky reality. He fell silent and stared out the window in search of distraction. Human habitation had begun to increase sporadically as they neared the village of Ashford Landing. An automotive garage here, a warehouse there and a sprinkling of newer bungalows along the highway.

"Working on it," he replied finally. "Now before we actually meet the Rural West guys, maybe you should tell me what they've got so far. Who's the victim?"

Sullivan didn't miss a beat, switching gears smoothly to return to the case. "So far nobody has a clue, which is suspicious in itself, because Ashford Landing is one of those tiny farm communities where people have lived forever. All Belowsky can tell is that he's not a country boy."

Green grinned. "His neck not red enough?"

"Not red at all. He's pale as a man out of solitary." Sullivan held out his square, freckled hand. "Not an honest callous to his name either. A local minister found him this morning, partially hidden in the tall weeds at the base of the church."

"Which coroner did they call in?"

"MacPhail should already be out there. I called him."

Green looked at Sullivan shrewdly. To have called in the city's foremost forensic pathologist instead of one of the regular coroners, Sullivan had to have some suspicion lurking in the back of his implacable mind.

"What the hell aren't you telling me, Brian?"

Sullivan's smile broadened, and he shook his head as if in reluctant admiration. "Okay, there are some things that bothered my buddy. But I don't want to tell you, because I want you to see the scene fresh, to make sure it's not just the rural boys' imagination working overtime."

Brian Sullivan expecting me to be the voice of rational restraint? That's a first, thought Green. Sullivan was the most pragmatic, down-to-earth investigator he knew, whereas Green was the one with the fondness for the wild blue yonder. But as soon as he laid eyes on the scene, he understood what Sullivan meant.

The village appeared suddenly over the crest of a hill—a small cluster of century-old buildings snuggled on the bank of the river. Glimpses of broad verandas and steeply pitched roofs showed through the canopy of trees, and battered pick-ups adorned the drives. Three old churches surrounded the square at the centre of the village. Two had tall, stately belfries, immaculate lawns, and freshly painted signs announcing the hours of worship. The third, the one surrounded by squad cars, yellow tape and gawking villagers, was abandoned and boarded up tight. Furthermore, the front door sported a padlock big enough for Green to see it clear across the road.

It looked as if no one had been near it in years.

Sullivan drew his car up behind the white forensics van, and the two detectives climbed out into the crisp fall air. Green leaned against the car to take in the scene. The village had looked idyllic from the hill crest, but close up, its faded signs and peeling paint bore witness to the harshness of rural life, and the big "For Sale" sign nailed to the wall of the deserted church looked as if it had weathered many storms. The diminutive limestone church sat amidst tall, withered weeds, bordered on one side by a small cemetery and on the other by woods. Its steeply pitched roof glinted silver in the noon sun, and a heavy stone archway framed its dark oak door.

There were a number of curious aspects to the scene. First was the obvious question of why that particular bell tower, which was the shortest and ugliest on the square. If the man had been looking for a view, there were taller, more promising ones, and if he had been looking for architectural charm, the red brick church across the square, with its stately gothic spire, offered far more. Secondly and more importantly, with all the windows boarded up and the front door padlocked, how the hell had the man got in?

A pair of Ident officers in white bunny suits prowled around in the grass at the base of the tower, obscuring the body from Green's view. Green recognized one of them as Lyle Cunningham, a neat freak with a passion for high tech gadgetry and sterile crime scenes. No doubt he wouldn't let either detective within fifty feet of the body, so Green was about to call him over when Dr. Alexander MacPhail himself emerged around the corner of the tower, closing his coroner's bag and plucking burrs from his pant legs. He cast Green a jaunty grin as he strode towards them, and his rich brogue boomed across the square.

"Well, this is a wee bonnie town, isn't it, lads? Nice drive into the country, with the maples turning and all."

Green braced himself as MacPhail engulfed his hand in a bone-crushing grip. "Seems a weird place to end it all, that's for sure," Green replied. "What does it look like?"

"I've left him to the crime scene lads for the moment, but I should get him on the table tomorrow morning. He's got a bloody great crack that smashed half his skull, creating lots of bleeding out through the ears, nose and mouth. He's lying face down, and the rock beneath his head has blood and hairs all over it. Bad luck, that rock. I'd guess the fall knocked him out, and over the hours the intra cranial bleeding killed him. Just a working theory at the moment, of course."

"Accidental fall or deliberate?"

"Well, I don't quite read minds yet, laddie. But if I were in the business, I'd have to say he jumped deliberately."

MacPhail's pockmarked face was deadpan, but the slight twitch at the corner of his lip gave him away. "Why?" Green asked. "Did he trace a suicide note in the dirt beside him?"

"No, but it's a wee bit difficult to fall off a tower that has a three-foot stone parapet all around the top."

Green glanced up at the tower, noting the thick wall around the top. "But I understand some of the wall gave way."

"It would still be quite a feat to fall off, unless of course the man was walking along the top, high on something. I'll do the usual tox screen for mind-altering substances."

"Still," Green persisted, "he could have been pushed."

MacPhail shrugged. "That's a job for your lads, I just get the body. However, I don't see any evidence of it. No defensive wounds, no scrapes on the hands. If someone was trying to force him up over that wall, I'd expect him to be grabbing what he could."

Including his assailant, Green thought, but knew better

than to tell MacPhail how to do his job. The pathologist would tell him soon enough whether there was tissue under the fingernails. "What's your estimated time of death?" he asked instead.

"When he was found at eight this morning, rigor was developing in his legs and feet. It's just dissipating now. Normally, that takes about twelve hours, but on a cold night like last night, that process would be slowed down. Body temp readings have the same problem in reverse. At first guess, I'd say some time last evening between four and midnight. But he might have taken several hours to die, so that doesn't help you much. I'll have to get inside him to see what the damage was."

Green glanced at Sullivan, but before he could even open his mouth to issue the order, Sullivan gave a curt nod. "Ident gave us a description and some shots of the body. The fall made a mess of half his face, but Cunny's going to pull one of his digital miracles, so soon we'll have a facial photo. But I've already got a street canvass in progress to see if anyone saw anything yesterday."

Green held his tongue. He knew Sullivan was a capable investigator who hated it when Green single-mindedly ran roughshod over his case. Instead, Green nodded his agreement. "Anything turn up yet?"

"No one saw the man. Or at least no one's admitted seeing him. But he's a stranger around here, and sometimes these small villages don't want to get involved." As if sensing Green's protest, he raised his hand. "I'll go over the ground again later myself. Turn on the Ottawa Valley charm."

Across the way, Green studied the villagers lingering near the scene. At this time on a regular workday, they were mostly old timers, who probably longed for the good old days when the village was served by a couple of friendly local boys from the Ontario Provincial Police detachment in Kemptville. To the old timers, Major Crimes detectives from the city would seem like alien voyeurs.

Not so to the children, who had grown up with TV crime shows and would probably be thrilled to be talking to real live cops. Once the children returned from school later in the day, Sullivan and his men might get an entirely different perspective.

He turned back to the pathologist. "What can you tell us about the victim?"

MacPhail didn't even need to consult his notes. "White male aged probably thirties, about five-ten, one fifty. No obvious marks or tattoos, no signs of illness or infirmity. Not someone you'd bring home to meet the wife, mind you. Stinks to high heaven, likely hasn't bathed or changed his clothes in over a month. Greasy hair, teeth full of debris. His clothes weren't his—the jacket's much too big and the trousers were held up with rope. He'd put layers of newspaper under his shirt to keep himself warm."

"A vagrant?" Green scanned the village thoughtfully. "Weird place for a vagrant."

"Well, that's the curious thing about our lad," MacPhail countered. His eyes twinkled and Green knew he was enjoying the tease. "He'd obviously hit a rough patch recently, but his physical health was good, and he was well nourished and cared for. There are no obvious indications of drug or alcohol abuse, and his teeth have enjoyed the care of an excellent dentist. This is not a street person, laddies. This is a respectable citizen whose luck just changed."

MacPhail's chuckle lingered in the air long after he'd tossed them a wink and strode off to ready his van.

Sullivan gestured to the notes he'd been taking. "If he's a respectable citizen, then someone, somewhere, will be looking for him. I'll run this description through missing persons to see if we've had a recent report that fits."

"Not too recent. Remember he hasn't washed in over a month. Start with reports from August and early September." Green scanned the quiet street. "What would bring a stranger to a village like this?"

"Maybe he was just passing through, on his way from Ottawa to Toronto, or back."

"And got a sudden urge to go into a church and jump off the tower?" Green shook his head. "This village is not on any of the major roads to anywhere. You have to make quite an effort to get here. No...I think he chose this place."

"Well, it would make a good place for a marijuana farm. Cops probably pass through here once a year."

Green laughed. "But that still doesn't explain the church. Of all places in town, he chose a goddamn boarded up church. What did it mean to him?"

"Maybe nothing more than a place to keep warm," Sullivan replied. "We've had heavy frost the last few nights."

Sullivan's practical mind had an answer for everything except the nagging doubt in Green's gut. On purely police procedural grounds, it was far too early to rule out the possibility of foul play. The lack of defensive wounds and the apparent randomness of the death said very little on their own without forensic examination of the crime scene and a thorough canvas of the town. Perhaps the man was an utter stranger to the town, perhaps not. Perhaps he had a personal connection to something—or someone—that had drawn him here.

"Ask the duty inspector if we can get the mobile command post down here and some extra men—"

Sullivan was drawing a sketch of the square, and he looked up skeptically. "Mobile command post? For this?"

Green grinned. "Why not? We've got an unidentified body, a possible missing person, a crime scene covered in blood, MacPhail, Cunningham... Besides, the big, huge, shiny truck ought to impress the hell out of the locals. And while you're getting it ordered up, I'll just wander over to talk to the man who found the body."

Before Sullivan could mount an objection, Green headed across the square to St. James' Church, the elegant red brick structure with an ornate silver spire. The minister of St. James had been making a routine check of the boarded up church when he discovered the body. If he had responsibility for keeping an eye on the place, perhaps he knew something about its history as well.

Green found Reverend Bolton in the rear of his church, ostensibly bent over his paperwork but actually keeping a keen eye on the drama through the leaded panes of his office window. The stubby man, who still looked a tinge green from his ordeal, blotted his glistening bald spot with a sodden handkerchief and blinked rapidly as he listened to Green's request.

"Oh, Ashford Methodist Church has been closed for over fifteen years now. When Reverend Taylor retired, you see... It was a small congregation of mainly old timers, and when he left, most of them came over here to St. James." He watched the Ident team doing a slow sweep of the tall weeds. "It's a lovely old building, really. We've tried to do various things with it over the years. Community suppers, day cares, even school plays, but the last while... Well, the stone interior just became too expensive to heat. So it's been up for sale, probably will be bought by some upscale couple from Ottawa."

"How many entrances are there?"

"Just the two. That front door and a small one out the back. Both are kept locked, of course."

"Who has the keys?"

"I have a set, which I gave to the police when they arrived. And of course, there's a lock box from the real estate company on the door at the rear."

"Would any of the former congregants still have keys?"

"After all this time? I shouldn't think so, but I can't be sure. Reverend Taylor was rather..." Bolton paused as if searching for tact. "Generous about such things, so it's possible. But you should ask him."

Green's eyebrows shot up. "Is he still alive?"

A ghost of a smile slipped across Reverend Bolton's lips. "Last I heard he was still preaching up a storm in Riverview Seniors' Home outside Kars."

Green jotted down the address, then paused thoughtfully. "Do you have any idea who the dead man was?"

"None at all. It's hard to tell, of course, but I don't think he's from around here, at least in my tenure. However, if you want someone who knows just about everyone who ever lived here, Reverend Taylor is your man. But—" Again that ghost of a smile. "If you're planning on going up to Kars to speak to him, you'd better have the afternoon to spare."

Three

Unlike Ashford Landing, which had so far managed to evade the spreading tentacles of modern Ottawa, the village of Kars had been overtaken by well-to-do urbanites seeking the privilege of green space and tranquillity at the end of a long day. Reverend Taylor's nursing home predated this gentrification, however, and squatted unadorned beneath scraggly, overgrown cedars at the edge of the highway. A few greying Muskoka chairs sat on the front veranda, but in the chill of October, none were occupied.

The two detectives found Reginald Taylor holding court in what the nurse euphemistically called the games room. The air was hot, stale and smelled faintly of urine. Most of the occupants lined the walls in wheelchairs and turned blank, disinterested stares towards the door when the two walked in. Four men were grouped around a table near the window, playing cards.

"Reggie," the nurse chirped. "You have visitors."

Four faces swivelled towards the door, eager for the diversion, but Green had no trouble distinguishing the object of their quest. Reverend Taylor was a bony, shrunken bird of a man with liver-spotted skin and a tangle of white eyebrows. He was impeccably dressed in black with a white clerical collar, and his pale blue eyes danced as if amused by some private joke.

The merriment died as soon as Sullivan explained to him

the reason for their visit.

"A body? In my church? Great Jiminy Cricket!"

"Not inside, Reverend. Outside. It appears he may have jumped."

"Oh dear, oh dear. I always tried to make it a sanctuary. There is so much pain and hardship in the world as it is, don't you think, Sergeant? Sullivan, is it? Catholic, I suppose. No matter, my son. We're all God's children, and the divisions we make are not the Lord's. Suffer the children and all that... One of my flock, you say?"

"Reverend, we don't know if it was one of your flock," Sullivan began. "That's—"

"No matter, they we're all my flock. Everyone was welcome to hear the Lord's word, that was always my belief, and—" The lilt of Newfoundland still clung to his vowels, and his grin held a hint of mischief. Green had never met a Newfoundlander without a rebel's sense of humour. "If it made some of the families uncomfortable, well, they just had to adjust. Tried to drive me out once before, too. Lucky for me the pastor at Rideau Church of God was a fool—"

Green laid Ident's digitally doctored photo of the dead man down on the card table. "Is this one of your flock?"

Taylor picked up the photo and gazed at it in a distracted way. His tangled brows knit further. "Well, of course, I haven't had a flock in several years. How many, Nancy? Three?"

"Eighteen."

Taylor looked shocked. "Nonsense. They drove me out, see, said I was too old, couldn't handle the demands. Nonsense. That pastor at Rideau Church of God wanted the crowd. He'd been driving away congregants with his thundering about brimstone and hellfire, so he thought he'd better steal mine—"

20

"Reverend, do you know this man?" Green repeated.

Taylor shifted his gaze back to the photo and eyed it with surprise. "This man's dead!"

"Yes, he jumped off the tower."

"Now why would he do that? I always welcomed people, even the sick, the poor, the deranged. There but for the grace of—"

Green swore a silent prayer of his own for patience. But before he could speak, Nancy jumped in. "Reggie! The police haven't got all day! Look at the picture."

Meekly, Taylor peered at the photo and slowly wrinkled up his nose, as if he could smell the man. "Seen better days, I'd say."

"Yes. Do you know him?"

"Never known them to be so dirty. Always a particular family. The mother kept them all well-scrubbed behind the ears, father wouldn't allow so much as a fart indoors. Hard to imagine it could be one of them."

"One of whom?"

"Could be, mind you. But with that beard and all that blood, well..." As if sensing Nancy's imminent tongue-lashing, he nodded at the photo with some vigour. "Could be one of the Pettigrews. Don't know which one. They all looked alike, and they were mere lads the last time I saw them."

"Were the Pettigrews a family in Ashford Landing?"

"Oh, not in Ashford Landing. They had a farm just north of town off Number 2. Nice spread, backed on the river."

Green glanced at Sullivan, who discreetly put his notebook away and slipped outside to verify the address. With any luck, they could stop by the farm on their return to Ashford Landing.

Green took out his own notebook and returned to the bright-eyed old man. "Did the Pettigrew family attend your church?"

"Pettigrews helped build it, every limestone block of it, back in 1896. Before my time, of course, but there have always

21

been Pettigrews at Ashford Methodist Church, until that pastor at Rideau Church of God started his hellfire and damnation. What did you say your name was, my son?"

"Michael Green. Inspector Green."

Taylor glanced at Nancy with twinkling eyes. "They make them younger eve ry year, don't they, Nan. All except you and me."

Green smiled. He was over forty, and a little grey had just begun to pepper his fine brown hair, but his skin was still unlined, and a spray of freckles across his nose gave him a deceptively innocent air. Which came in handy when he wanted to go unnoticed.

"Irish too, are you?" Taylor persisted. "Mind, I've nothing against the Irish. Worked side by side with us to build up this country, and I've no patience for those who say otherwise."

Green hesitated. In the city, his Semitic nose sometimes gave him away, but out in the country, Green suspected few of the old-timers would have ever met a Jew. Moreover, the reverend's concept of religious diversity seemed to be more than a century out of date, and Green wasn't sure the man's welcoming attitude would extend that far. Instead of responding, he plucked the photo from the Reverend's reluctant fingers, thanked the man for his help and headed gratefully towards the fresh outside air.

Sullivan was just coming back from the car. Across the road behind him, a solitary tractor was chugging slowly along an open field, and the smell of manure wafted over the road.

Green wrinkled up his nose. "Let's hope this Pettigrew family grows corn, not cows."

Sullivan laughed. "That's fertilizer, Green. Great stuff! The Pettigrew farm will be knee-deep in it, no matter what they grow."

Fortunately, when Green and Sullivan turned down the long lane leading up to the Pettigrew farm house, there were no tractors to be seen. The country air was sharp and clean, despite a faint overlay of turpentine, a smell Green was all too familiar with these days. A minivan and a dusty turquoise Sunbird sat in the gravel drive and as Sullivan drew to a stop behind them, a tiny poodle burst through the front door, yapping.

A young woman strode out, waving her arms. "Chouchou, stop! *Assez!*"

The dog raced around the car like a frenzied cotton ball, growling and snapping every time Sullivan tried to open the door. Green knew better, having become somewhat more versed in the canine psyche since acquiring his oversized Humane Society reject. He showed the woman his badge through the window and sat in the car waiting for her to capture her dog. By the time she pounced on it and shoved it under her arm, she was panting as hard as it was. As she approached the car again, the odour of turpentine grew stronger and Green saw flecks of white paint on her hands. She leaned against the car, her chest heaving and her cheeks flushed. Even in tattered jeans and T-shirt with a paint smudge on her nose, she was a sexy, vibrant woman.

"Sorry, officers. We just moved in, and Chouchou is..." She ended the explanation with a Gallic shrug. Her accent was slightly French Canadian, more in its cadence than its words. "He'll be all right once he gets to know you. What is this about?"

The two detectives exchanged quick glances before Sullivan took the lead. "We're looking for Mr. or Mrs. Pettigrew."

She looked puzzled. "They were the previous owners, but they don't live here any more."

"Can you tell us where we might reach them?"

"We only met them one time. We communicated through a real estate agent."

"*Qu'est-ce qui se passe?*" A reedy young man appeared around the edge of the house carrying a leaf rake. He was smiling, but behind thick glasses his gaze was wary. "What's going on?"

"It's the police looking for the former owners."

The detectives climbed out of the car and introduced themselves. Sullivan handed them his card, then indicated his notebook. "For our paperwork, could you give us your names?"

Jacques and Isabelle Boisvert, the woman said, but they could be of little help since they had only met one of the sons.

Sullivan pulled out the photo. "Is this the son?"

Jacques took the photo and recoiled in dismay. "This man is dead!"

"That's why we're anxious to reach the family. Have you the name and phone number of the real estate agent you dealt with?"

Isabelle fetched a business card, which Sullivan took back to the car to make the call. The husband was eyeing the photo with almost morbid fascination.

"Could that be the son?" Green prompted.

He shivered and shook his head. "This man is more aged. The man we met was Robert Pettigrew, and he was only in his twenties. No beard, very pleasant-looking."

"Perhaps this is the father. You never met him?"

"He was in hospital. He had a stroke, the agent said. That's why the son had to sell the farm so fast." He cast an anxious glance at the vast unkempt meadow that surrounded them. In the distance, a copse of maples flamed red and gold against the blue sky. "The whole place is falling to pieces. Like nobody takes care of it since twenty years."

Green appraised the house with his new expertise in

disintegrating buildings. On closer inspection, he could see the tell-tale signs. The house was a stately, red brick Victorian with a steeply pitched roof. Its intricate wood trim had once been white but was now a weathered gray, and its windows were caked with grime. Roof shingles were lifting, and the front porch listed dangerously to one side.

Isabelle had taken the photo and was studying it thoughtfully. As if hearing the bitterness in her husband's voice, she gave his arm a quick squeeze. "We will make it beautiful, I p romise you. Why don't you take Chouchou in the back to work with you, and I will walk these gentlemen to their car."

With one last weary glance at his wife, Jacques slumped back around the house with the dog under one arm and the rake in the other. An oddly lifeless man to have snagged such a tantalizing woman, Green thought. Quietly, she gestured to the photo as she walked.

"I have seen this man. I didn't want to say in front of Jacques, because he is negative enough about this place. He's from Vanier, and he finds it very isolating here."

I'll just bet, Green thought. It would be a massive culture shock to move to this pastoral desolation from the close-knit clamour of the francophone inner city. "Where did you see this man?"

Isabelle nodded towards the right of the grounds and began to walk. About a hundred feet in front of the house was a rundown, square-timbered barn, and beside it, a wooden shed of similar vintage. But in the far corner of the yard opposite was an overgrown thicket of brush. It was here that Isabelle stopped.

"Yesterday, after Jacques left for church, Chouchou began to bark at something. It was fog outside, and frost on the ground, but I'm positive it was this man. He was in the brush here, ducking down, trying to hide. I thought he was a bum, and I yelled at him. He took off."

"In what direction?"

Isabelle gestured towards the maple woods behind the farm house. "He went into those trees, and it's the last I saw of him."

"What's beyond the trees?"

"The river. But there is a path along the shore through the trees, and I guess he escaped that way."

Green peered through the dying foliage of the thicket where the man had hidden. Raspberry canes and scrub had been allowed to grow undisturbed for years, but there were signs that someone had been there recently. A path had been trampled into the centre, and the weeds had been flattened as if someone had lain there. Gingerly, Green got down on his hands and knees and crawled into the thicket, praying that he wouldn't encounter any crawly things. In the middle of the thicket, charred wooden planking had been strewn about, and the grass had been dug up in little patches all over.

It looked for all the world as if someone had been searching for something.

*　　*　　*

Green gazed out the car window at the passing fields, deep in thought. In the distance, the ribbon of maple trees was slowly fading into the horizon.

"We should send an eager young constable out there to see where that path through the trees leads to," he said.

Sullivan took his eyes off the road long enough to follow Green's gaze. His eyes revealed nothing behind his mirrored sunglasses, but his lips twitched in a smile. "It leads to Ashford Landing."

"How do you know?"

"That's the way the country works. Farmers usually leave a border of trees along the river, and in the old days they'd bring their produce to the village either by boat or along the river's edge in the shade. The Boisvert farm is about two kilometres from town. Perfect distance for foot paths."

Green looked at the straight, flat road ahead of them. Why would the man go along the shore, he wondered, and have to contend with mud, cow crap, underbrush and swamp when he could walk straight along the road? Green could think of at least one good reason—to avoid being seen.

"So in all likelihood," he said, "when our guy ran away from the farm yesterday morning, he got to the river and headed to Ashford Landing. Two kilometres, you said? That should have taken him no more than half an hour, which means he should have reached town before noon. MacPhail places the death after four p.m."

"But remember he could have fallen earlier and bled for hours."

"Okay, but he still might have been lurking around town for a couple of hours, which means he could have been seen."

They had reached the outskirts of the village and Sullivan eased his foot off the accelerator, allowing them to coast over the crest and down into the tiny commercial centre. They passed the general store and the gas station before spotting a big yellow real estate agency sign on the lawn of a Victorian manor house painted a striking Wedgwood blue.

Sullivan had reached Sandy Fitzpatrick on his cell phone from the car, interrupting him in the middle of a showing. The agent had agreed to meet the detectives back at his office, but there was no answer when they rang the doorbell. An old silver Grand Am was tucked at the rear of the house, but the main drive was empty. Through the bay window, Green could see a large office with maps papering the walls and print-outs littering every surface. Looking up at the rambling size of the old home, he guessed that Sandy Fitzpatrick probably lived above his offices.

Sullivan was just returning to the car to check on the street canvassing when a late-model red pick-up revved around the corner and screeched into the drive. Out leaped a tall, muscular man whom Green estimated to be in his mid thirties. The man rushed at the detectives, his hand extended heartily.

"Sorry, officers. The house business—never a dull moment!" He lifted a huge ring of keys from his belt, selected one and unlocked the door with one expert twist. Inside his cluttered office, Green and Sullivan took the client chairs while Fitzpatrick went behind his desk. He flipped on his computer and punched the answering machine button before he'd even sat down. Then, as the first of sixteen messages began to drone, he looked at Sullivan sheepishly.

"Sorry, force of habit. No secretary, no partners, just me always rushing to stay on top of the business." He paused the machine but couldn't keep his eyes from straying to his email box briefly before he swung around.

"Okay!" He clasped both hands together on the desk before him like a man salivating to make a deal. "Is it about the body? It's the talk of the town."

Green couldn't resist. "And what's the town saying?"

"Some homeless guy?"

"No rumours as to his identity?" Green asked.

"None I heard. But what's it got to do with the Pettigrew place?"

Green didn't reply, reminding himself that it was Sullivan's case and he ought to let him decide how to play it. Sullivan chose to play it casual.

"Who's handling the sale of the church? Your firm?"

Fitzpatrick's face fell. "Oh no! That's a firm from Ottawa. I used to list that place, but...no one's been able to sell it."

"But you can access the key if you have a client. You have the combination to the lock box, right?"

"Well, I can get it. We can all get it. But I hardly ever show it. People want waterfront properties, not a musty old rock pile in the middle of town."

Green glanced around the office. Despite the country clutter, it sported the latest in electronic gadgets. There were no pictures of wife and children, but Fitzpatrick clearly loved his expensive outdoor toys. Snowmobiles and four-by-fours were everywhere, and one photo showed him posing with a friend in front of a sleek, white motorboat, holding up a fish that must have been three feet long. Slimy-looking thing, Green thought with distaste, but the two men were grinning from ear to ear.

"I guess the waterfront business has been good to you, Mr. Fitzpatrick," Green remarked.

"Please, call me Sandy. Good investment, in today's times. People are snapping it up all over Ontario. If you detectives are interested—"

Sullivan stepped in to head off the sales pitch. "What can you tell us about the Pettigrews?"

Sandy looked startled at the sudden change, then his face took on a regretful air. "What can I say? Sad, sad situation. The great-great-grandfather hacked the farm out of the wilderness himself back in the early eighteen hundreds, and his grandson built that brick house in the 1890s. Raised dairy cattle, owned the creamery here in town, had the best stud bulls in the county. Now they're all gone, and the farm's been bought by a civil servant from Ottawa, who's not going to raise a single head."

"What can you tell us about the more recent Pettigrews?" Sullivan asked. "Did you know them?"

"Oh yeah, everybody knew them. I went to school with the

Pettigrew boys, and the adjacent farm is still in my family, thank God. What do you want to know for?" His jaw dropped. "Oh my God, was the dead man a Pettigrew?"

"Who's been living there recently?"

"Just—just the old man. And Robbie off and on. He's the youngest. There were five boys, so it gets confusing. But all the others...well..."

"Do you know where the others are?"

Sandy stared across the table at them in silence, his hearty façade quite gone. "If you think one of them is the body in the churchyard, I want to know, because they used to be friends of mine."

Sullivan laid the photo on the desk without a word. Sandy stared at it fixedly, his colour slowly draining from his face.

"Holy crap," he muttered. "What a mess."

"Can you recognize him?"

Sandy wagged his head back and forth helplessly. "It might be one of the boys. It's hard to tell from this, and I haven't seen them in a long time."

"Have you got their current addresses? Or any idea where they are?"

Sandy's eyes strayed to the photo again, and he stared at it in bewilderment. "When I was growing up, they were a happy family. Religious and strict, but happy. I used to love to play over there. But they've had more tragedies than any family was ever meant to bear—one by one they left home, until in the end all that remained was Robbie and his father."

"Could this be Robbie?"

Sandy shook his head firmly. "Robbie's much younger than the others. In his late twenties, I'd say. But I haven't seen any of the others since they were in their teens or early twenties, so it's impossible to know. I mean, that's twenty years ago."

Sandy eyed the photo again with a shiver of distaste. "Poor Robbie. Now he'll have one more thing to contend with. Some guys never get an even break."

When Green and Sullivan emerged from Sandy's office, it was past five o'clock and the autumn sun was sinking fast. Green realized a quick check with both home and office was in order, to ensure that no major crises had occurred in either place while they'd been vacationing in the country. Sullivan, meanwhile, wanted to check on the progress his team had made in the village.

The massive white truck that served as a mobile command post had arrived and sat on the grassy verge opposite the church. On the outside, it looked like an oversized chip wagon, but inside it was stocked with the latest in surveillance and communications devices. The two detectives logged in with the scribe before settling down at the work stations. The harvest from phone calls and email checks was meagre, however. On Green's end, he was happy that Bob had not knocked the house down and that no murders or grievous crimes had cropped up in his absence. Sullivan was less delighted to learn that virtually nothing useful had turned up, either in the canvass of the town nor in the intensive search of the church grounds. Although the name Pettigrew had surfaced a few times, no one could be certain who the dead man was.

But no one would be surprised if it was a Pettigrew at the bottom of the tower. It was a cursed family, they said.

Sullivan logged off, stifled a yawn and headed to the door. "Time to get back to the city, Mike. We've got the current address on this Robbie, so I'll take the photo to him after I drop you off. Hopefully, he'll be able to ID his own brother and we can wrap this up, pending MacPhail's autopsy report and the tox results. We've found no one who saw an altercation or another individual near the church, and the victim had no defensive wounds on his body, so it's looking like a self-inflicted. There's no evidence to suggest foul play was involved."

"Except the broken wall and the torn piece of jacket," Green countered. "That could suggest a struggle."

Sullivan shrugged. "Not much of one, according to Ident. More consistent with him trying to climb over the wall."

Maybe, Green thought, but there were a few more questions that needed answering before he would be willing to sign off on it. Such as why had the man returned, what was he searching for at his parents' farm, why had he chosen that particular church?

And perhaps most importantly, how did he get in? Ident reported no evidence of forced entry, the huge padlock hadn't been touched in years, and the back door had been locked when the police arrived. It was the self-locking kind that the victim might have pulled shut after his entry, but unless he had the skill to crack a combination lock, how had he unlocked the door in the first place?

All in all, it had been an intriguing day, Green thought as they drove back into the city. Manure aside, the air had been crisp and fresh, the fall colours spectacular. The pace out here was slower and the sense of history more vivid than the life he was accustomed to, yet it was important for the Major Crimes Squad to be sensitive to the difference. He felt less hurried and discouraged than he usually felt at the end of a typical office day, and he was quite looking forward to an evening with his family. Even the prospect of the dismantled kitchen did not bother him. Maybe they'd all go out to dinner and spend a bit of real time together.

But when he opened his front door, he found himself just in time to overhear the full blast of adolescent wrath.

"Forget it! You had no fucking business going through my things, and I'm not giving it back! Even if you ground me for a hundred years!"

Four

Sharon Green had staggered through the front door an hour earlier, her head pounding and her feet on fire. Hospital budget cuts were going to do her in. Psychiatric nursing had always been emotionally draining, but as the patients got sicker and their inpatient stays briefer, it was the physical exhaustion she noticed most. She had spent much of her shift trying to wrestle a three hundred pound depressive out of bed into a bath, and she felt rancid from head to toe.

Hannah's bedroom door was closed, but the pulse of rock music shook the entire house. Something the girl had in common with her father, Sharon observed, surprised yet again by how similar they were, despite having been apart all Hannah's life.

Sharon knocked on Hannah's door and waited for an invitation, well aware of her tenuous status as stepmother. A grunt answered her, but in her frazzled state, that was enough. She peeked in.

"I'm ducking into the shower," she said. "Would you please watch Tony for a few minutes?"

Hannah was sitting cross-legged on her bed, writing something which she snapped shut at the sight of Sharon. She smiled, not at Sharon but at Tony, who was squirming in her arms.

"I'll take him out," she said unexpectedly. "I want to mail a letter anyway."

Sharon knew better than to question the motive for this minor miracle. It was enough that Hannah was volunteering to do something helpful.

Two minutes later, Sharon peeled off her clothes, then stopped at the entrance to the bathroom with dismay. It looked as if a hurricane had hit. The walls dripped moisture, the window and mirror were steamed up, three soggy towels lay scattered on the floor, and Hannah's school clothes were in a lump outside the shower where she had stepped out of them. Sharon gritted her teeth. Resolutely, she opened the window, picked up the towels and tossed them into the hamper. She resisted the urge to fold the clothes; instead she scooped them up, carted them to Hannah's room and tossed them on the bed. A gold chain slipped out and fell to the floor.

When she retrieved it and saw what it was, she hesitated. Mike would not be thrilled, but Hannah had been entirely raised by his ex-wife with, as the ex-wife was fond of pointing out, no help from him. If Ashley had seen fit to give Hannah an elaborate gold crucifix, who had the right to protest? Sharon turned the cross over and saw there was an inscription, delicate and worn, but still legible.

"To Derek, with all our love, Mother and Dad."

She frowned. Hannah was a petite girl with elfin features and sparkling blue eyes. Sharon knew she had already cast her social net wide in the four months she'd been in Ottawa, but Sharon hadn't realized she'd snared a boy in that time. Snared him so thoroughly that he'd given her a precious piece of personal jewellery.

Sharon put the crucifix on the dresser and headed into the shower. She said nothing when Hannah returned, waiting instead until the girl wandered into the kitchen an hour later, drawn by that unerring instinct of teenagers and pets for the impending arrival of food. Sharon offered her a carrot stick, which Hannah ignored.

"So who's Derek?"

Hannah's eyes flew wide in surprise. "What?"

"Derek. The boy who gave you the pendant."

"Pendant?" Hannah seemed genuinely puzzled, then outrage replaced the surprise on her face. "You searched my room!"

"No, I cleaned up the bathroom."

"But it was in my pocket!"

Sharon leaned against the counter, sensing that she was handling the situation all wrong. She sought for a way to salvage the scene. "Hannah, I wasn't trying to be nosy. It fell out, and I wouldn't mention it but—"

"Then don't!"

"But it's obviously something very meaningful from the boy's parents, and I don't think-"

"He gave it to me!"

"I know he did, and I'm sure his heart was in the right place."

But Hannah was having none of it. She turned red, as if her very freedom were being challenged, and took a deep breath to launch into her counterstrike. At the very moment of that counterstrike, Green walked in. Hannah took one look at him and flounced out of the room. The whole house shook when her bedroom door slammed.

Green drew Sharon into his arms and kissed her black curls. "So how was your day?"

"Hellish," she replied, snuggling into the warmth of his arms. He smelled of raw earth. "And that was before I came home to that."

"And what was that?"

As she gave him a brief summary, his expression grew rueful. "Boys," he muttered. "I was hoping for a little more training time before we faced boys."

"She's a pretty girl. But she's got the attention span of a flea, Mike. I'm sorry, but she'll dump this poor Derek next week, and then he'll be out a valuable crucifix."

"Then next week we'll mail it back to him."

She swatted him, chuckling. "Coward. There's an important principle at work here, which I think Hannah should learn."

"When I was a kid, I hated to be told I was wrong."

"What do you mean, when you were a kid?"

It was his turn to chuckle. "Touché. The point is, I usually knew. And if people gave me enough space..."

"What's enough space?"

"Till tomorrow?"

In fact, an hour was all that was needed. Hannah didn't emerge from her bedroom for dinner, but when Green tapped on her door afterwards, he was greeted not by silence or cursing but by a surprisingly subdued "Come in". He found her sitting on her bed, writing. She didn't smile, didn't even glance up, but at least she was calm.

"So where is this crucifix?"

She flicked her black nails at the dresser. "I think *she* put it up there."

Green picked up the delicate chain and turned it over in his hands. The gold was ornately carved, and the inscription on the back was in old-fashioned Gothic script. Sharon was right; there was no way this was a proper gift for a girl. He remembered his own first clumsy attempt at impressing a girl. He'd stolen his mother's Queen Elizabeth coronation spoon, the only silver finery in his parent's humble home, and given it to blonde, untouchable Susan Fielding in his Grade Five class. Susan and her friends had all laughed at him.

"I guess this guy Derek really likes you."

She snorted. "You're both as bad as Mom was. Always jumping to conclusions, thinking there's got to be sex at the bottom of everything."

"So he doesn't like you?"

"I don't even know who the fuck Derek is! A kid I know found it and gave it to me."

Green liked the sound of that even less. "Found it?"

Hannah cast him a sidelong glance. "Spoken like a true cop. That's right, Mike. He rolled poor Derek on his way home from church and ripped it right off his neck."

"What are you planning to do with it?"

"Nothing. I can hardly give it back to the kid. It would hurt his feelings."

As opposed to Derek, who is probably in deep mourning, Green thought, but wisely refrained from comment while he considered the situation. It was a strange choice of words Hannah had used. What boy would give a girl someone else's crucifix and expect her to say nothing? Slowly the answer came to him.

"This is one of your special needs kids, isn't it?"

"The detective strikes again," she muttered. When he didn't rise to the bait, she nodded slightly. "He's a nice kid. I know he'd never steal it."

"But if Derek lost it, he's probably looking all over for it."

"Kyle was so proud when he gave it to me."

"Hannah, there must be a way. We'll enlist his parents' help if we have to. Do you know where he lives?"

"Some two-bit town called Ashford Landing."

For a moment, Green was struck dumb. Until today, he'd barely heard of the two-bit town. To have two unrelated events occur in that same place on the same day seemed an impossible coincidence. He tried to hide his excitement as he closed the crucifix in his palm.

"Come on, let's look up Kyle's address. I feel like a drive in the country."

She suddenly came alive, leaping off the bed and snatching the chain from his grasp. "No way I'm turning up there with my father!"

"I'll let you do the talking if you like."

But she was backing away, shaking her head. "I see Kyle tomorrow. I'll give it back to him."

"But we need to make sure it's returned to Derek. We need Kyle's parents."

"He's not stupid, you know."

"He's a child."

She rolled her eyes. Sensing her resistance had more form than substance, he turned towards the door. "I'll even let you listen to your own music in the car."

*   *   *

He had occasion to regret that gesture as they barrelled down Highway 416 with Nine Inch Nails cranked up to top volume. Even Green's spunky new Subaru seemed to shudder. Any conversation was out of the question, which perhaps was the reason for the volume in the first place. Hannah sat rigidly in the passenger seat, staring out the side window.

The blackness was absolute once they turned onto the back road towards Ashford Landing. They passed the Pettigrew farm on the left, and a kilometre further south, Hannah suddenly pointed to a blue number sign as they flew by.

"That was it."

Green pulled on the handbrake and executed a emergency skid turn that had Hannah hanging onto her seat. He grinned at her. "Cop school. Never have much chance to use it."

As he nosed the car down the narrow lane towards a farmhouse twinkling in the distance, he felt that peculiar excitement that came with being on the scent. He didn't know the connection yet, but this boy's farm was right next door to the Pettigrew's.

When they approached the house, they were greeted by a pair of shaggy black dogs of dubious lineage, whose loud barking brought a middle-aged man to the door. Green shouted an introduction and waited until the man had banished his dogs back inside before getting out of the car. The man's wary scowl broke into a smile as he turned his attention to Hannah. He had that sun-burnt, grizzled look that Green associated with the Texas desert, but when he opened his mouth, he was pure Ottawa Valley.

"You're Ky's teacher! He talks about you all the time, loves school for the first time ever." He ushered them inside through a narrow, slanting hallway that smelled of pumpkins and into an old-fashioned living room. Lace mats covered the heavy wooden tables and quilts protected all the chairs. A modest needlepoint picture with the words "Bless this house" hung framed over the dining table, and the only adornment in the living room was a large wooden cross hanging in the centre of the main wall.

"Mother!" the man shouted. "Ky! Look who's here."

A stout, greying woman of about fifty emerged from what Green assumed was the kitchen. She looked considerably less enthusiastic at their arrival, and Green saw her silently taking in Hannah's blue hair and multiple body piercings. Her thin lips pursed.

Kyle bounced into the room like a goofy, overgrown puppy, smacking into furniture and grinning from ear to ear. Apart from the childlike gaze in his pale blue eyes, Green thought he looked like any vibrant, attractive young teenager. His sun-bleached hair, deep tan, and burly chest hinted at hours hefting hay bales in the field.

"Ky, sit down," his mother snapped.

He subsided on the sofa, his puppy eyes fixed on Hannah. The mother turned to Green with stiff formality. "How do you do, I'm Edna McMartin. My husband Jeb, and you know Kyle." She whipped the quilt off the sofa under the cross and waved a stubby, ringless hand. "Please sit down. Jeb, perhaps you can fix our guests some tea?"

Hearing the forced enthusiasm in her tone, Green shook his head. "Thank you, Mrs. McMartin, but we don't want to intrude. My daughter—"

Hannah silenced him with a glare that would do a veteran teacher proud, then turned solemnly to Kyle. She uncurled her hand to reveal the chain. "Kyle, this is very beautiful and I thank you very much for giving it to me—"

Edna McMartin stiffened. "Eh?"

Hannah kept her eyes on Kyle. "But when I looked at it carefully, I realized it belonged to someone else."

The mother snatched it from Hannah's hand, and Kyle shrank back on the sofa as if hoping he could disappear.

Edna looked appalled. "Where did you get this!"

"I think he found it," Hannah replied.

The mother leaned across and glared at her son. "You steal it? You know how I feel about that."

"He found it," Hannah repeated, but Green could hear the quaver in her voice. She's handling herself beautifully, he thought with surprise and pride, but that accusation has shaken her.

He stepped in to help. "It's not a question of theft, rest assured. We just think the boy who lost it would probably like it back. Do any of you know who Derek is?"

Edna turned the crucifix over to read the inscription, then shook her head sharply. "Nope. Never heard of a Derek."

"Anybody named Derek in the area?" Green persisted.

"I just said there wasn't."

The father had been frowning thoughtfully. "Wasn't that the name of the oldest Pettigrew boy?"

"Oh, but he's been gone for years. No." The mother handed the crucifix to Green with an air of finality. "Kyle must have found it in the city."

At the mention of Pettigrews, Green's mind was already racing ahead, but he tried to sound gentle. "Did you find the chain in the city, Kyle? Or out here?"

"He doesn't understand distances," said his mother. "For him, there's the school, the bus and home."

"Where did you find this, Ky?" Hannah asked him quietly.

He sneaked a glance at his mother, then shrugged.

"At the farm or at school?"

"Don't know."

Green leaned forward. "Do you think you could show me tomorrow when it's light out?"

Kyle shrank back. "I have to go school."

"What good is all this?" the mother said. "It's just an ordinary crucifix. Look, the inscription's almost worn away. Someone was probably throwing away some old family junk. Happens all the time when people clear out these old places they've lived in for generations. Kyle loves garbage, Mr. Green. Dollars to doughnuts, that's where he got it."

Once Green and Hannah were back on the main highway, and he didn't have to feel his way through the narrow back roads, he reached across and turned down the Nine Inch Nails.

"Would you do something for me tomorrow?" he asked.

Hannah cast him a wary glance.

"Kyle trusts you. Would you come out here with me after school and get Kyle to show us where he found the chain?"

"Why?"

"It's part of an investigation."

"And why should I help you with an investigation?"

He could have said it was because an unidentified man was dead, and there was a very real possibility this chain belonged to him. But instead, he tried to think like a teenager. "Because it might be fun."

* * *

At eight o'clock the next morning, Green parked his car in the underground parking lot of the police station and made a mad dash for the elevator, clutching a bagel in one hand and a cup of Starbucks highest octane coffee in the other. When he disembarked on the second floor, he was relieved to see Brian Sullivan still at his desk, scrolling through his emails. Sullivan was an impossibly early riser and liked to get his investigations rolling before most of the world was even awake. Green signalled towards his office as he strode by.

The Major Crimes Squad room bustled with activity as the new shift checked in and reviewed the fruits of a night on the streets. In his office, Green was greeted by a pile of phone messages and post-it notes as well as a full voice mail box. The implications were clear; a middle management inspector abandoned his desk for an entire day at his own peril.

He was flipping through his phone messages for dire

emergencies when Sullivan loomed in his doorway. He was already shrugging his jacket over his massive linebacker frame, and he grinned at the sight of Green's overflowing desk.

Green silenced him with a scowl. "How did the ID go on the Ashford Landing John Doe?"

Sullivan shook his head. "Robert Pettigrew wasn't home last night. But the autopsy's set for ten, so I'm sending over the new detective. Might as well get her feet wet. I've got Bob Gibbs trying to track down the dentist who used to work that neck of the woods. I'm just on my way out to see Robert Pettigrew again. Ident's cleaned up the photo, so he should be able to identify it."

Green took the crucifix out of his desk. "I'd like to see if he can identify this, too. Apparently one of the older brothers was named Derek."

Sullivan reached to take it, but Green pulled it away. "I'd like to do it." Seeing Sullivan's raised eyebrow, he explained about Hannah's involvement and the fragility of their key witness to the discovery.

Sullivan surveyed Green's desk. "Suit yourself, Mike. But I'd say you're good for at least two hours here, and this can't wait."

"Half hour tops. Then I'll be set to go."

True to his word, half an hour later Green logged off his computer, rounded up Sullivan, and together they set off. Robert Pettigrew lived on the tenth floor of a shabby apartment block in Alta Vista which would have been tolerable had it been on the north side overlooking the grassy shoreline of the Rideau River. Unfortunately, his minuscule apartment faced west over four lanes of Bank Street and the Billings Bridge Mall parking lot. Stale grease permeated the hallways.

The moment Robert Pettigrew opened his door, Green was struck by his resemblance to the dead man. In front of them stood a younger, handsomer, clean-shaven version, but the blue eyes and the sharp cheekbones were the same. There could no longer be any doubt that the man on the slab in the morgue was a Pettigrew.

Robbie introduced himself with a moist handshake and a nervous laugh. When Sullivan explained the purpose of the visit and produced the photo, he blanched and sank onto the sofa.

Sullivan took the lead. "Do you recognize the man?"

"No. Yes. Well, it looks like my father when he was younger."

"Is it one of your older brothers?"

Colour began to return to Robbie's face. "I haven't seen my brothers in many years. Ohmigod, let me think." He stood abruptly and carried the photo over to the light. While they waited, Green absorbed impressions about the room. It was neat and uncluttered, but the furniture was heavy, dark and worn, the carpet on the floor stained and threadbare. There were no pictures of family, or smiling children, or even his father. On the wall was a single framed print of Van Gogh's *Sunflower*—a splash of cheer in an otherwise bare and melancholy room. The room had a makeshift feel, as if Robbie had never wanted to live there.

Slowly, Robbie shook his head. "I thought it might be Tom, because he lives on the streets, and I imagine washing facilities would be somewhat limited."

"The streets here in Ottawa?" Sullivan asked.

"Toronto. Last I heard he was living in a cardboard box under the Gardiner Expressway."

"How old would Tom be?"

"Well, he's twelve years older than me, so that makes him forty. In fact—" Robbie looked surprised, "his fortieth birthday was just last week."

"But you don't think it's Tom?"

"It's hard to tell from this, but Tom has a scruffier look, like he's been battered a thousand times. He's an alcoholic."

"The photo's been touched up, so that might not show," Sullivan said. "Did Tom ever sustain any broken bones, because those can be identified in the post mortem. As can scars or tattoos."

"I only saw him every few years, usually when he was in trouble. I confess I never looked very closely."

"What about your other brothers? I understand there are five of you?"

"One's dead. Died in a car crash fourteen years ago." A spasm of pain crossed Robbie's face. He withdrew a photo album from the bookcase beside the TV. "I haven't seen the other two since I was eight, but I do have some pictures we can look at." When he flipped open the album, the two detectives crowded around him, curious to get initial objective impressions of their own. Robbie leafed slowly through the pictures of smiling clusters of boys surrounding birthday cakes, perched atop tractors, posing with prize calves. Not exactly the cursed and tragic family that Sandy and the villagers had described yesterday, Green thought.

"I haven't looked at these in a long time," Robbie said. "It always feels surreal to me, like someone else's family." He gestured to a photo of a smiling blonde woman showing off her dress. "I can't believe my mother ever smiled like that. As a child, all I remember are long stares and silence. Hours and hours of silence. Anyway...there's Tom." He stopped at a photo of a teenage boy, handsome in the slick, big-haired style of the eighties. He had a saucy grin on his face and a possessive arm around a girl with stunning black hair cascading to her waist.

"Good-looking guy," Sullivan observed.

"Yeah. Dad always said Tom had a mesmerizing way with women, which somehow passed me by." He managed a smile that warmed his mournful eyes. "Although I don't think he's had much more luck keeping them in the long run than I have."

"What about Derek?" Green interjected, unable to restrain his curiosity. "Any pictures of him?"

Robbie flipped through some pages. "His university graduation picture is the last—ah-hah!" He spread a page in triumph. A proud, self-conscious grad smiled out of the picture. The deep-set blue eyes were almost identical to Tom's, although the hair was lighter brown and the jaw line softer. But the striking difference was in the personality. Tom shone through as cocksure and sensual, Derek as quiet and deep in thought.

Sullivan held the photo side by side with the dead man's, and they all studied it in silence. "How old would Derek be now?" Sullivan asked.

Robbie narrowed his eyes to calculate before replying forty-two.

"When was the last time you heard from him?"

Robbie shrugged. "I've never heard from him. I was only eight when he went away to graduate school in California, and we had no real relationship. My parents heard from him every now and then, but I don't know when was the last time."

"Perhaps we might ask your father if he's heard from him lately, and if Derek mentioned coming home?"

The young man seemed to think a long time before answering, as if debating the wisdom of disclosing family matters. "My father can't speak," he said finally. "He's had a serious stroke that left him without speech and paralyzed on one side. I think he understands a little, but he can only say one or two words with great effort."

Sullivan had stopped taking notes, no doubt regarding the

father's health as irrelevant, so Green jumped in before he could change the subject. "When did this happen?"

"About three months ago. He's still in hospital; the doctors at first thought he wouldn't survive, and later they said he'd never be able to go home again. That's why I sold the farm. I work here in the city, and I couldn't manage the farm. Anyway, I always hated the place."

Green could see Sullivan starting to fidget. Sullivan was a no-nonsense, straight-ahead type of investigator who liked to stick to the point, gather the facts and move on. No dallying, unless he was playing a suspect on the line, and no wandering down side alleys. Green, however, felt there was a strange mystery in this family. The earlier photos painted a picture of a close, happy family who loved to celebrate together. But something had happened to change all that, and suddenly the eldest son moved to the opposite side of the continent, never to return, another son became a drunk, a third had died in a car crash, and a happy home had turned to silence. Now, twenty years later, had that prodigal son returned? What had drawn him back, and what—or who—had he encountered upon his return that he had ended up dead?

"Any special reason why you hated the place?" Green asked gently.

Robbie had been gazing at the picture of the farmhouse, taken years ago when the porch was straight, the trim white and the gardens lush with flowers. "Because my parents hated it. Because all they ever did was scream at each other, and my brothers left me all alone to cope with them." He snapped the photo album shut and thrust it back in its slot. "I never cared to see my brothers, detectives, because they never cared for me. I hear from Tom about once a year, always when he needs me to bail him out of some mess. Bad debts, or a failed business scheme, or a bar brawl. I'm not a rich man. I'm a produce manager for Loblaws, I have two ex-wives and one little girl, and as you can see, I barely have a place to live. I've lent Tom money half a dozen times and never seen a penny back, plus he's never once come up to help me with Mom or Dad."

His face was growing red as the pent-up anger spilled out. "But then last week, out of the blue he calls me and freaks out when I tell him I sold the house. He hasn't been back to visit or help out, but suddenly he's swearing at me and saying I had no right to sell it, and he had important stuff in the basement there, and..." He broke off as a thought occurred to him, and he waved at the dead man's photo in disgust. "That's probably Tom, coming up to get his important stuff and being so goddamn drunk he fell off the church."

"What was the important stuff?" Green asked.

"Who the hell knows? I told him there wasn't a goddamn thing worth having in that house when I sold it. Just a bunch of old boxes full of junk."

Green removed the crucifix from his pocket and held it out. "Do you recognize this?"

Robbie checked himself, as if embarrassed that he had lost control, and he took the chain with a puzzled frown. "Did you find this on the body?"

"No, but it was found in the vicinity. Derek is an unusual name, and the engraving looks old."

"I don't recognize it, but I hardly remember Derek, let alone what he wore."

When Green asked if any of the rest of them had been given crucifixes by their parents, Robbie shook his head. "I believe my parents used to be very religious, but they weren't much for jewellery, especially expensive stuff like that. We had no money to spare. I know Derek had to work two jobs and win a scholarship to go to university."

Sullivan had already closed his notebook and was edging toward the door, but Green took the photo album out again and began to examine the photos of Derek with his magnifying glass. No sign of a crucifix. Perhaps it was under his shirt, rather than being worn as a fashion statement, as they were today. He felt vaguely dissatisfied that he couldn't connect this loose end, but he was still convinced that it connected somewhere. Patience, he told himself as he rose to join Sullivan at the door. When Hannah found out from Kyle where Derek had lost his crucifix, that might shed some light on what had led him from his childhood farm house to his death in the church yard. It was only once they were back in the car heading across Billings Bridge towards downtown, that Green remembered.

"Jesus, Brian. There was another son. We forgot the fifth son!"

Five

For the first time since her impetuous decision to purchase the Pettigrew farm, Isabelle Boisvert felt overwhelmed. A surly Jacques had gone into the village for supplies, and she was sitting on the front porch with her mid-morning coffee, taking advantage of the rare October warmth to contemplate the bounty of her land. But all she could see was work. The porch sagged beneath her feet, its wood planks rotting away, and across the expanse of barren weedy yard, the two wooden outbuildings were collapsing beneath the weight of time. And inside its spectacular red brick exterior, the house was just as bad. The plaster walls were crumbling, and all the beautiful oak woodwork had been painted over with cheap white paint that had cracked and flaked.

In the distance, the maple trees by the river shone crimson and gold. She tried to remind herself that this was why she'd bought the property. She'd known it would be a labour of love, but owning a hundred acres of land and forest with over a thousand feet of wooded river frontage had seemed like a dream worth labouring for. Jacques had been reluctantly persuaded by its investment value, but she hoped to raise horses, perhaps one day have an equestrian school and make enough money that they could both quit their civil service jobs and dispense with the frustrating commute to the city altogether.

For now, to pay for all the repairs, they needed their jobs more than ever. To save money, she and Jacques were trying to do much of the work themselves. Unlike Jacques, she had grown up in the country and hoped that working with her hands would somehow return her to her roots. But today she didn't know where to start. Jacques wanted to attack the interior of the house, where they would be confined for most of the long, upcoming winter months.

But the warm weather would soon be over, and with it all chance to tackle the outside. They hoped to have a professional builder restore the main barn in the spring, so she could use it for her horses. But the little tool shed looked beyond repair, and even worse was the eyesore of bushes and burnt planking that sat at the edge of the yard. Jacques was anxious to bulldoze it over and build a garage for the cars before winter struck, but that cost money that was sorely needed for other things. It looked as if no one had spent a penny on the place in years.

She didn't know how Mr. Pettigrew had earned his money once he no longer farmed the land, but the man had managed to consume an astonishing quantity of booze. They had found closets full of empty bottles everywhere and had spent a whole day simply carting bottles to the local dump.

Once, long ago, someone with skill and devotion had ministered to the house, for beneath the flaking paint, the woodwork was intricately hand-carved and the hardwood cabinetry bore an expert craftsman's touch. But then, quite abruptly, it seemed as if the family had stopped caring. The basement had been abandoned in a half-finished state with pine planking erected on half the walls, but only two-by-four framing on the rest. It was all dried and warped now, and someday she would have to rip it all out and start from scratch.

But not today. Today she would tackle the charred,

overgrown eyesore in the front yard that was ruining her view from the porch. That way she could have a huge autumn bonfire like the ones she remembered from her childhood.

She stretched, tossed the dregs of her coffee on the ground and headed for the tool shed, where she'd seen a number of battered tools, perhaps among them the axe and crowbar she would need for the job. However, inside she found a small scythe, a hammer, and a handful of rusty saws, but no axe or sledgehammer big enough to do the job. She searched the barn and house to no avail. Making a note to buy a decent axe, she set to work with a shovel, hacking away at the woody stems and prying loose the roots. In less than an hour, she had a pile of branches and planking ready to burn.

She was just getting down on her hands and knees to wrench out a stubborn root when a flash of turquoise caught her eye, and she saw Jacques' Cavalier speeding down their lane in a plume of dust. She felt an odd mix of feelings. Frustration that he persisted in driving on the country roads as if he were on the Queensway, delight at the prospect of his company, and apprehension that she might be in for another hour's worth of bitching about country life. He'd left that morning in a foul humour, threatening to move in with his brother Jean Marc in Orleans.

When he leaped from the car, however, his eyes were wide, and he chattered in staccato French as he removed grocery bags from the car.

"This house, Isabelle! Everyone in the village is talking about it! That man who died at the church was one of the Pettigrews. A hundred years ago they owned all the land from here to the village, and they used to be big leaders. In the church, in the town. That little church the man died in, that was a major one in town, but there was a split in the movement when a new priest came. They talk like it was yesterday, but it was twenty-five years ago. Some went to the Anglican Church and some—"

She took some bags from him, set them on the counter and silenced him with a kiss. When Jacques began to talk religion, he lost her. "Is this important?"

He was not to be deterred, and his tone acquired an urgency. "What's important is that this family, the Pettigrews, they helped build that church, but they left it too, and everyone says that's when things started to get really bizarre. One of the sons went so crazy they had to lock him up. The mother was afraid he was possessed, and this house—"

Isabelle looked at him with alarm. Jacques had a deeply religious core and had not totally shaken off the strong Catholic indoctrination of his childhood among the priests. If he started believing that the house was haunted—or worse, possessed—she might never be able to persuade him to feel at home.

She slipped into his arms and took his face in her hands. "*Chéri*, this is our home now. We'll take it apart, every board and wall, and we'll make it ours."

A frisson passed through him. "But they are everywhere! Their initials are still carved on the windowsills, their names are glued to the bedroom walls. And the worst thing—" He paused. "Isabelle, they said the wife hung herself in the very room where we are sleeping!"

*   *   *

Fifteen minutes after leaving Robbie's apartment, Sullivan was inching the Impala through the Glebe in bumper to bumper traffic. To save time, Green radioed ahead to Gibbs, but before he could even relay his request, the young constable's stutter burst over the wire.

"I—I'm afraid I struck out on Derek Pettigrew's dentist, sir. Seems the man who used to treat the family died about ten years ago, and the old files have been destroyed. So we have no dental ID."

Green sighed. That meant they would have to identify the body by process of elimination. He instructed Gibbs to find out as much background as he could about the Pettigrew family. Gibbs was Green's favourite gofer, eager, tireless, relentless and intelligent to boot. By the time the two detectives reached the Major Crimes Squad room, he had not just the full names, but the dates and places of birth and death of four generations of Pettigrews.

"I'm sorry I don't have all the current addresses yet, sir, but I'm working on it. None of them are in the system."

Green had doubted they would be, for until amalgamation a few years ago, Ashford Landing had been under the jurisdiction of the Ontario Provincial Police. He advised him to check with the OPP.

"I already did, sir." Gibbs smiled and met his eyes. The kid's finally getting some confidence, Green thought with relief. Gibbs had a wonderful investigative nose, but he was scared of his own shadow, which was a major drawback in Criminal Investigations. "They've nothing on them either, sir. Except for one son, Benjamin, victim of a one-car fatal in 1990."

"Any particulars?"

"It was labelled driver error, but the accident occurred at one-thirty in the morning, so alcohol might have been a factor. Although County Road 2 is pretty dark and deserted at that time of night."

County Road 2 is also pretty straight, Green thought, remembering their recent drives along the road leading to Ashford Landing. He looked at Benjamin's date of birth and did a quick calculation. Benjamin had died on his twenty-first birthday, possibly on his way home from one too many celebrations. Green felt a twinge of sorrow for the beleaguered family. Had this been the tragedy that had turned their lives upside down?

He returned his attention to Gibbs's notes. Benjamin had been the second youngest son, but still seven years older than Robbie. The mother had died twelve years ago, two years after Benjamin. Gibbs had not yet been able to track down any additional details beyond the name and birth date of the remaining three sons. Derek, Tom and Lawrence. Green pointed to their names.

"Concentrate on Derek, but just to be thorough, see if you can locate the present whereabouts of all three—or at least their most recent known address. Lawrence would be the fifth son we forgot to ask about. Check if Robbie Pettigrew or any of the villagers know where he went. Let Brian know if you find anything useful."

After Gibbs had scurried off, Sullivan eyed Green with disapproval. "You just gave him the work of two officers. You know, just because he'll do it, it doesn't mean you should ask him to."

Green smiled. "That's why you're going to give him a new partner. The new woman you just got from General Assignment? Sue Peters? I think she'd be a great fit for Gibbsie."

Sullivan laughed without humour. "Where did you get that bright idea? She'll scare him half to death."

The idea had only just occurred to Green when he saw the new confidence in Gibbs. It was about time he took on a more senior role and began training others in that wonderful investigative nose. And who better than the cocky young detective who was clawing her way resolutely through the ranks. Learning to dot every i and cross every t under the meticulous tutelage of Bob Gibbs ought to slow her down a touch. As well as maybe make a decent investigator out of her.

But he said none of that to Sullivan, who was clearly irked by Green's cavalier invasion into his territory yet again. "It'll do them both good," he replied instead, tossing a wink over his shoulder as he headed for the third floor. "I'd like a quick update after my meeting before I go home. And I'm leaving at three."

"Three!" Sullivan's tone registered his disbelief, for Green almost never left before six.

"I have to see a kid about a crucifix."

* * *

Hannah flounced into the passenger seat and immediately changed the radio station from Green's classic rock to extreme rock, casting him a look that dared him to object. Ignoring the bait, Green pulled out of the school drive and accelerated up Carling Avenue towards the Queensway. It was half past three, and the autumn sun was slanting through the window onto her face. She jerked the visor down and hid behind dark glasses.

"How was school?" he ventured neutrally.

"Kyle wasn't there today."

"Oh? Sick?"

She shrugged. "Seemed fine yesterday. Till you started asking him all those questions."

"Well, we'll try to make this like a game today. Make sure you explain to him that he hasn't done anything wrong."

"He understands English, Mike. He's not an idiot. I mean—" She broke off, flushing.

"I know he isn't, but I'm a police officer, and he may think that means he's done something wrong. Tell him we just want him to help us figure out who the chain belongs to."

To her credit, Hannah tried her best when they arrived at the McMartin farm. Kyle was in the barn, looking perfectly healthy as he mucked out stalls. The reek of manure clung to his clothes, and he seemed oblivious to the flies that swarmed around him. Green was struck by how big and muscular he was in his overalls and rubber boots. A boy's mind in a body that was fast becoming a man's. Green's impression was reinforced by Kyle's reaction to Hannah, which was pure adolescent male. Red-faced, tongue-tied and tripping over his limbs.

But as soon as she mentioned the crucifix, he started to wag his head back and forth.

"I don't remember. I get mixed up."

Green watched him carefully. "What were you doing when you found it?"

"Walking."

"Morning or afternoon?"

Kyle began to shake his head when Hannah stepped in again. "Was lunch finished?"

A nod.

"Was dinner finished?"

"No. Not started."

"Good." She smiled and squeezed his hand. "Were you walking home from the village?"

"No."

"Were you walking to the village?"

Kyle squirmed and looked away, shaking his head.

Green picked up the cross-examination technique. He pointed towards the woods in the direction of the river. "Were you walking over there, Kyle?"

"Kyle's not allowed to go in the woods, Mr. Green," came a sharp voice from behind them, as Edna McMartin strode into view from the interior of the barn. Her grey hair stood on end and wisps of straw stuck to her clothes.

Kyle shook his head vigorously. "I didn't. I didn't go there."

Her eyes were hostile, and Green felt all chance for cooperation slipping through his fingers. He thought he knew why; they had not informed her of their arrival nor asked permission to speak to her son. Kyle had come out to greet them and, hoping to keep the interview as casual as possible, they had simply slid right in.

He apologized to her as humbly as he could and explained the importance of pinpointing the discovery of the chain. "We believe the dead man was probably Derek Pettigrew and that this chain was lost by him shortly before his death. We're trying to trace his movements leading up to his death."

Edna McMartin fixed Kyle with a firm, unwavering gaze that Green suspected would see through anyone's subterfuge. "Did you go to the woods near the river, Ky?"

He swallowed and shook his head. "No, Mom. Never."

"Then where did you find the chain?"

"I was walking to the village. Through the field." Kyle pointed across a stubbled field towards the distant church spires of the village. Green studied him thoughtfully. The boy was lying; he had earlier denied this. But why?

"Why is Kyle not allowed to go in the woods?" he asked the mother casually.

"Because of the river, of course," she answered in a tone that implied a silent "you idiot."

"Of course. Have you lived on this farm long?"

"Long?" She snorted. "Is all my life long enough?"

Green felt as if he had hit a gold mine, if he could only figure out how to mine it. "Then you would have known the Pettigrew boys before they all left."

Her gaze grew wary. "Some. We stay pretty busy on the farm."

He turned abruptly towards Hannah. "Sorry, honey. I need to have a few words with Kyle's mother inside. Do you think you and Kyle can amuse each other out here for a while?"

Poor choice of words, Green thought with a grimace as he ushered the reluctant mother into her house. She seemed as uneasy about leaving them alone as he was, no doubt for opposite reasons.

"I don't know what I can tell you," she said as she perched on the edge of her sofa, looking ready to bolt at any moment. Unlike last evening, she made no effort to remove the quilt or offer him a drink. "I haven't seen any of the older children in years. And I never had much to do with him—" She jerked her head in the direction of the Pettigrew farm. "—since he started pickling himself in booze and bawling at the moon at three in the morning. Could hear it clear across to the village some nights."

"Were you friends when the wife was alive?"

"Well, close enough when the boys were at school together. We were in the same church, and my Sandy was friends with their Lawrence—"

A distant bell of recognition rang in Green's head. "Sandy Fitzpatrick? The real estate agent? He's your son?"

Her lips formed a tight, wary line. "How do you know Sandy?"

Green gave her the short explanation—that Sandy had provided Robbie Pettigrew's address. That seemed to satisfy her, for she nodded and actually volunteered some information. "Sandy's father is dead, fell under the baler. Jeb McMartin is my second husband."

Green absorbed the coincidences of village life. That made Sandy and Kyle brothers, despite the probable twenty-five year age gap. Both were burly and full of health, although beyond that he could see no resemblance.

Edna flushed, as if having two husbands somehow made her a harlot. "His boy needed a mother, and I needed a man about the farm. This life is hard, Inspector. You take from it what you have to."

Green nodded sympathetically. "I understand life was hard for your neighbours as well. What can you tell me about Lawrence? Do you know where he is?"

"St. Lawrence Psychiatric Hospital in Brockville, last I heard."

"What happened to him?"

"Went crazy. His folks locked him up."

"How long ago was that?"

She pursed her lips as if dredging her memory. "In Grade Eleven. I remember because he and Sandy were in the same grade, and Lawrence just stopped coming to school. Wandered around the place talking to himself, or suddenly you'd turn around and there he'd be standing, staring at you. Gave everybody the willies." As the bearer of grim news, she seemed to lose her frostiness. "They tried to get him help up in Ottawa, and then one day they packed him into the family's old pick-up and drove straight to Brockville. I don't think the mother ever recovered, and then when her Benji was killed, well, that did her in."

Green had a sinking feeling. A cursed family, the villagers had called them. "What do you mean?"

"Killed herself. Took years building to it, mind. Sinking deeper and deeper, with him not helping a bit, and poor little Robbie just raising himself. About ten, twelve years ago, I guess she figured he was raised enough, and so she called it quits."

*　　*　　*

Green struggled to steer with one hand as he punched numbers into his cell phone with the other. Extreme rock pulsated through the car, and Hannah was bobbing her head with a secretive twinkle in her eyes.

"Do you want me to drive?" she shouted.

"In your dreams, honey."

She pulled what he recognized as a classic Hannah pout. Pro forma, with no outrage behind it. "Back home I had my learner's permit."

"And we'll have this discussion when you're back in regular school."

"I like Alternate Ed. The kids are way cooler, and I get to do this part-time work in the real world."

He flicked off the radio and turned his attention to Gibbs, who had finally answered his phone. It was nearly five o'clock, but Green had known the man would still be hard at work. Green filled him in on Edna's revelation about Lawrence Pettigrew.

"I'm ahead of you, sir," Gibbs said. "One of the villagers told me, and I've already contacted the hospital personnel."

Which is why I love you, Green thought with admiration. "What's the news?"

"He was in St. Lawrence Psychiatric Hospital from 1984 till 2000, but he's been in a supervised group home since then until just a couple of months ago."

"What happened a couple of months ago?"

"He graduated to monitored independence, sir. Whatever that means. I'm trying to reach those people now."

"Good. Let me know as soon as you find him. We're looking for an absolute positive sighting in the past forty-eight hours to rule him out."

Green rang off and found Hannah eyeing him with the

faintest smile on her pixie face. She was so tiny and innocent-looking, it was hard to believe she packed such a punch.

"If I hadn't been in Alternate Ed, I wouldn't have met Kyle. And if I hadn't met Kyle, you'd never have found out the truth about that gold crucifix."

"Okay, I'll bite. What did he tell you?"

"Without his mother breathing down his neck, he told me the truth about where he found it."

It was Green's turn to smile. "I thought he might."

Her eyes narrowed suspiciously, and Green's smile broadened. "He found it in the woods on the way to the village, didn't he?"

She nodded. "There's a path running along the river, which starts at the next farm and runs past the McMartin farm into the village. He found it somewhere near the village."

"On the ground?"

"Yes, just lying in the leaves."

Green considered the implications. If Derek had lost that chain twenty years ago, it would probably have been found by other travellers or buried under layers of leaves and debris during the intervening years. To be found so easily by a boy strolling along the path, it had to have been dropped there recently. Perhaps on the very day the mystery man was spotted at the farm by Isabelle Boisvert.

Green winked at her. "I'll make you a sleuth yet. Do you mind a little side trip?"

"Where?"

"To talk to Kyle's older half-brother. He was a friend of the Pettigrew brothers years ago."

"But Dad!"

It was the first time she'd called him Dad, and his jaw dropped before he could stop himself. Quickly, she scowled.

"I've got homework to do and friends to call."

"Fifteen minutes, tops. Promise." And without giving her time to protest, he pulled into Sandy's drive.

The realtor was even more frazzled than he had been a day earlier. Before Green could explain his visit, Sandy launched into a grilling of his own.

"It is true? They're saying it was Derek in the church yard!"

"Who's saying?"

"Everyone. I heard it from Harvey at the grocery store, who heard it from my stepfather."

"You saw the picture. Did it look like Derek?"

"I haven't see him in twenty years, and I was only seventeen when he left." Sandy scrubbed his hands over his face distractedly. "I always assumed Derek was off having a successful life somewhere. But all the boys looked alike. Miniature clones of their father. It was their personalities that differed a great deal."

Green settled into one of the client chairs and pulled out his notebook casually. He'd left Hannah in the car, blasting out the latest Disturbed album. "I understand you were Lawrence's friend. What can you tell me about him? What was life like back then?"

Sandy drew two deep breaths as if forcing himself to settle. He twirled his pen restlessly while he gathered his thoughts. "Lawrence... Such a sad case. We used to play together all the time, build forts in the woods and pretend they were starships. He was a gentle, sensitive, imaginative boy who was cruelly teased, not only by the other boors around here but by his own brother Tom. Tom was all brawn, no brains, and proud of it. He ran with a pack of troublemakers in town who used to beat Lawrence and me up regularly."

"Did Lawrence become schizophrenic?" It was a diagnosis that seemed to fit the symptoms Green had heard.

Sandy's face hardened in anger. "It was his father drove him over the edge. The old man shoved religion down all the kids' throats, but some of them took it more to heart than others. Lawrence started obsessing about sin and worrying that people were damned to hellfire and brimstone if they didn't purify themselves. Can you imagine—a house full of healthy teenage boys and Lawrence was obsessing about sin? He used to hide their condoms and spy on them. I tried to help, but as he got sicker, he started to retreat more and more. Stopped coming to school, shut himself up in the shed for hours on end, performing his rituals. It was spooky. Finally, it got so bad the family just snapped and committed him."

"Was this before or after Derek went away?"

"Right after. I think that's why they went ahead with the hospital. Derek had always protected Lawrence and stood up for him, especially against Tom. Look, these were country people, they didn't understand what was happening to Lawrence. None of us did. It's only afterwards I did some reading about schizophrenia, but back then we were just scared and angry at him."

"Except Derek?"

"Well, Derek was—" Sandy paused as if searching for words. "I was only a kid, but I remember how smart he seemed. He was in university, and he knew so much about the world. When he left, I think Lawrence probably flipped out, and the family grabbed the chance to ship him out of their hair."

"Have you seen or heard anything about him since?"

Sandy shook his head. Green sensed a little regret, even shame, in his tone. "Not a word. Sometimes folks would ask the Pettigrews how he was doing, but they never said much, just that it wouldn't be good for him to have visitors. Not that anyone wanted to visit the poor guy."

"What about Derek? Ever see him?"

Sandy's expression grew shuttered. "No, but he always said he wouldn't come back."

"You mean he discussed it with you?"

"Oh no, that's just what I heard. He hated the farm. Country wasn't his thing. Beneath him."

"Did he have any friends here that he might have kept in touch with?"

"University friends, maybe? But no one here in the village. Although of course, I hardly knew him."

Outside, Hannah leaned on the Subaru horn, making Sandy jump. Green moved to get up and fancied he saw relief cross the other man's face. Green thanked him for his help and then paused for one last question.

"Can you think of any reason or circumstance that would have drawn any of the brothers back home right at this moment, after an absence of twenty years?"

Sandy had risen to usher Green out, and now he hovered restlessly in the doorway. "Their father's illness, perhaps? Or selling the family farm?"

It was possible, Green thought as he made his way out to confront Hannah. But as far as anyone was willing to admit, only one of them besides Robbie knew their father was ill and the farm sold.

Tom.

* * *

Isabelle could not return to her work in the yard until late in the afternoon, after a lunch break and a stint helping Jacques strip the blue flowered wallpaper from their bedroom. He had attacked the task with a frenzy, as if determined to banish the

65

mother's ghost before he spent another night in the house. He'd been right; all the bedrooms held the memories of decades of family life. In one bedroom, they discovered lists of girls' names carved on the window sill, and on another sill "DP loves..." with the initials vigorously scratched out.

"A teenage love affair that ended badly," Isabelle joked as they sanded down the marks.

Jacques pointed to the lengthy list of girls on the other window. "This guy evidently didn't take his *grandes amours* so seriously."

After two bedrooms, even Jacques agreed they'd both breathed enough dust for one day, and he headed into the city to check paint stores. The afternoon was still crisp and sunny, so Isabelle retrieved her shovel and returned to the thicket. Tearing up the weeds and decaying planks, she encountered more slugs and earwigs than she ever cared to, and she was about to give up in disgust when her hand struck something hard. She dug around it and levered the shovel under it until she finally unearthed a small tin can with the lid rusted on tight. It rattled when she shook it, as if there were several loose objects inside. Soot smudged her hands where she had gripped it, and the label was illegible beneath the black. She studied the hole it had come from. This was no accident. The hole was deep and clearly covered by charred floorboards. Someone had deliberately lifted a floorboard and buried the can underneath.

She remembered the man she'd seen rummaging around here in the thicket. Perhaps he was looking for this! She felt a flutter of excitement. It might be jewellery or coins, perhaps something even more valuable. This is an old home; an ordinary artifact might be worth a lot of money. Whether she kept it or turned it over to Robert Pettigrew, she would decide later, once she'd seen what it was.

With the help of some oil and a screwdriver, she began very slowly to work the lid loose. It was stubborn and loosening it took an interminable time. Finally, with one last pop, the lid came off. Isabelle peered inside and her eagerness died abruptly.

Six metal bottle caps, a white feather, a box of condoms, two slips of paper, a brass key, and the final object—a small white sphere. She turned the sphere over in her fingers curiously until she was looking at it head on, and saw two tiny holes and the remnants of a beak. It was the skull of a tiny bird.

Isabelle snatched her fingers away as if they'd been burned. The bird skull tumbled into the dirt next to the can. Horror crawled over her skin, and she sat back on her heels, staring at the object, in the grip of an irrational fear. Had the man come back to the farm for this? For a dozen condoms, a bunch of useless junk and a bird skull?

She scooped up the contents, returned them to the tin and pressed the lid down tightly before heading into the house to find Sergeant Sullivan's card. She wasn't sure what the significance of the tin was, but she knew the police had better have a look at it.

Six

When Green arrived at the station the next morning, Brian Sullivan's desk was deserted, but a young woman was parked outside his own office, clutching an envelope of material to her generous chest. She wore a hideous black and white checked pant suit and clunky black shoes and made no attempt to tame her frizzy red hair, but nevertheless, she managed to look cute. She looked about fourteen years old, although Green knew from her file that she was twice that.

Her baby blue eyes lit at the sight of him, and she stuck out an exuberant hand. "Inspector Green! Detective Sue Peters, remember?"

He took her hand in his, felt the smooth, firm pressure of her fingers. It lingered a little long, he thought, making a silent note to beware. He opened his door and nodded to her package. "You have something for me?"

"Yessir. The Sarge—Sullivan, I mean—told me to bring you this stuff. Thought you might like to see it." She followed him inside, making no effort to detach the envelope from her breasts.

"And where is Sergeant Sullivan?"

"Got a call, went out to Ashford Landing." Without an invitation, she kicked the guest chair out and plunked herself down in it.

Green surveyed the mountain of paperwork on his desk and the blinking message light on his phone. "What's the material about?"

"Stuff from Ident, mostly pictures from the Ashford Landing scene. The Sarge said there wasn't much new, but you'd want to look at it all anyway." Still she clutched the material as if it were the Crown jewels.

He nodded to his desk brusquely. "Thank you. Just leave it there, I'll look at it in a minute. Did the sergeant assign you anything else to do?"

Her lips curved up in a grin. "I'm working with Gibbsie, t rying to find those three brothers. Quite the nice little riddle, eh, sir? Which one's the guy who took the swan dive off the tower?"

Green glanced through his open door into the squad room to see Gibbs hunched over his computer, tapping furiously. "That's the basis of a lot of detective work, Peters. The sooner we know who the man is, the sooner we can begin tracing his movements and figuring out how he died. You'd better go help, Detective."

It took her a couple of seconds to get the hint, but finally she parted with her prize, dropped it on his desk and headed over to Gibbs. Green uttered a short, silent apology to the faithful, hard-working detective, waited until Peters was well out of sight, then snatched up the envelope.

Fi ve minutes later, he tossed the reports aside with frustration. Sullivan was right; not much there. Yet even the lack of evidence was telling. Not the slightest trace of blood had been detected on the top of the tower, which made it unlikely that any of the victim's abrasions had been sustained in a struggle up there. The contour and markings on the fatal head wound matched those of the rock beneath his head, confirming MacPhail's theory that the fall itself was the cause of death. The small piece of fabric that had snagged on the parapet had been sent to the RCMP lab for formal analysis, along with the jacket from which it had presumably ripped, but Cunningham had found the torn section at the back of the hem where it seemed to fit.

Green fed the CD of crime scene photos into his computer and watched as his screen filled with meticulously ordered shots—overviews, middle views and close-ups of every single item of evidence found at the scene. Green studied the views of the body, trying to picture it in the physical surroundings of the church. The man lay on his stomach with his legs splayed and his head facing the tower. His head was twisted to one side, almost touching the stone base. Ident had done a very thorough physical search of the vicinity and had photographed a dozen cigarette butts, a decaying tennis ball, a few old candy wrappers and an ice cream cup. Everything looked at least a month old.

The next series of photos was a scrupulous record of the church tower, from each latent fingerprint on the ladder to the colourful collection of bird droppings on the parapet. The fabric from the jacket had been found on the top of the wall directly above the body. Green studied the photo carefully. The fabric had snagged on the inner corner of the wall where it had crumbled, leading Cunningham to speculate that in the act of hoisting himself up over the wall, the victim had pressed against the wall, dislodging some old mortar and tearing his jacket. Cunningham was still trying to match all the latents lifted from the ladder, but he was leaning towards suicide.

Green leaned back in his chair and shut his eyes, trying to visualize the victim's last movements, but the photos weren't enough. The suicide theory didn't feel right yet. Once Ident had finished there, he needed to go to the scene, to walk through the steps the man had taken, in order to see the things he'd seen and imagine the thoughts he had. Maybe then Green would understand whether the man had jumped of his own accord.

Meanwhile, it was a waiting game while the detectives gathered facts, and reluctantly Green turned his attention to his mountain of paperwork. He was at it for less than an hour and had made his way through only a fraction when Bob Gibbs knocked diffidently on his door.

"Sorry, sir. Ah... Angela Hogencamp, the woman from the St. Lawrence group home, is on the line. Lawrence Pettigrew has disappeared. Are we going to send someone down to interview them?"

"Put her through." Green shoved his paperwork aside with relief and snatched up his phone the moment it rang. The woman at the other end sounded as if she smoked two packs a day and had seen every depravity known to man. After preliminary introductions, Green asked her what she meant by "disappeared".

"Six weeks ago. He didn't show up for his meds and routine blood work."

"Six weeks ago! Why was no one alerted?"

There was a chilly pause. "Who should we have alerted, sir?"

"The police."

"Lawrence wasn't in custody. He's a voluntary patient living on his own, and he's free to stop treatment any time he chooses. What's the Ottawa police's involvement, sir?"

Green rethought his approach, for he wanted cooperation from this woman, and right now she was in classic "cover-your-ass" mode. "I apologize, Mrs. Hogencamp. I didn't mean to imply you were derelict in your duties. We've had an unusual sighting of a man who bears some resemblance to him. I know Lawrence was in hospital for close to twenty years, and I'm concerned he might not have the street smarts to survive on his own."

"As are we, I assure you," she replied in a tone only slightly thawed. "We have been searching all over for him, and the Brockville police have in fact been notified. But he's not top priority for them, being but one of many chronic psychiatric cases they've had to contend with over the years. He's not a danger to anyone but himself."

Green's ears perked up. "Are you saying he's suicidal?"

"I didn't mean to imply that. Merely that, as you said, he's rather childlike. He's been in hospital since 1984. After twenty years of illness and institutional life, as well as years of electroshocks and strong anti-psychotic medication, I'm afraid there aren't too many brain cells left."

She tossed the observation off with a casual resignation that matched her smoke-weary voice. From Sharon, Green knew that psychiatric staff, like police officers, saw the grim underbelly of life every day, and that the woman's sensitivity had probably been a casualty of her years spent battling the pain and wasted lives of mental illness. "Would he be delusional? Hallucinating?"

"Not right away. He still would have had a supply of pills for a while, but then he would have gradually become less coherent."

"Did you notify his family?"

The woman snorted, triggering a prolonged coughing fit, which left her hoarse and gasping. "We tried the number on file, but it had been disconnected. Not that it would have mattered much. His family hasn't visited him in years."

"Did anyone else visit him?"

"Former patients, occasionally. But we've checked, and none of them has seen him."

72

"Might he have tried to go home?

She paused. "This was his home."

"Would he know how to get to the farm where he grew up? Did he ever talk about it?"

"Not once." She hesitated, and her voice softened. "I shouldn't really be telling you this, but when the ward was closing, the team looked at moving him back home, or at least to a group home nearer home. He regressed badly at the suggestion, and his father wanted nothing to do with it. Refused to even come meet our team. Lawrence knew his family had rejected him. I can't imagine he'd want to go back there ever again."

Green had encountered many mentally ill people over the years, and he knew how crucial family support was to their recovery. He was beginning to feel very sorry for this poor, misunderstood, stigmatized young man. Shunned first by the village, and then by his own family.

"Any idea why they rejected him?"

"Why do families reject the mentally ill? Afraid of them, ashamed of them? Tired of dealing with them, want to be able to take that trip to Florida? You'd be surprised what a dumping ground the hospital is, Inspector."

Cynicism aside, she had a point. He asked a few more questions about Lawrence's personal effects and finances, both of which were virtually non-existent, then told her he'd be asking the Brockville police to show her a photo and some clothing to see whether they might belong to Lawrence. She had thawed considerably by then, and she heaved a deep, regretful sigh. "If it is him who died, I wouldn't be surprised. Not that he wanted to die...but he didn't really have anything compelling to live for. Wasn't actually living much at all."

Once he'd hung up, Green sat at his desk a moment, recalling the chronic schizophrenics he'd met in his career.

Mostly street people, adrift from the anchor of meds and family support. It's true that by normal standards they hadn't much compelling to live for, but even the street people clung to the lives they had, deriving pleasure and pride from simple moments and never setting their sights or their hopes too high. If Lawrence had killed himself, the questions remained. Why there? Why now?

He opened the door to his office and was pleased to spot Sullivan just emerging from the elevator. He beckoned him inside. Sullivan dropped into the guest chair, stretched his long legs out, unsealed a plastic evidence bag and plunked an object on a piece of white paper on the edge of Green's desk. Bits of dirt fell from what looked like a blackened tin can.

"Okay, I'll bite," Green said, reaching into his desk to slip on nitryl gloves. "What's that?"

"Someone's secret treasure chest. Isabelle Boisvert found it in her yard, right around where our dead guy was digging. Looks like he buried it there."

The can rattled as Green picked it up. "Have you looked inside?"

Sullivan nodded. "Someone had a ve ry weird idea of treasure."

Green pried the lid off and spread the objects carefully on the sheet of paper. For a moment, they both contemplated the collection in silence. The bottle caps could be explained away, as could the feather, the key and the condoms. Children collected the oddest trinkets. But the bird skull gave him pause. A child might have a passing fascination with a dead animal, might even keep a skeleton for a while, but to store it with their treasures suggested a fascination with the macabre that was a little over the top. And where was the rest of the body? The skull was perfectly intact, almost as if the bird had been decapitated with surgical precision.

What sane, normal child decapitates a bird and stores the head in their treasure box?

Only a crazy one. Green unfolded the slips of paper and popped each inside its own evidence bag. One was a smudged fragment of paper torn from a notebook "S Bus 4:30, meet me 3:00 our place". The other was a page from a love letter written to a girl named Sophia, asking for her forgiveness and begging for another chance. The two were in different hands—the former a tight, sophisticated script and the latter a ragged scrawl.

Sullivan had been silent during Green's perusal of the contents, and as he returned the objects to the can, he was aware of Sullivan's questioning gaze. "This is Lawrence Pettigrew's stuff," Green said by way of answer. "Apparently he used to confiscate his brothers' condoms and try to interfere with their sex lives. I don't know what the rest of this stuff means, but it's beginning to look as if Lawrence might be our John Doe. He's disappeared from Brockville."

"What about Derek's crucifix?"

Green shrugged. "It's possible Lawrence stole it, or expropriated it." He gave Sullivan an update of what the group home supervisor had said. "We'll fax John Doe's photo down to Brockville PD and ask them to run it by the group home staff. If the ID is positive, we'll need to send someone down."

Sullivan nodded. "I'll send Gibbs and Sue Peters. Give her a chance to see how we put together corroborating evidence to make an ID."

"Her and Gibbs in the car together for two hours?" Green winced. "Cruel and unusual punishment for our Gibbsie. I think you should go with her."

Sullivan frowned at him. "I've got a bunch of other cases on my plate."

"But I think Sue Peters can learn a lot from you. And she

needs all the help she can get." And with her on the case, CID needs all the help it can get as well, he added to himself.

"She's got to learn some time, and this is a case she can't really screw up," Sullivan said.

"Still, it is your case."

Sullivan raised his eyebrows. "Oh, is it now?"

"Yeah, and you can use your Irish charm on this Mrs. Hogencamp. She's a little skittish, and we need her nice and chatty. Peters would shut her up tighter than a clam."

Sullivan shrugged and hauled his large feet off Green's desk. "First, I'll fax the photo down to Brockville and make sure our dead guy is Lawrence. Then I'll go tell my staff sergeant that the inspector might be ordering me into the boonies for the day just to ID a suicide. Make him feel important." He restored the tin can to the evidence bag and carefully resealed it. "If I take Peters instead of Gibbs, he'll think he's done something wrong, you know."

"I've got other plans for Gibbs."

*　　*　　*

Green had hoped to get to Gibbs before the office grapevine did, but by the time he had a free moment, it was too late. He found the young detective hard at work at his computer, but his avoidance of Green's eyes betrayed his hurt. Green was reminded once more of what a good cop Sullivan was; he knew his men, and despite his bear-like physique and his country boy manner, sensitivity was his greatest strength. Green did not have Sullivan's tact, nor his ease with emotion. He simply pulled a chair up to Gibbs's desk and leaned over.

"So? Any luck?"

Gibbs stared at his screen without answering for a moment,

then seemed to draw himself together. He straightened his long, gangly form and picked up his notes.

"What do you want first, sir? The success or the failure?"

"The failure. Then we've nowhere to go but up."

Gibbs didn't smile. "Derek Pettigrew's whereabouts are a complete mystery. Not only can I find no one who's seen him in the past few days, but no one's seen him, period. It's like this guy dropped out of sight twenty years ago. There's no record of anyone with that name and birth date being registered at Berkeley or any other California university."

"He could have gone to some other state or moved anywhere in North America."

Gibbs cast him a brief, triumphant glance. "But no one with that name and birth date has ever filed a tax return or applied for a passport in either the U.S. or Canada."

Green tried to make sense of this latest surprise. Plenty of people dropped out for lots of reasons, most of them nefarious. Criminals eluding the authorities, people escaping an unpleasant past or unsavoury associates, occasionally children or spouses hiding from their families. Certainly the Pettigrew family had been far from exemplary, and Derek had broadcast that he was never coming home again, but nothing the investigation had uncovered so far suggested he'd go into hiding to avoid them.

"Do we have any record of this guy in our system? Some young offender stuff from long ago—suspicious contacts, anything that suggests he may have gotten in over his head with some bad guys? Can you check with the OPP and the RCMP?"

Again that faint look of triumph. "I've checked that, sir. So far, nothing. He was an excellent student all through school and university, although he changed his major from physics to philosophy in his third year."

Green contemplated that information curiously. Changing

from a hard science to the intangible study of truth suggested that Derek had undergone at least a mild identity crisis in his penultimate year, which had forced him to rethink his goals and aspirations. But such soul-searching was common—indeed, almost a rite of passage—for a serious student. Remembering Derek's quiet, thoughtful grad photo, Green could see such a youth being drawn to the fundamental truth-seeking of philosophy.

Changing one's intellectual identity, however, was hardly the same as changing one's physical one. In any case, he would have had to register at Berkeley as Derek Pettigrew if he'd hoped to get in.

"Bob, can you get Berkeley to check their admissions for 1984? See if in fact Derek Pettigrew applied and was expected to attend?"

Gibbs reddened as an irrepressible smile crept across his face. His Adam's apple bobbed. "I've put that request to them already, sir, but it will take a while."

"Good work. And I wouldn't classify this as a failure. We've learned some very peculiar things about Derek Pettigrew. Keep it up. Now—the good news?"

"Tom Pettigrew. He's been much more visible. Toronto Police have a long sheet on him, mostly summary offences like theft under and causing disturbances. He's also had a few businesses go belly-up, and he's reneged on payments to creditors. Toronto faxed me this."

He unfolded a long print-out and Green scanned down the list of Tom's contacts with the Toronto police. They showed the sorry state of Tom's life. Police contacts had been few in the first ten years, but over time he had become involved more frequently in brawls, public intoxication, loitering and disturbing the peace. He'd been in and out of the Don Jail five times in the past year alone, but only one stint had been substantial; thirty days for his fourth conviction for theft under. Shoplifting from a liquor store on Jarvis Street.

Scanning to the bottom of the list, Green saw that his most recent incarceration had been only a month ago, for causing a disturbance. He'd been released the next morning. As if reading his mind, Gibbs pointed to the entry.

"I'm trying to contact the officer who handled the case, sir, to see if he knows where Tom is living. He's listed as no fixed address, but he probably has his unofficial place. The officer will call me when he gets on duty this evening."

Gibbs had thawed considerably as he related the fruits of his labour, and now Green smiled at him. "If and when the Toronto police find him, I want them to pick him up, and I want you to go down there to interview him."

"By myself, sir?"

Seeing a mixture of pleasure and apprehension on Gibbs' face, Green shook his head. "If Toronto finds Tom before Brian heads back from Brockville tomorrow, I'll send Brian on to meet you in Toronto. Always better to have two officers in on an interview."

Gibbs smiled like a puppy who'd been tossed a treat. Sometimes I handle things not too badly, Green thought, but we really must do something to toughen this boy up.

*   *   *

With both Gibbs and Sullivan dispatched, Green tried to settle back down to his paperwork, but the excitement of matching overtime requests with policy directives paled in comparison to the lure of missing Pettigrews. His thoughts returned to the strange tin can Isabelle Boisvert had unearthed in the thicket in her yard. Green recalled that the ground had been all dug up in patches over the interior of the thicket where the dead man had been seen, suggesting that he was searching for something. The tin can was caked with dirt and firmly rusted shut, as if it had been buried long ago.

Assuming it was poor crazy Lawrence who had hidden the tin before he was sent to the psychiatric hospital, and assuming none of the other family members had known of its existence, it was almost certainly Lawrence who had been snooping in the yard and Lawrence who lay dead at the bottom of the church tower. The supervisor in Brockville had said he'd been missing for six weeks, and MacPhail had indicated that until recently the man had been well cared for. Which Lawrence certainly would have been, courtesy of Ontario's health care system.

Had Lawrence left Brockville and made his way by bus, thumb or foot all the way back to his childhood home? If so, why? What in that strange tin can collection had he been desperate to retrieve after all these years? Why had he fled to his old church? And most importantly, had he in his despair been driven to jump, or had someone pushed him?

Green pondered the contents of the tin can. A feather, a half dozen caps, some condoms, an antique key, a note, and a fragment of a love letter to a girl called Sophia. The handwriting of the letter had an uneven, childish quality, with spelling mistakes galore. Perhaps Lawrence had written the letter when he was a young, bumbling teenager hopelessly in love with Sophia. And perhaps he had kept that love alive through twenty years, dreaming of the day he returned to find her waiting for him.

Except she wouldn't have been waiting, of course. While he languished in a psychiatric hospital, suspended forever in adolescent yearning, she had probably married, borne children, and become deeply immersed in a rich, demanding family life.

Green's instincts quickened. It was a long shot, perhaps, but it made sense. What else but a woman could draw a man back to his despised and long-abandoned roots, and what else but a woman could plunge him into suicidal despair?

He glanced at his watch, which registered nearly one o'clock. A lunch break was in order, combined with an impromptu visit to the troops still conducting interviews in Ashford Landing. And perhaps a short side trip of his own to find out the identity of Sophia.

Seven

Sandy Fitzpatrick was a man whose eve ry emotion showed on his face, an unfortunate trait for someone engaged in sales but a windfall for Green. Even before Sandy skidded his pick-up to a complete stop in the gravel outside the Boisve rt house, his bewilderment and alarm were etched on his ruddy face.

Green had phoned him en route to ask him to meet him at the farm and had himself arrived only five minutes earlier. Isabelle had been showing him where she'd found the tin, and they were both knee-deep in the tangle of brush and dying raspberry canes when Sandy arrived. He vaulted down from his truck, dressed in a hunting vest, big rubber boots and thick work gloves. As he clumped over towards them, he replaced his alarm with his familiar hearty grin.

"Is there a problem, Isabelle? I hope you're not doing all this work yourself!"

Before she could answer, Green extended his hand amiably. "Sandy, thank you for coming. You used to visit here as a child, so your recollections might be ve ry useful to our investigation. Do you recall what if anything was located here?"

Sandy's brows shot up. "Here in this brush? Why?"

"Mrs. Boisvert found some remnants of burned planking which suggests it may have been a firepit."

"It was a shed. Built as a carriage house originally, but it burned down years ago."

"What was the shed used for?"

Sandy shrugged. "Nothing much. Balers and plows and that, back when the farm was more productive. But for years before it burned down, it was pretty much..." He looked at Isabelle sympathetically. "I know it's an eyesore. If you like, I can get a construction buddy of mine—"

"What was it used for twenty years ago?"

Sandy coloured as if embarrassed. "Well, when we were kids, we all used to play in it, pretend it was a fort or a secret hide-out. It was mostly filled with hay, and there was a beautiful antique horse carriage. The leather was all cracked, but with the right care... Anyway, we used to bring old blankets inside and have sleep-overs."

"We?"

"Lawrence and me. Lawrence loved that shed, and when he got sicker, he hung out there more and more, although the other boys liked it too. To get away from their parents."

"When did it burn down?"

Sandy scratched his nose with his massive glove. "So long ago I can't remember."

"Before or after Lawrence was sent away?"

Sandy stared off towards the river as if the answer could be found in the ribbon of gold and red along the edge. He looked uncomfortable at being forced to dredge up old times. "About the same time," he said finally. "I'm not sure exactly, because I'd stopped coming here."

"Why?"

"Well...my mother was the protective type, and she got it in her head that Lawrence was dangerous." With that admission came some anger. "But now that I'm thinking about it, that shed burned down right about the time Lawrence was taken away, because I remember seeing the smoke. It was early May, and the leaves were just budding on the trees, so you could see a lot easier across the fields. The shed was old, and the hay inside was dry as a bone, so the place went up like a bonfire."

Green pondered the implications. He sensed that something bad had happened that spring of 1984, something that had so upset the family that they had committed their child to a mental hospital and severed all contact with him. Something that had so frightened Lawrence that he panicked at the mere mention of returning home.

Had the shed burned down accidentally, or had Lawrence set it on fire? "Did Lawrence or any of the other boys play with fire in there?"

"Not Lawrence. But Tom smoked in there. Their mother was very strict, and she wouldn't have any smoking or drinking in the house—"

"I thought the father was a heavy drinker."

"That was later. In those days, he was a real holy roller. He used to—" Sandy paused as if weighing the wisdom of revealing such private details, then once again anger seemed to urge him on. "He used to keep all the boys in line with a strap. Most of them toed the line, but Tom fought him every inch of the way. He'd sneak out to the shed to smoke, did marijuana there too, with his gang of loser buddies and all the girls he could get his hands on. The horse carriage came in mighty handy."

Green went to his car to retrieve the tin can. Before he could even open the evidence bag, Sandy's eyes widened in astonishment.

"Lawrence's magic box!"

Green spread the items out on the hood of his car. Each of them had been bagged individually now to prevent contamination, but the contents were still clear. He picked up

84

the bird skull and asked if Lawrence ever killed small animals.

"Oh, no, Lawrence loved birds! He loved to watch them fly overhead. He thought they were angels from God. When he was little, Lawrence thought God sat on those fluffy clouds up there next to Jack in the Beanstalk." Sandy smiled wistfully at the memory, then picked up the bag with the feather. "He collected bird feathers because he thought they could ward off Satan, and when he got sicker..." His smile faded and his eyes grew sad as he fingered the bottle caps. "He developed strange rituals to drive away Satan."

Green's instincts began to tingle. "What sort of rituals?"

The sharpness of his tone must have betrayed him, for Sandy drew back, furrowing his brow. "He wasn't a violent person, wouldn't in a million years hurt anyone. He'd only cut himself. He thought the feather could purify him and keep evil away. It sounds...creepy, I know, but it was only a tiny bit of blood."

Creepy doesn't begin to describe it, thought Green, but he kept his expression neutral. Close scrutiny revealed a few flakes of rusty residue on the feather, similar in colour to the smudge on the torn note. Green had assumed the note was simply dirty, but now he grabbed his magnifying glass for a closer look. This time he detected the fine circular traces of a fingerprint in the smudge. Finally, something Ident could sink its teeth into! He looked back at Sandy, pondering the significance of a fingerprint etched in blood on a torn fragment of a note. The first question was—whose blood?

He slid the note out of view casually. "Did he ever try to purify anyone else? His brothers, for example?"

"I remember he drove his brothers crazy. He prayed over them, confiscated their things. He stole cigarettes and porn magazines the boys had hidden in their rooms. He spied on their girlfriends."

All of which could create a powder keg in the household, Green reflected. "Did he himself have a girlfriend?"

Sandy's eyebrows shot up and a smile broke his taut features. "Good Lord, no. Lawrence would never know how to handle a real live girl."

"Could there have been a girl he loved from afar? Or imagined he had a relationship with?"

"It's possible, I suppose. But why...?" Sandy's voice trailed off as his gaze travelled from the tin can to the tangled brush. "The body is Lawrence, isn't it?"

"Possibly." Green picked up the evidence bag containing the love letter. "Do you remember a girl named Sophia?"

Sandy looked sad as he studied the letter. "There was a girl in our grade, who lived in Richmond. Pretty girl with long black hair."

"Last name?"

He shrugged. He'd been scrutinizing the letter, turning it over. "I seem to remember she was Tom's girl, though. I don't think Lawrence wrote this."

Green handed him the scrap of paper with the fingerprint. "This is another handwriting, maybe to the same girl. Could that be from Lawrence?"

Sandy stared at the simple note. "Holy crap," he whispered.

Green waited, but Sandy didn't elaborate. Simply shook his head as he handed the note back. "What?" Green prompted, wondering if he'd recognized the smudge for what it was.

"I...these shreds of the past, they seem to speak volumes."

"What volumes?"

Sandy shrugged and pulled his gloves back on his hands vigorously. "I was just a kid, but it makes you wonder what all was going on. All those horny boys, pretty girls, secret liaisons, the father going on about sin—"

"And Lawrence wandering around in the middle of it, crazy as a loon," Green finished grimly. More than ever, he was convinced that Lawrence's return, and his death, were linked to events long ago. "Where might I find this Sophia?"

"I haven't seen her in years. Not since high school."

Green scooped up the evidence bags and returned them to the car. "Then let's check your high school year book. That will give us a name."

When they arrived at Sandy's house, they discovered the real estate office open and Edna McMartin firmly ensconced behind the desk. She was holding forth on the phone, arguing with someone about pies for the church bake sale. Sandy had to wait while she cast her vote for pumpkin, then she signed off and turned to her son with a smile. Which, Green noted, he didn't return.

"Church business again, Mom? On my business phone?"

Her jaw thrust out. "Sandy, you won't make any money if you never have anyone in the office to answer inquiries. I've taken three calls already this afternoon."

"That's what the answering machine is for, Mom."

"People don't like talking to machines," she countered. "I made one appointment for you, which I'll take if you don't have time." She fixed her gaze on Green pointedly, and her smile vanished. "Buying a country house, Detective?"

Sandy glanced at Green. "Perhaps we should do this upstairs."

Edna was instantly alert, her shrewd eyes narrowing. Ready to protect yet another of her babies from my intrusion, Green thought, even if this baby was nudging forty and clearly unappreciative of her efforts. Yet the friction might be interesting, and many a secret inadvertently slipped out in the heat of a family dispute. Besides, no one in the village was likely to know more about the Pettigrew secrets than their long-time neighbours.

Green dropped into the client's chair and looked up at Sandy casually. "Why don't you bring all your yearbooks down here, and I'll keep your mother out of trouble."

Sandy opened his mouth to protest but thought better of it. Flushing, he turned around and clumped upstairs.

"Yearbooks?" Edna's lips pursed warily.

"We're trying to gather some background on Lawrence Pettigrew." He smiled amiably. "I understand Sandy was a good friend of Lawrence growing up, but at some point you forbade your son to go over there anymore. Why?"

Her eyes grew shuttered, and she folded her arms over her chest. Green held up a soothing hand. "Not being critical, just wondering."

"Because the boy was a dangerous lunatic."

She was still bristling, so Green cast about for a means to soften her. "I know he was schizophrenic, and I'm not questioning the family's decision. I'm sure his illness was very hard on them. But I'm wondering if you know what happened. Perhaps Lawrence's mother confided in you?"

"What does all this matter now? Lawrence is dead. That's what you're saying, isn't it? He's thrown himself off that old church tower, and as far as I'm concerned, good riddance."

Green kept his expression friendly with an effort. "Why did you forbid your son to go over there?"

She pressed her lips together stubbornly, but he waited her out with his notebook poised and his gaze steady. Finally she seemed to relent. "Even Katherine was afraid of him. And afraid for Robbie, who was only a young lad. She told me one day Lawrence threw out all the knives in the house because knives were evil. Another time he cut up Derek's sheets because, well, frankly, they were dirtied. But the final straw was Tom's centrefolds. Tom had them taped on his wall, and

Lawrence slashed all the girls' bodies with a razor. Would you want your small child growing up with that?"

Dismayed, Green stopped writing. The deeper he dug in this family, the more sinister the picture became. Edna was watching him as if daring him to come to the madman's defence.

"No, I wouldn't," he replied truthfully. "Do you recall the circumstances surrounding the fire that destroyed the shed?"

She had just begun to relax, but now she stiffened in surprise. "What the dickens has the shed got to do with anything?"

Green explained about Lawrence's recent visit to the place where the shed had been.

"They burned it down," she said. "That shed was Lawrence's special hideout. And after they shipped him off, they got rid of all his things. Clothes, books, belongings. Burned every last one of them, like they were contaminated by the devil."

There was a thumping on the stairs, and Sandy burst back into the room with a slim volume open in his hands. "I found her. Sophia Vincelli." He handed Green the book and jabbed his finger at the photo of a beautiful, porcelain-fine girl with long black hair falling in a sheet below her shoulders. The same girl who had been clinging to Tom in the photo Robbie Pettigrew had shown them.

"Tom's girl," Edna said without hesitation.

"One of Tom's girls," Sandy amended. "Come on, Mom, they usually only lasted a week."

"Oh, but she was a beautiful girl. I remember her from that school play in your Grade Eleven year. She played Ophelia. I'm surprised you don't remember her, dear. All you boys were cross-eyed over her."

Sandy rolled his eyes so quickly that Edna didn't notice, but Green smiled to himself, suspecting Edna rarely missed the chance to remind her son of all the ones who got away.

Sandy parried the thrust with practised ease. "For all the good it ever did any of us," he replied. "If she was dating Tom Pettigrew, she was way out of our league. He'd already dropped out of school by then and was working. Tom always picked off the best ones, only to break their hearts and dump them when the next one came along."

His mother leaned over to peer at the yearbook. After a moment, she tapped the picture thoughtfully. "I know Tom was a ladies' man, but I seem to remember this one was different. Katherine Pettigrew told me it ended badly for Tom. The girl simply vanished one day, probably ran off with someone else. Broke Tom's heart. That's why he left town. Of course, she was Italian."

She made the pronouncement as if it explained everything, but Green's thoughts were already running ahead. To another person who had also inexplicably vanished, to the bloody note in the elegant hand "S. Bus 4:30, meet me 3:00 our place". To a crucifix that had ended up in Lawrence's hands twenty years later.

He had an idea how they might all fit together, but only a vague, uneasy idea what they might mean. First, he had to see the crime scene for himself, to try to put himself in Lawrence's mind. Then he needed a long talk with the most sensible, psychologically insightful person he'd ever known.

* * *

The sun had almost dipped to the horizon, casting a searing orange glare over the barren field. The autumn chill was already stealing in, and Isabelle's breath formed frosty swirls as she bent over the ground. She swore at the gathering darkness, which would cut short her efforts long before she felt she'd done justice to the task. Rationally, she knew the pond could wait, but her frustration needed an outlet, and shovelling was as good as any.

After Green had left that afternoon, she and Jacques had had a pitched battle over what to do with the tangled eyesore at the edge of the yard. He'd been spooked by the story of decapitated birds and bizarre blood rituals and had wanted to raze the site at once and pour a slab of concrete over the whole mess. She was not inclined to disagree, but in his vision of their future home, he saw a double car garage on that spot, whereas she did not want to look out the window at the backside of a garage and favoured instead a lush garden complete with pond, water lilies and exotic fish.

But before she knew it, Jacques had Sandy Fitzpatrick's buddy on the phone and was arranging for the foundation to be poured next week. "Fine," he had snarled when she protested, "if you want your damn pond, you have one week to dig it yourself, but if that mess is still there next week, the garage goes up." Isabelle had been so fired up with adrenaline and fury that she had snatched up the shovel and crowbar and marched straight out to the yard.

By the time the sun finally slid out of sight, she had accumulated a vast pile of raspberry canes and charred timbers and was plunging her shovel deep into the sandy soil. Time and time again, her shovel thudded against rock or hit a wayward root from a distant tree, so she thought little of it when it struck something hard once more. She shifted her position a few inches and tried again. This time the shovel sank deep but became stuck underneath something. Swearing, panting and drenched in perspiration despite the cold, she wrenched the object free.

It was a long shaft with bulbous ends, brown and pitted beneath the dirt. She turned it over, straining to see it in the failing light. A bone. She shivered a little as the sweat ran cold down her back. Probably a cow or moose long buried in the dirt, she told herself as she tossed it onto her pile and retrieved her shovel. She probed more carefully this time, almost reluctantly, and was rewarded with nothing but dirt and sand. She was just beginning to return to her former vigour when her shovel clanged against something hard again. She probed the length of it, dug and pried as she explored an unmoveable object only three inches wide but over three feet long. Far too long to be a bone. Cautiously, she knelt by the hole and explored by touch. Felt the cold, hard surface of metal. Relieved, she began to tug and twist. Finally, she had freed it enough to reach down and pull it out. The long shaft broke in her hands, rotten from years underground, but the end, heavy and covered with rust, had retained enough of its shape to be recognizable.

It was a huge axe, pointed at one end and brutally blunt at the other. A peculiar fear crawled over her. Glancing up sharply, she saw how dark the night had become. How full of shadows. She swallowed and tossed the axe aside with disgust. Not one goddamn axe anywhere on the farm, not even a hatchet in the tool shed, and here's this thing, cast aside and forgotten as if it were of no use whatsoever.

What other buried treasure am I going to find in this dilapidated, mistreated heap of junk we bought?

She told herself it was too dark to see any more, so she wiped off her tools, returned them to the shed and headed towards the house, steeling herself for Jacques' mood. Instead, the scent of cinnamon and apples hung in the chilly air, and when she walked in, Jacques greeted her with a cup of hot cider, a strong, warm embrace, and a kiss that reminded her why she'd married him in the first place. And chased away the taste of fear from her throat.

Eight

The Mobile Command Post was gone, but a squad car was still parked on the square outside Ashford Methodist Church. The patrol officer guarding the scene was nowhere in sight, however, and the heavy oak door to the church was still padlocked shut. Carrying the evidence bags containing the contents of Lawrence's tin can, Green ducked under the yellow police tape and mounted the stone steps to the door. Brown leaves had accumulated along the base of the door, and an intricate network of spider webs clung to the corners. No one had opened this door in a long time.

As a precaution, he slipped on nitryl gloves before stooping to examine the lock with his magnifying glass. Rust had caked around the hole, suggesting no one had tried to insert a key in quite some months. But the size of the hole looked about right. He took the brass key from its evidence bag and inserted it into the keyhole. It was stiff and balky, but with some gentle coaxing, he was able to work it in all the way. He was about to turn it when he heard a shout.

"Hey! What the hell do you think you're doing?"

He spun around and spotted a uniformed constable striding around the corner of the bell tower, bunching a stream of discarded yellow tape in his hands and scowling at Green from beneath thick black brows. A cop's scowl, honed to intimidate and control. When Green identified himself with his badge, the scowl rapidly gave way to alarm.

"Sorry, sir. I thought everyone was finished here."

"Where the hell were you?" Green countered. "This scene is supposed to be secure."

"Ident released it this afternoon, sir. I was just clearing things up." The young man's forehead puckered. "Is that a problem, sir?"

Green shook his head. Cunningham was as obsessive and meticulous a forensics specialist as Green had ever encountered. He and his partner had had two days to process the scene and if Cunningham said they were done, they were done. Besides, that meant Green could finally prowl around all he wanted.

Green hastened to reassure the officer before dispatching him to continue his clean-up. Once the officer had disappeared back around the bell tower, Green returned his attention to the key in the padlock. The mechanism was badly rusted, and for a few moments the key wouldn't budge, but finally, with one strong twist, the lock clicked open. As Green unhooked the padlock and slowly pulled open the door, a wave of cold, musty air rushed over him.

He stepped through into the interior, rendered dank and gloomy by the boarded windows. Slivers of sunlight pierced through the cracks and cut shafts through the dusty air. There was a small ante-chamber with a table and a door off to the right, presumably to the bell tower. Beyond the ante-chamber, the church opened into a rectangular sanctuary with a vaulted ceiling crisscrossed by thick, black beams. Green's footsteps echoed on the stone floor as he walked the length of the interior. It had been stripped bare of furnishings except for a black wood stove sitting in the corner with an empty wood box beside it and a rusty axe propped against the wall. Over the altar hung a plain wooden cross. Green stood a moment before the altar, trying to picture the room full of pews and people, with the mischievous Reverend Taylor ministering to his flock and the Pettigrew family swaying happily to the hymns.

Green turned slowly in place. Lawrence had the key to this church in his treasure chest. Stolen, or freely lent? Reverend Taylor had a soft spot for society's lost souls. Perhaps it was the key Lawrence was searching for in the Boisvert yard that morning. But since he'd been scared away before finding it, then how had he gained access to the church?

The lure of the unanswered questions—the how and why— drew Green like a magnet. He walked back through the sanctuary towards the bell tower, trying to gather the few fragments he'd learned about Lawrence into some form of understanding. He needed to get inside the man's head, to see those last few moments of his life as Lawrence had seen them. But as Green entered the tower, he sucked in his breath with dismay. Dim daylight slipped in through the arched openings where the cast-iron bell hung, but otherwise the tower was dark. Fastened to the interior stone wall was a metal ladder which reached up past the massive bell to a trap door above. The climb was probably thirty feet; to Green it looked like a hundred.

Just contemplating it made him dizzy. He'd hated heights ever since his childhood, when his friends had made a game of chasing each other up the rickety fire escapes and over the tenement rooftops of Lowertown. He'd slipped, breaking his collarbone and subjecting himself to weeks of painful immobility. Now his palms turned slick and his legs jellied as he gripped the bars. The silence was broken only by the cooing of pigeons up above and the pulse of his own heartbeat in his ears. He was so alone. Surely, it was unwise to make the climb with no one there to get help should he fall, or should the ladder break away from its rusty anchors and crash to the ground.

He shook the bars to test the ladder's stability. Flakes of debris floated down, but the ladder was rock solid. "Coward," he muttered aloud, and the curse echoed around him. If the Ident team could go up and down the ladder half a dozen times, then so could he.

Gingerly, he planted his foot on the bottom rung and began his ascent. He kept his body pressed to the wall and his eyes fixed on the stones in front of him, forcing his feet to follow one step after another. Soon he was level with the old bell, which hung motionless in the fading light. Lawrence might have found this seclusion comforting, but when the bell rang it would have been deafening inside this small space.

Green raised his eyes to the trap door and felt his stomach churn. He would have to hold on with one hand and pry open the door with the other. Fear hammered in his ears as he forced himself upwards. The platform above was wooden but supported on all sides by a small stone ledge. Glued to the wall, he groped overhead to feel the contours of the door, found the hinge, the opposite edge, the slight gap where the door abutted the floor. He pushed. Nothing. The goddamn door weighed a ton. He gritted his teeth, leaned into it and pushed again. It lifted six inches before slamming back down with such force it nearly knocked him off the ladder. He clutched the bars, gasping for breath. What the fuck am I doing, he thought. I'm not some muscle-bound farmer used to tossing bales of hay into the barn. I'm a pencil pusher, for God's sake. Much as I hate it, much as I mock it, I spend most of my days on the phone or on my ass in a committee room chair. Even when I was a kid, my idea of serious exercise was jumping my bike over the potholes on Nelson Avenue.

But I'm here. I've come this far and going down will be even worse than going up. If I go up one more step so I can get my shoulders and back behind the push, maybe I can work a miracle.

He pushed, grunted, pried and slowly forced the door up far enough to wedge it open with the stick that had obviously been left inside for that purpose. Not daring to look down, he crawled through the opening and rolled over onto the roof.

Late afternoon sun nearly blinded him. He lay on his back, blinking at the blue sky and thanking God for the feel of solid wood beneath him. On all sides, the stone parapet was covered with lichen and stained with a century of bird droppings. He stood up in disgust, wiping the stains off his jacket as he surveyed the scene.

The stone wall rose to about hip level, affording a sense of both security and privacy. Down below him on one side lay the village square, the cars catching the sunlight as they cruised down the main road. On the other side stretched a view of golden trees and vast fields bisected by the river. In the distance, if he looked hard, he could just make out the reddish smudge of the Boisvert's old farmhouse. A person could stand here virtually unseen, divorced from the world below and yet witness to it all. A spymaster's dream.

Here the teenage Lawrence could have sat in isolation, safety and peace. At the top of God's house, in the palm of God's hand. Here, sharing this private spot with his favourite feathered creatures, his angels of God, he could have spied on the world, seen who went where in the village, who came and went through the oak door below.

He would have felt all-knowing, all-powerful. Perhaps even messianic.

Was that what had lured him back all these years later? Not

a girl but a yearning to reconnect with his spiritual past, to capture once more the power and inspiration that this special place had given him in his troubled youth? Perhaps when he first left Brockville six weeks ago, he had simply wanted to come home, but as his medication wore off and his delusions gained hold, had he remembered this sanctuary, where he communed with the angels and talked directly to his God? Perhaps he hadn't been looking for the old love notes at all when Isabelle Boisvert spotted him, but for the antique key that would get him back in here.

A century of ice and rain had gouged deep cracks in the wall. Green examined the spot where the top had crumbled. MacPhail was right; a mere few inches had broken away, hardly enough to cause an accidental fall. Furthermore, anyone trying to force a person over the wall would have a major task lifting them over the lip and preventing them from scratching and kicking everything within sight. Yet there were no signs of a struggle. The lichen was nearly undisturbed, and many loose pieces of stone were still in place.

It looked as if Lawrence's jump had been intentional, and Green felt a wave of sorrow for the man. What had happened? Had God failed to come to him? Had he suddenly realized the futility of it all? Twenty years later, looking not through the rosy lens of an impressionable, delusional teenager but through the dimmed lens of a burned out schizophrenic, had he realized he would never hear God, and that his angels were nothing more than pigeons pecking out a pointless existence on a smelly little roof?

A pigeon swooped in, landed on the wall opposite him and fixed him with beady eyes. Green watched it a moment, wondering if Lawrence had seen it that afternoon, read meaning into its random pecking at the lichen and into its frankly hostile stare. Then the bird shook its wings, gave a soft coo and lifted off again, sailing high above the square.

Green tracked it until it was nothing but a white speck over the distant trees. Such freedom. Had Lawrence watched it fly away, felt the tug of freedom as Green had. What was it the St. Lawrence supervisor had said? That after twenty years in hospital, several hundred electroshocks, and a ton of mind-numbing drugs, Lawrence had very few brain cells left? Had he thought, in his primitive, child-like way, that he could fly free like the birds? Spread his imaginary wings and fly straight up to heaven?

The sun dipped below the horizon, sapping the warmth from the air and bringing Green back to reality with a jolt. He reached out his hand to steady himself. Shook his head incredulously at his own folly. What was it about this place that unleashed such spiritual ravings? He was an investigator, not a psychic trying to communicate with the dead. This was a crime scene, not a seance.

Green leaned over the edge of the wall and peered cautiously down at the spot where Lawrence had fallen. The grass all around had been trampled, and blood still stained the stones. He remembered the photo of the body splayed in the grass, and now, looking down from above, he realized something was odd. Why would the head be facing the tower rather than out? If Lawrence had jumped of his own accord, he should have fallen feet first and pitched forward so that his head was facing out. To have landed face down with his head towards the tower, he would have had to twist in mid flight. Green had never known a jumper to do that.

As he leaned over, the rough surface of the wall scraped his suit. He backed away, brushing mortar dust and lichen from the front of his jacket. At once, another inconsistency struck, him. The back of Lawrence's jacket had snagged on the inner edge of the wall. But if Lawrence had been preparing to jump, he would probably have stood facing outward to clamber up onto the wall, in which case he'd be more likely to snag the front hem of his jacket rather than the back. If he'd then swung himself over the wall and sat on the edge, perhaps gathering the courage to jump, he'd be more likely to catch the back hem on the outer edge of the wall, not the inner.

They were minuscule inconsistencies, certainly not enough to dispute the suicide idea altogether. It was possible the man had hoisted himself backwards over the wall, or that his back hem had draped over the entire top of the wall as he slid off the edge. But there was a much more obvious way the back hem of his jacket could have snagged on the inner edge of the wall. If the man had his back to the wall and had pressed hard against it. Perhaps been pushed with enough force to rip the fabric.

They were very thin threads on which to hang a murder theory. But as long as they were there, he owed it to Lawrence to follow it through. After he returned the tin can to the evidence room, he'd get all the latest intelligence from the troops, and he'd go home to Sharon.

Now more than ever, he needed her sane, experienced understanding of the deranged mind.

*　　*　　*

When Green finally made it back downtown, it was past six. He dropped into the forensics lab in the hope of finding Cunningham still at work over his fingerprint files, but there was no one there. He tagged Lawrence's tin can back into the evidence room and left a requisition for Cunningham to fingerprint every item in it and to send the reddish stain to the RCMP lab for analysis. Any fingerprints and blood were to be matched to the dead man. Another small step towards unravelling the mystery, thought Green as he prepared to go home.

One final minor detour, he promised himself as he made his way up to his office. Just to see what the troops have uncovered. Both Gibbs and Sullivan had gone home, but their email updates were waiting for him, along with Dr. MacPhail's preliminary findings from the post mortem. Gibbs reported, with his usual apologies, that he was still waiting for word on Tom Pettigrew from the Toronto officer who'd released him, and that he had no useful leads on Derek's disappearance. Berkeley, California, had responded snippily that according to its archived records Derek Pettigrew had been accepted but hadn't registered in his program. To date, all other avenues that Gibbs had explored proved to be dead ends.

Physical examination of the victim's body during the post mortem had revealed no signs of bruising suggestive of coercion or struggling, and although a lot of dirt had been extracted from beneath his fingernails, none had been identified as human tissue. It did not appear as if Lawrence had put up any resistance. Based on the condition of the victim's brain on autopsy, MacPhail refined his estimate on the timing of his death. Death had been caused by extensive intra cranial bleeding due to the trauma sustained in the fall, but that amount of bleeding would likely have taken four hours, give or take. Death most likely occurred between six p.m. and midnight, but the fall probably between two and seven p.m.

Still a big window of time, Green thought, but at least a time when people would have been out in the village, walking their dogs, playing ball or attending Sunday services at the other two churches. It was worth another canvass of the village, with a focus on that time span. Sullivan's email expressed the very same thought. Inquiries would resume in the morning.

A later email from Sullivan, logged shortly before five o'clock, reported that the St. Lawrence group home supervisor had been unable to make a positive ID from the dead man's photo. Mrs. Hogencamp thought it could be Lawrence, but she didn't recognize the clothes, and on a matter as crucial as a man's death, she was not willing to commit herself. Green flipped through his notebook for the supervisor's number. As he reached for the phone, he glanced at his watch. Nearly seven o'clock. Sharon would have long since given up waiting for him and would have fed herself and the children dinner, assuming she had a kitchen in which to prepare it. Bob had skipped yesterday, leaving both fridge and stove in the middle of the floor, but had returned with a vengeance this morning, bringing a crew of four and a truck full of cabinets. A promising sign, Green had thought at the time.

His fingers hovered over the phone pad. He ought to call Sharon first to show his support. When you have a toddler entering the terrible twos, a teenager who'd never left them, a massive mutt and a kitchen in non-functional shambles, you do not need a spouse who stays out well past the family witching hour without so much as a call. To drive her point home, Sharon had done it to him a few times. Empathy was not always his strong suit, but he'd got the hint eventually.

Sharon's tone when she answered told him he'd done the wise thing. She sounded perilously close to murdering someone. Bob, perhaps, whose hammering could still be heard in the background.

"Yeah, he's still here," she said. "Or rather he's here again. The hinges he brought this morning were all the wrong size, so he had to go back for new ones." There was a slight pause. "You're not still at the station, are you?"

"Listen," he said hastily. "Why don't you pile everyone in

the car—well, except Bob and Modo—and meet me at Swiss Chalet in half an hour. Sounds like we can't inhabit the kitchen anyway."

"Hannah's not going to like that. Chickens once breathed, you know."

"Then she can stay with Bob and Modo. Come on. Nice, succulent, barbequed chicken and ribs combo, fries drenched in sauce..."

She surrendered and hung up even before he'd finished his pitch. Laughing, he returned to the task at hand.

The St. Lawrence group home supervisor sounded relieved when her co-workers managed to track her down and put her on the line. "I've been thinking about that photo all day," she explained. "It was so unreal looking. It's not just that I want Lawrence to be alive, but I want to be sure."

"We wouldn't rely solely on your impression, Mrs. Hogencamp—"

"Please, Angie."

The name took him aback. Neither the name nor her anxious tone went with the two-pack-a-day, world weary cynic he'd pictured. He relinquished some of his formality. "I know it's a hard call, Angie. We'd bring one of your staff up to identify the actual body, but before we put any of you through that, we'd like to be reasonably certain. What did you think?"

"The man in the photo had a beard and longer hair. Lawrence is clean-shaven, and he is heavier. His face is rounder."

"But you haven't seen him in over six weeks. In that time, he could grow a beard and longer hair, and he could easily lose ten pounds, especially if he was on the streets."

"I know. That's why I'm saying I just can't be certain."

"All right, what about his clothes? The brown cords don't ring a bell?"

"That I'm sure of. The last time I saw him it was summer. All summer he wore the same khaki pants and white T-shirt. If it was cool he'd put on a navy windbreaker. He's had the same clothes for years. We'd practically have to tear them off him to wash them. So when he moved out of hospital, I helped him buy a whole bunch exactly the same—half a dozen white T-shirts and khaki pants. Lawrence is very set in his ways. Don't try throwing him a curve ball, he doesn't cope."

Green thought back. The dead man had been wearing a T-shirt blackened by grime and newspaper ink but conceivably white in its former days. However, it was a thin thread to hang an ID on.

"What about personal effects and accessories? Any watches, rings...jewellery?"

"Oh, he has a crucifix."

Bingo, Green thought, asking her to describe it.

"It's an ornate gold cross on a chain. It's not his," she added quickly. "It's apparently his older brother's, but he's had it since he first arrived at the hospital. He loves that thing, wears it night and day. Never lets it out of his sight."

"Do you know how he came by it?"

"The family didn't say, if I recall. They just said that anybody who tries to take it away from him had better watch out."

*   *   *

It was ten o'clock that evening before Green finally had the chance to catch Sharon alone. He returned from walking Modo to find her sprawled in his old vinyl easy chair in the living room, with her feet propped on the coffee table and her eyes closed. She looked done in. The house was quiet, Tony

asleep and Hannah closeted in her bedroom with her music miraculously turned down low. Only the bass beat pulsed through the ceiling.

Modo padded into the living room to flop down in her usual spot at Sharon's feet. Even that did not rouse her. Green vacillated in the doorway, loathe to disturb her, when he saw a faint smile curve the corners of her mouth.

"Okay, Green," she said without opening her eyes. "Fix me a cup of tea, and I'll listen."

He hesitated, wondering what had given him away. She regarded him through eyes at half mast. "You have that look in your eye—Detective Green on the scent. What is it you want to know?"

Humbly, he went into their ravaged kitchen, found the kettle and brewed up a pot of Sharon's favourite Darjeeling brand.

"Don't forget to scald the pot," she called from her chair. O ye of little faith, he thought. After five years of her exacting tutelage, he knew how to make a perfect cup of tea. When he brought it to her, complete with a saucer and oatmeal cookie, she took a sip and grinned at him.

"Just keeping you on your toes. Okay, I probably have about half an hour of consciousness left, so shoot."

Cradling his tea, he sat on the chesterfield opposite her, p ropped his feet next to hers on the coffee table and summarized the case. Even though her eyes were closed, he knew she was absorbing every word.

"I'm not ruling out homicide, because that piece of jacket bothers me," he said as he finished. "But everything points to suicide. We have no signs of a struggle—no blood or disturbance up on the top. No defensive wounds, no abrasions on his hands to suggest he even grabbed at the wall to stop

himself from falling. No witnesses to anyone else being in the area at the time. MacPhail's pretty sure it's suicide. Even Cunningham, who likes every minutia of physical evidence to fit, thinks it's suicide. Lawrence's group home supervisor says he hadn't much to live for. And with his crazy delusions, he could have been thinking anything."

"So what do you want me to do?" she murmured. "Add my guess to the others?"

He was about to protest, but stopped himself. "You've worked with schizophrenics for years. I want you to help me understand this guy. Would he be likely to kill himself, and if so, why? Or could he be so crazy that he'd jump off, thinking he could fly?"

Her eyes were still closed, but a smile crept across her face. "That's what I love about you. You don't ask much. As to your first question, the answer is yes. Schizophrenics kill themselves all the time. It's a devastating disease that robs both its victims and their families of normal, happy lives. It torments them with voices, fears and obsessions they can't escape. Sometimes they make a very lucid choice to end it all."

"But I thought there are medications nowadays."

"Modern psychiatry has made amazing strides in treating this disease, at least to improve the quality of life, especially if it's caught early. But in his case, after all these years of illness, what the disease hasn't destroyed of his mind, our more primitive treatments probably have. Besides, you said he was off his meds, so he'd already be falling back into the grip of his delusions."

"In which case he might not realize the consequences of his jump? He might think he was immortal?"

"Given the place he chose for his jump, I'd say that's as good a possibility as the other." She opened her eyes to take a sip of her tea. His exasperation must have shown, for she

wiggled her toes to stroke his foot, the only exertion she could manage. "I know you want to understand why he jumped. That's what I love about you. That driving force to solve the riddle of a case, to untangle people's lives. But we will never be able to get inside his head that much."

"I suppose. Still, it helps to know that, psychologically, suicide is possible. Even likely." He ceded the point reluctantly. "Much more likely than murder, twenty years later when his family had all moved away, and no one even knew he was in town."

She nodded, emitting an appreciative sigh as she took another sip. "There is an in-between possibility, you know. If he suffered from paranoid delusions, he might believe others were out to get him. Instruments of the devil, or something. I had a patient once who genuinely believed I was a witch, and she was terrified of me." She shivered. "That was scary."

He leaned forward, his own tea forgotten. "So what's your in-between theory?"

"Well, simply that something scared him so much he jumped off the tower to escape."

"Something? You mean someone." His thoughts were racing back to the crime scene, to the scrap of fabric on the wrong side of the wall.

"Who knows? Perhaps something he saw—or someone—triggered his fear. Or perhaps it was all just a hallucination. Remember, by this time he was getting pretty sick."

Green struggled through fatigue to grapple with the elusive speculations she was tossing out. So much hinged on Lawrence's mental state, but as Sharon said, no one could ever really know that. He grabbed onto the facts he had. "But his group home supervisor said with the meds he'd been on, he might still be in fairly good shape."

She shook her head dubiously. "In good shape for him, honey. But some schizophrenics are hit worse than others, and he sounds like one of the sicker ones. His illness struck him early in his teens—a bad sign—and he had to have electroshock, which is a drastic treatment normally used as a last resort. Plus it's unusual for St. Lawrence to keep someone hospitalized for almost twenty years. He'd have to be resistant to almost all the treatments they tried, and they had to think he presented a serious ongoing risk."

"Risk to what?"

"To himself. Or to others."

"What if his parents just didn't want him to ever get out?"

She shook her head. "You know as well as I do that they don't have that power. Especially before Brian's Law came out in 2000. Lawrence couldn't have been held indefinitely against his wishes."

Green himself had been a detective on the major crimes squad when popular Ottawa sports broadcaster Brian Smith had been shot dead by a schizophrenic who had refused treatment. The outrage of the community had spilled into the legislature as well, making it easier for doctors to force treatment on those without the power to judge wisely for themselves. But it was still a difficult feat unless the patient consented.

"What if he wanted to be kept in too?"

"He'd still have to be pretty sick, Mike. A lot of patients are afraid to leave hospital because it's the only home they know. But part of the staff's job is to help them get ready."

He pondered the situation. The vague, uneasy feeling he'd had earlier after discussing the past with Sandy and his mother began to crystallize. "What if he did something really horrific?"

"He'd have gone to a forensic facility."

"Only if people found out." He sat forward excitedly. "Bear with me, honey. See if you see the same thing I do." He picked

up a set of Tony's playing cards from the table and began to talk, laying them down, one for each point, as if arraying his forces.

"First we have the father lecturing about Satan and using the strap to drive evil out of his boys' lives. Second, we have at least two older brothers engaging in sex and other sins. Third, we have a boy spying on his brothers and believing he's the agent of God's will. Fourth, we have this same sick boy believing he can purify souls by bizarre blood rituals. And finally, we have a brother who seems to have disappeared from the face of the earth. You add to all this the fact that the family put Lawrence away for good, they burned down the shed he loved, they threw out all his things, the father and brother became drunks, and the mother killed herself."

By the end, Sharon was sitting straight up, wide awake. "Something horrific, you said. What, Mike? What exactly are you thinking?"

As she posed the question, Green looked at his six cards and recognized the uneasiness that had been lurking in the back of his mind. About Sophia, Derek, blood-stained notes and the jacket that was torn on the wrong place.

"I think he may have killed his brother," he said. "And maybe somebody wanted revenge."

Nine

The next morning, much to his own surprise, Green was already in his office on the phone before Brian Sullivan even arrived at work. Sullivan usually arrived at the first hint of dawn, freshly scrubbed and sunny. Today he lumbered over to his desk an hour late, balancing his coffee and turning on his computer before he'd even shed his coat. He looked like a man who'd rather be somewhere else.

Green beckoned him through his open door, then held up his hand for silence as a voice finally came on the line. He had reached St. Lawrence Hospital's administrator before she'd even showered from her morning jog, and she was not pleased. She had an entire day of labour negotiations booked for that day, she informed him, and had absolutely no time to speak to the police. No need, Green assured her blithely. When my detectives arrive, they will only need to speak to the physician in charge of Lawrence Pettigrew's care and to the staff who treated him, as well as examine his file. The woman sputtered about confidentiality and privacy laws, but again Green was ready for her. You will have the necessary paperwork, he replied with more conviction than he felt. Legally, it was unclear who was Lawrence's official next-of-kin, given his father's current mental state, but Green hoped that Robbie Pettigrew's signature together with Sullivan's Irish charm would do the trick.

After Green hung up, Sullivan fixed him with bloodshot eyes over the rim of his Tim Hortons coffee, looking very short on Irish charm. "You're not still serious about the Brockville goose chase."

Green bristled but sidestepped the ill humour. Everyone was entitled to a bad day. "Now more than ever."

"Mike, I've got work backed up the wazoo."

"I'll fix it. The visit has three main purposes, but whatever else you can dig up, hey, that's gravy. First, find out if Lawrence had a history of violence, either when he was admitted twenty years ago or during his stay. Second, find out if he ever talked about returning home and why. Third, bring the supervisor Angie Hogencamp up here to confirm the ID."

Sullivan nodded, tossed back the last of his coffee and lobbed the cup over Green's desk, nailing his waste basket dead centre. "Gibbs says you also mentioned going to Toronto. Seems like an awful lot of manhours for a case MacPhail called a probable self-inflicted."

"I'm not convinced it was self-inflicted. Besides, it's not just Lawrence's death I'm concerned about. It's the older brother's disappearance."

"And you think...what?"

Green shrugged. With Sullivan in this mood, there was no way he was going to share his tenuous theory. "I'm still putting the pieces together."

Sullivan stuck his foot out and kicked Green's door shut. "The guy took a dive, Green. End of case. It's a case I could have handled with my eyes shut. I just asked you along for the ride in the country. The guys out in the sticks grumble that the central brass don't give a damn. They've had four different inspectors out there in the past year. I didn't expect you to turn it into a major investigation!"

"Then you've forgotten who I am."

Sullivan raised his eyes to the ceiling, as if appealing for patience. "No, I haven't fucking forgotten. But I've got a stack of other cases out on my desk which I have to assign. I'm the officer of record on this case, so I'd appreciate knowing all the facts. I won't walk into an interview with a bunch of hospital tight asses without knowing exactly why I'm there."

The two stared each other down. Green was the first to look away, not because Sullivan was tougher, but because he was right. As Green summarized his discussion with Sharon, Sullivan listened with an expression that betrayed nothing. But at the end he shook his head.

"Green, that's absolute bullshit."

Green flushed. He knew it was a tenuous theory, especially in the sober light of second thought, and he hadn't had time to plug all its holes, but he had hoped for a more open reception. "Something terrible happened, Brian," he repeated doggedly. "And the family tried to erase all signs of it."

Sullivan shook his head incredulously. "I've seen some weird family shit in my career, and not much of what people do surprises me any more. But I grew up in a big family, remember? Five boys, two girls. And I can tell you if the crazy one murdered the family hero, there's no way any of us would have protected him. If we didn't kill him ourselves, we'd sure as hell turn him in."

Green pondered that problem. Being an only child, he couldn't fully grasp the dynamics of a large family or the notion of conflicting loyalties, but he could imagine the anguish the Pettigrew family had endured in making their decision. He groped ahead, trying to put himself in their shoes.

"But Lawrence was also one of their own. They knew he was crazy and wasn't responsible for his actions. Or it could

have been fear of all the publicity, the protracted pain of a trial, the shame of insanity in the family or even the gossip in the small town. Who the hell knows! I just think they chose their own private form of justice, and they made sure Lawrence would never, ever be free."

Sullivan was still scowling, but this time his tone was less dismissive. "But you don't have a body, Green. You don't even have people wondering if there's a body."

"We've got a suspicious disappearance. Derek Pettigrew has dropped off the radar screen."

"Didn't the drunk—Tom—didn't he hear from him?"

"We have only his word on that. He was twenty at the time of the blow-up, so he could have been part of the cover-up. Besides, this historic murder could tie into the death we are investigating. If Lawrence did kill Derek, then there might be a line-up of people wanting to pay him back. Hell, the whole goddamn village might know who did it, and they aren't planning to tell us a thing!"

"Mike, if the family was going to kill him, they'd have done it right then and there, not waited twenty years!"

"Things change," Green countered, not sure he had an explanation himself, nor a decent list of suspects. "The kids were young, the parents were alive, maybe the revenge took twenty years to fester before something triggered it."

Sullivan frowned. "You're talking about Tom."

"Or Robbie."

"Robbie was eight years old!"

"And now he's twenty-eight—a disillusioned, damaged young man whose childhood was ruined and who is now quite strong enough to throw the culprit off that tower."

"But Robbie barely remembered Lawrence!"

"So he says," Green countered. "But remember how he

never mentioned Lawrence when we interviewed him? And I don't remember seeing a single photo of Lawrence in that album, which is why we forgot to ask about him."

Sullivan looked as if he'd been flattened by a steamroller. Which perhaps he had, thought Green ruefully. He held up a conciliatory hand. "I'm not saying it happened, Brian. I'm not saying Lawrence was even murdered. I'm just saying we still have unanswered questions, and we shouldn't be closing the case till we've answered them. So your first step is to confirm that the dead body is actually Lawrence and then to find out all you can about what happened twenty years ago that led to his committal."

Sullivan rubbed his square hand over his cropped blonde hair, making it stand on end. Green, who was familiar with his every move, knew he was about to cave. "Mike," Sullivan said in a weary, last-ditch effort. "This is a goddamn fishing expedition. We can't even get to the murders we have bodies for, let alone one that the family is denying ever happened."

Green hesitated, reluctant to add more wild speculation to Sullivan's already overloaded plate. "Maybe that's because they're hiding something more," he muttered.

"What?"

This time Green didn't respond. He was thinking of the two love letters in different handwriting, of a beautiful black-haired girl who had left town at the same time. He had only the vaguest fear of what might have happened to her, but it was too early to even voice it aloud.

"Suit yourself," Sullivan muttered finally, thrusting his chair back to stand up. He was too much of a professional to sulk, but Green watched with dismay as he strode across the room to snatch his jacket off his chair. There was an anger to his movements that went far beyond the minor spat they'd

had. Behind closed doors, they often shed their disparate ranks and argued about a case, just as they had in the old days together in the field. But their disputes rarely bubbled over into the more personal sphere.

Green sat at his desk fearing what was at the root of Sullivan's mood. The station was alive with rumours about promotions and a major shake-up in assignments. Sullivan had been a sergeant for seven years, but in recent years his hopes of rising higher had always been thwarted by politics. Besides being an anglophone with only rudimentary French, Sullivan was a white male at a time when that was a major roadblock to promotional hopes.

Green wondered if Sullivan had heard something that he, Green, had not. Green was often the last to hear the rumours; all his ambitious middle management colleagues knew he was content to stay where he was, anxious to avoid being promoted any further, and utterly useless as an ally or co-conspirator in the climb up the ladder. He had an anxious thought that the Deputy Chief might even be planning to move him to a totally different posting like District Inspector, where he'd be expected to oversee patrol operations about which he knew absolutely nothing. Banishing that crazy thought from his head, he phoned Ident to ask if they'd made any progress on the fingerprints, either on the ladder or on the bloody note.

"Green, I'd tell you if there was," Cunningham exclaimed. "You want any old answer, or do you want the right one? I've got a dozen cases on the go here."

"Just asking. I'm bumping this up to a higher priority."

"Oh yeah? Well, I can tell you one of the nice latents we got off the ladder is the dead man's, which is no surprise. The stained print on the note isn't."

"I want you to pull Thomas Pettigrew's prints off the

115

system and see if they match anything. Hang on, I'll get you his FPS number." Green rummaged on his desk for the printout Gibbs had taken off the police computer. With the requisite grumbling about workloads and Green's lack of appreciation for the complexity of forensic work, Cunningham agreed to look into it.

On a roll, Green summoned Bob Gibbs and gave him Sandy Fitzpatrick's yearbook. If anyone could track down a person from a stone-cold, twenty-year-old trail, it was Gibbs. He would revel in the challenge.

"We're looking for Sophia Vincelli," Green told him. "Her family lived in Richmond twenty years ago and may still. Once you've found her, let me know directly, and we'll take it from there. Sergeant Sullivan is on assignment out of town for the day."

No sooner had Gibbs loped out of the office with the yearbook under his arm than Green's phone buzzed. It was the clerk of Superintendent Jules, Chief of Detectives.

"The Superintendent would like to know if he could have a word with you this morning. Does ten thirty suit you?"

Adam Jules was a man of manners and protocol, but Green was not deceived by the courtesy; it was an order, not a request. Green's mouth went dry. He wanted to ask the reason but knew that was not part of the protocol. Nor was negotiating a different time. Jules was a meticulous man, and if he said ten thirty, that was what he meant.

The Chief of Detectives was sitting at his desk poring over a procedural manual when his clerk ushered Green in. He had acquired gold-rimmed reading glasses a few months earlier and these were perched on the bridge of his fine aquiline nose. He peered over them, pressed his lips together in his idea of a smile and rose to offer Green his hand.

"Michael, thank you for coming." He closed the procedural manual and came around his desk to sit in one of the four chairs clustered around a coffee table by the window. With a fluid flick of his manicured hand, he invited Green to sit.

A coffee table conversation, thought Green with alarm. Always a bad sign. He forced himself to sit down and wait. Adam Jules was a man of few words, but each word spoke volumes. This time, however, he seemed to be having trouble getting started. He removed his glasses, folded them with precision and slipped them into the breast pocket of his jacket. Pursed his lips, gazed out the window. Like the rest of the senior brass, he had a spectacular view of the Museum of Nature, which rose like an elaborate Scottish castle in the middle of a grassy square across the road. Grey clouds massed on the horizon beyond the ramparts. Green hoped they weren't an omen. His hand strayed to his tie, checking to see if the knot was crooked. It felt too tight. He pulled at it gently. Waited.

Jules drew in his breath. His cheeks were tinged pink, and Green realized that beneath his almost unreadable exterior, Adam Jules was upset. "The announcement of the latest assignments and transfers will be released this afternoon, but I thought it only fair to let you know..."

He paused. Green's heart plummeted.

"That as of next week, I will be assuming command of the Eastern Division, and—"

"What!"

"I've been transferred to Eastern Division."

"Out of CID?" Green asked stupidly. He was dumbfounded. Jules was a career detective who knew and had performed every job of the detectives under his command. He'd been Green's boss at one level or another for almost all of Green's investigative career. CID without Adam Jules was unthinkable.

Jules grew pinker as he nodded. As Green's astonishment subsided, he realized this move had not been Jules' wish. The Police Chief had obviously decided that his top advisers needed to know all aspects of policing and that no single officer could monopolize a field.

"I'm sorry, Adam. Truly sorry. You'll be greatly missed." Green's thoughts raced ahead in alarmed contemplation of possible replacements. "Can you tell me...?"

Jules made a slight face. "Inspector Devine. Her promotion will be announced tomorrow."

Green's heart sank still further. He suspected his horror showed on his face, for Jules smiled faintly. "She's an experienced detective."

She is that, Green thought. Experienced in working a room, feathering a nest and putting a favourable spin. Barbara Devine had spent about two years in each of the units she'd worked, just long enough to lodge her toe firmly on the next rung in the ladder. Things couldn't get any worse. Then again, he thought, perhaps they could. He hardly dared ask the question.

"Is there anyone else in my section I need to know about?"

Jules managed his tight smile again, and Green knew he wasn't fooled. "There are those who argued the inspectors should be moved around to allow new people a crack at each job. New blood, new perspectives. I persuaded them that with a new Chief of Detectives at the helm, we needed to keep the experienced CID people in place."

Relief and gratitude flowed through Green, mixing with the regret he felt at losing Jules. At least he himself had been spared for now. "It's the only job I'm good at, Adam."

Jules cocked his head. "You might surprise yourself some day."

"What about the NCOs? Any changes there?"

Jules nodded. "You have a new staff sergeant in Major Crimes."

Which was no loss, because the current one was close to burn out. "Someone I know?"

"Gaetan Larocque, from Organized Fraud. Good man."

Green felt a new wave of regret. Larocque was a good enough investigator, seasoned and hard-working. But Fraud was a far cry from Major Crimes, and as far as Green knew, he hadn't done a homicide investigation in years. But that wasn't the worst of it. If Gaetan Larocque got his promotion to Staff Sergeant, that meant Brian Sullivan had been passed over yet again, by a man five years his junior.

* * *

Isabelle Boisvert was heading down County Road 2, still a good half kilometre from her turn-off, when she spotted something moving in her front yard. At first she thought Jacques had decided to take another day off from the office, but as she drew nearer, the sunlight flashed off a metal object far larger than the Sunbird. It was a dump truck.

She shoved her foot harder on the accelerator and felt the minivan sputter in response. She took the turn at top speed and slewed the minivan down the lane, bumping over ruts and showering gravel in her wake. She reached the front yard just in time to see the truck dump a massive load of crushed stone onto the ground. She leaped out of the minivan and stormed towards the truck, her shouts futile over the rattle of the stones.

The company name Scott Construction was stencilled on the cab door in faded red. A burly man with a John Deere cap, wrap-around sunglasses and tattooed biceps the size of Douglas firs, was perched inside, peering over his shoulder at

the gravel in the back. Behind him, where the tangle of shrubs had been, was a gaping hole bordered by a square of rough cut pine planks. It was into this enclosure that the truck was dumping the gravel, releasing clouds of gritty dust.

Isabelle hammered on the driver's window. He turned to her, surprise showing on his face through the dusty glass. In the next instant, he switched off the hydraulic lift and rolled down his window.

He touched his cap. "Mrs. Boisvert?"

"Yes. Just what the hell do you think you're doing?"

He jerked a massive thumb towards the pit. "Phil Scott. I spoke with your husband last night, eh?"

"But you weren't supposed to do this till next week. Not today!"

"I know, but we had a look at it this morning. It's not a big job, and I had a bit of time to spare. Sandy Fitzpatrick said it would be okay to go ahead."

"This was Sandy's idea?"

"Well, no. But we had a look at it, eh, and we just thought... I mean, Sandy said you shouldn't have to be out here yourself digging it up with your bare hands."

Isabelle scanned the yard in dismay. Except for a few stray canes of raspberry still strewn on the ground, there was no sign that the thicket had ever been there. Nor the axe and the cow bone. She felt her autonomy being bulldozed by a pair of Neanderthal country men.

"But what happened to all the wood?" she blustered. "I was going to have a bonfire."

"Oh, we took that this morning. Brought my little cat in and loaded the truck up. Raspberry canes and that don't make a good fire anyway, eh?"

He was leaning out the window, his tone the essence of

courtesy but his eyes unreadable behind sunglasses. He made it sound as if their actions had been completely sensible—just country folk offering a helping hand—and indeed Jacques had arranged the job the night before. Damn him for not informing Phil Scott of the change in plans.

"Well, Phil, I appreciate you trying to help, but we're not sure about the garage yet. I'm kind of thinking of a pool here."

Scott brightened. No doubt seeing the dollar signs. "A swimming pool?"

"No, just a little fish pond."

Scott leaned his chin on his tattooed forearms and peered solemnly around the yard. "Bad place for a fish pond. Wind likely whips through here pretty strong, straight across them fields. You'd be better to put the pond in the lee of the house. Put a patio and all in there too. That's where the Pettigrews used to have their firepit and picnic table."

Isabelle looked at the pile of gravel sitting in the centre of the yard. He was right, damn him. In her frustration, she had wanted to build a place of beauty where the ugly thicket had been, but it made much more sense to integrate the pool into a garden at the side of the house. Besides, considering all the spooky remnants of the past that she had unearthed in that spot, it was comforting to think that the whole mess was well buried beneath a foot of stones.

"I'll help you dig your pond over there next week if you like," Phil offered. "No extra charge than what was agreed last night. It'll be nice to see this old place come to life again."

Ten

The flat monotony of farm fields whipped by as Sullivan drove down Highway 416 towards Brockville. His hand was steady on the wheel, and his gaze was fixed straight ahead, inscrutable behind his mirrored sunglasses. He knew Sue Peters was probably bursting with questions, but she betrayed no hint as she fiddled with the car radio for the sixth time. He let her fiddle. It was going to be a long drive, an hour each way even if he broke the speed limit, and he had no wish to fill it with idle chit-chat or station gossip he'd heard a hundred times. He had more important things to occupy his mind. A good buddy in the Deputy Chief's office had tipped him off on the promotions list last night, and this morning Sullivan was nursing the first hangover he'd had in years. He had forced himself past the rage stage now, past the "fuck them I quit" stage, past the hurt stage and the betrayed stage. He was now taking a cold, hard look at his future. He knew he'd come to a fork in the road, and like it or not—mostly not—he had a choice to make.

That's what he really wanted to talk about—this endless loop of doubt and discontent that ran through his thoughts—but there was no one to talk it over with. Not Green, who'd tell him that promotions sucked and he should stay in Major Crimes anyway. Certainly not this poised and assertive young woman beside him who, if she played her cards right, would

reach Staff Sergeant before he did. She probably thought it mattered that they go down to Brockville, do a good job, unmask this historic murder, and tie the two deaths all up in a neat bow for the Crown.

But it didn't matter a flying fuck.

Because even if there had been a murder twenty years ago—a big if—the alleged murderer was now dead, the mother was dead, the father was a vegetable, the only other remaining son was a useless drunk, and Robbie Pettigrew needed to know this secret like he needed his guts reamed out. What good was going to come of it, compared to the harm? Sullivan knew villages like Ashford Landing. A horrible secret like this would reverberate forever, condemned from the pulpit and whispered in the grocery aisles for years to come.

He steered the car onto the 401 on-ramp and joined the torrent of transport trucks and speed demons racing along the Montreal-Toronto corridor. Not trusting his booze-sodden reflexes, he maintained a steady one hundred and ten kilometres an hour, as if the appearance of patience and calm could make him feel that way.

The Brockville police station was a squat, square building just off the 401 on their way into town. After a brief courtesy call and a chat with the officer who'd taken Lawrence's photo to the group home, Sullivan and Peters headed south through the historic core of the town, which had stood guard on the St. Lawrence River opposite New York State for over two centuries. Picking up the original river road, they headed east towards the hospital.

As they turned onto the grounds of St. Lawrence Psychiatric Hospital, Sullivan did a double-take. He had expected an insane asylum built over a century ago to look more like the Bastille than an exclusive country resort, and was

surprised to find a graceful, rambling, red brick castle set back amid rolling lawns and trees overlooking the river. Once he and Peters entered the front door, however, the worn tiles and chipped paint told a more accurate tale. Like many historic hospitals, it had been slated for closure by the belt-tightening Ontario Conservatives after gradually losing its clientele to better drug treatments and outpatient clinics. But people still got sick, and like most cops, Sullivan was all too familiar with what happens when a philosophical ideal, however noble, gets translated into real life. Of necessity, St. Lawrence Psychiatric continued to limp along, underfunded and shrunken in size, serving the revolving parade of chronically ill who fell through the gaping cracks in the supports.

Green had paved the way, and less than five minutes after Sullivan identified himself at reception, he and Peters were ushered into the office of the Chief of Psychiatry, a man who looked like he'd risen from a slab at the morgue. Dr. Roddingham peered down his beaked nose at the signed release form from Robbie, clucked his tongue and shook his head.

"You have to understand, Sergeant, I get several requests a month from investigators and lawyers wanting access to confidential files on the flimsiest of evidence. Psychiatric patients are the first to be suspected if anything happens in the community, and their rights fly out the window. So I insist on very strict protocols to safeguard our patients' rights. I need a death certificate and a subpoena, at the very least a legal document attesting that this Robert Pettigrew is the official next of kin."

Sullivan sighed. Green and his goddamn wild goose chases. "We don't suspect Lawrence of doing anything, and we're not looking for evidence to be used in court. We believe the man is deceased, and we're looking for information on his recent activities and his state of mind when you last examined him."

Sullivan paused before trying to slide the next sentence by unnoticed. "As well as for information about the circumstances of his original admission."

Dr. Roddingham proved more alive that he looked. His cadaverous eyes narrowed. "Why?"

Why indeed, thought Sullivan wearily through the jackhammers in his head. He fished for straws. "Because that may shed light on the reason for his return, and who he may have visited on his return."

Roddingham's eyes narrowed further. "You think he may have been murdered?"

"No, sir," Sullivan countered quickly, thinking just what he needed—another overactive imagination. "We're just questioning whether he was frightened or upset by someone. I understand he hadn't seen his family in twenty years."

Roddingham seemed to be weighing his position, no doubt sorting through the maze of regulations governing disclosure. He tapped his lips absently as if to stop himself saying anything.

"As to the former request, we will need his treating psychiatrist to answer that. As to the latter, we will need his old charts. I will not permit you to inspect them, but I will see if there is any useful information I can share." He reached for the phone and issued two terse orders to his secretary. He winced, apparently at one of her answers, and hung up. "Dr. Assad will be with us shortly from another wing. The chart will take a few minutes."

Dr. Assad must have broken the record for the hundred yard dash, Sullivan reflected, for his footsteps could be heard clattering down the hall overhead, and barely a minute later he burst through the door, dark-eyed, dishevelled and struggling for breath. He was a small man with a pencil mustache and goatee that made him look like a rat. As he listened to

125

Roddingham's request, his nose twitched as if testing the air for danger. He made all the right noises when he heard about Lawrence's death, but protested at the suggestion of suicide.

"There was nothing in his behaviour to indicate that!" he exclaimed. "He's only been in my care for four years since he moved to the group home, but I read his previous psychiatrist's discharge note carefully. Last spring, when we moved him to independent living, he was as good as he was going to get after almost twenty years of institutional care. Mentally he was a child, but then we'd never let him grow up. Worse, we regressed him—"

"Dr. Assad." Dr. Roddingham's voice, though deceptively quiet, cut like a whip. "The police merely want to know if, in your professional opinion, he might have been suicidal."

"I have no way of knowing, I haven't seen him since June. I'd have to examine him, which of course is not possible now."

"June!" Peters exclaimed before Sullivan could shut her up. He decided to let the challenge lie.

Assad pressed his lips together in a thin line. "I have three hundred outpatients on my caseload, madame. The treatment for his illness is medication, and my job is to ensure the drug and dosage are optimal. Medically his condition was stable; all that was needed was routine monitoring and lab work."

Sullivan reasserted control. "What about his life, his friends? What was he doing with his time?"

"We discussed symptoms and side effects, not living habits. In any case, he'd be more likely to confide that sort of thing in the group home workers who monitored his progress."

The door opened to admit Roddingham's secretary, carrying several thick, dog-eared charts which she plunked on Roddingham's desk. With visible relief, Assad seized the most recent and began to leaf through it. Buttressed by his paperwork, his voice took on a new confidence.

"My latest chart note is dated June 19—oriented in all three spheres, no hallucinations or disorganized speech. Not very talkative, flat affect. Certainly no signs of trouble there. I recommended he continue his olanzapine."

"What do you mean by flat affect?" Sullivan asked.

Roddingham took over as if the role of professor was second nature to him. "Affect is visible emotion. Schizophrenic patients, especially in the chronic phase of their illness, often have a flatness to them rather suggestive of robots. They lack spark and spontaneity."

Must be contagious, Sullivan thought wryly. "So you're saying he was neither happy nor sad."

"Not overtly. Of course—" Roddingham paused and blinked his reptilian eyes slowly. "There's no telling how he felt inside. He may have felt quite empty. That's not uncommon either."

"Ten per cent of schizophrenics do kill themselves," Assad added helpfully.

Sullivan eased into the topic of Green's interest carefully. "What about delusions? I understand he had been quite preoccupied with good and evil."

Roddingham had begun paging through one of Lawrence's earlier charts and did not look up when Assad cast him a glance for guidance. Without any, Assad chose to equivocate. "He was always a religious man, with a simple view of right and wrong. However, I would call his interest obsessional, not delusional."

"But if he stopped taking his medication six weeks ago, could he not become delusional again?"

Assad's eyes lit as he saw a way out from under his burden of responsibility. "Of course, without monitoring and treatment, I can't predict what he might do. That's very possible."

"Was there a potential for him to become dangerous?"

Roddingham looked up with alarm and clearly decided it was time to resume command. "Off the record? Certainly he has the potential. He's a paranoid schizophrenic, and it depends on what form his delusions and hallucinations take. However, the vast majority of schizophrenics are not dangerous, and the law does not allow us to lock up indefinitely a patient who might someday, potentially, become violent." He perused a chart slowly. "In his earlier charts, there were numerous incidents of agitation when he had to be restrained to protect himself or others. But there is no record of his actually inflicting physical harm."

Sullivan nodded casually at the file Roddingham was studying. "What do the records say about his admission? Did his parents report any incidents of violence?"

Roddingham paused to scrutinize something in the chart and looked up with surprise. "On the contrary. Here's your answer. The reason they gave for wanting him committed was that he tried to kill himself."

Sullivan's headache receded before his sudden surge of interest. "What were the circumstances?"

"He tried to hang himself. Very nearly succeeded, from the look of it. Still had the marks around his neck when he arrived."

* * *

Sullivan shut his eyes and leaned his head back against the plastic booth at McDonalds, letting the shriek of small children wash over him as he waited for Peters to bring their food. He had taken one look at the crowd lined five deep at the counters and quickly accepted her offer to help. If she wanted to score some Brownie points with him, who was he

to stop her? Thankfully, she'd been quiet on the drive from the hospital to the McDonalds near the police station, which allowed him to gather his thoughts, but he knew she was brimming with questions she was too proud to ask. He'd soon have to turn on his teaching skills. How many years had he been breaking in rookies? Too many, for sure.

Sue Peters was an army brat who'd grown up in a house full of brothers on army bases around the world. She seemed comfortable in the company of men, but Sullivan suspected a small part of her still felt she had something to prove in a man's world. She was determined to look good, even at the expense of asking how. He'd seen it before in cops of both sexes who thought they always had to be in control, and he wasn't keen to be the one to break her in.

Something thumped on the table, and he opened his eyes to see Peters shrug off her jacket and drop into the booth opposite. She slurped her coke with a flourish.

"What do you think of that shrink, eh, Sarge? The Arab guy? Weasely bastard, I don't think he remembered our guy at all!"

Sullivan winced. Where to begin? With the Arab, the shrink or the Sarge? He chose to start with her prejudices.

"Dr. Assad has a large caseload. I suspect he wanted to make sure he had his facts straight before he committed himself. And Detective," he leaned his large frame towards her to make sure he had her attention, "exact language is essential in investigative work. Dr. Assad is a psychiatrist, not a shrink, and his ethnic background is of absolutely no relevance to this investigation."

To her credit, she flushed as she busied herself dousing vinegar on her fries. Finally, she shrugged. "I didn't mean anything by it. All the guys..."

"All the guys don't. I don't. All we have is our reputation for professionalism and objectivity, Detective. In court and with witnesses, without that reputation we're useless." He took a large bite of his Big Mac, leaving her to mull that over for a few minutes. After he'd polished off more than half his burger, he picked up his coke and leaned back, feeling slightly revived and ready to begin.

"What did you make of the interview back at the hospital?"

She met his gaze levelly, as if she was still smarting from his reprimand. "They didn't tell us much, considering the guy's been living in that place over half his life. Makes you wonder if he was much more than just a number in a bed." She shook her head. "What a pathetic, wasted life."

"I think you'll find the group home can tell us more this afternoon. That staff would have lived with him day in and out. But we did learn one useful thing."

"What? That he tried to kill himself?"

Sullivan nodded. "It isn't quite what the Inspector was looking for, but it does confirm his suspicion that something had happened in the family back then."

"Maybe he just went off the deep end for no reason. After all, he is a psycho."

Sullivan fixed her a silent glare, and she threw her hands up in frustration. "Another word off limits? Sarge, how can we do this job if we don't blow off some steam among our own kind? I wouldn't use psycho on the stand."

"Disrespect is disrespect. Just as I'm Sergeant, not Sarge."

Two spots of colour flamed her cheeks, but she said nothing, lapsing instead into a frosty silence that lasted the rest of his Big Mac. He cursed his hangover and his own stupidity in choosing to bring her along. Christ, how the hell had she made the force, let alone detective?

"Peters, you have a choice here this afternoon," he said. "You can grow up, act like a professional, and set your investigative mind to this case, or you can catch a cab to the Voyageur bus station, and leave me to do my job." He picked up the tray and stood up. "I'm going to the john. Your choice if you meet me outside in the car. Or not."

He knew she'd be in the car, of course, but he hoped she'd leave the attitude inside. Sure enough, when he emerged from the building, she was sitting obediently in the passenger seat, staring straight ahead. He knew her pride had taken a beating, so he refrained from comment. As he eased the car into gear, she took out her notebook. Her tone was subdued.

"I'd like permission to conduct the interview with the group home supervisor, sir. At least the first part."

"Why?"

"She's a woman. She might feel more comfortable with me."

Sullivan wondered if she was implying he was a blunt, lumbering oaf, but decided she'd never in a million years be that subtle. "What questions do you plan to ask?"

They worked on her list of questions as they drove to the group home, which was located in an older, blue-collar neighbourhood not far from the hospital. Peters gradually relaxed as she put her mind to the task, and Sullivan was able to catch a glimpse of a promising investigative mind. He nonetheless reserved his decision on the interview until he had gleaned his initial impression of Mrs. Hogencamp.

He wasn't sure what he expected a group home supervisor to be like—a stout, no-nonsense matron, perhaps—but the reality took him aback. She was a wiry, frenetic bird of a woman whose fiery henna hair clashed with her pink spandex jumpsuit and her red finger nails. She looked as if she belonged in an aerobics studio, but they found her in the kitchen of the old converted

home, shepherding her bewildered assistants through the preparation of dinner with a gentle, patient hand.

The minute Peters introduced herself, however, Mrs. Hogencamp stiffened, and Sullivan could almost smell her fear. Of what? he wondered as she ushered them out of earshot into a small office at the back of the house. On closer viewing, he saw that she was older than her attire would suggest; fine wrinkles webbed her eyes, and her skin was beginning to crepe around her neck. Her voice had the texture of coarse gravel. Given her defensive stance, he decided to handle the initial questions himself.

"It's beginning to look like the dead man up in Ottawa may in fact be Lawrence Pettigrew," he began gravely, explaining that they had already talked to the doctors at the hospital. "Any information you can give us about his recent activities would be helpful."

She studied her red nails. "Poor Lawrence. I don't know what I can tell you. He was fine the last time I saw him. The doctors had judged that he was well enough to live independently and he was to come here once a week for a group."

"What date did you last see him?"

"August twenty-fifth. He had an appointment here September eighth, which he didn't keep, but unfortunately I was on holidays and there was some new staff, so no one became concerned until he missed the twenty-second as well. That's when we began searching for him and notified the police."

Peters peered at her notebook. "Didn't you say he had a group here once a week?"

"Normally. But we're short staffed in the summer."

Sullivan saw the beginnings of a frown on Peters' face, and he hastened to intervene. "What was his demeanor when you saw him in August?"

132

Mrs. Hogencamp consulted a book on the desk, but Sullivan suspected it was a delaying tactic. He was sure she'd reread the entry a dozen times since Green's initial call.

"He seemed a little depressed," she conceded. "I—I thought it was because I was going on holidays."

"What do you mean?"

She flushed slightly. "I've known Lawrence for years. I nursed on his ward before I came here, and I've always had a soft spot for him. No one ever came to visit him. I guess what I'm saying, Sergeant, is that the staff and patients on his ward became his family. He became upset when one of us left."

"Upset enough to kill himself, in your opinion?"

"I wouldn't have let him go that day if I'd thought that." Her indignation cost her, for she broke into a fit of coughing which left her breathless. "He was just sad, in his vague, blunted, schizy way."

"Did he say what he planned to do in the next few weeks?"

She gave a wheezy smile. "Lawrence was heavily medicated, and he'd been ravaged by the disease. He didn't plan or set goals the way we do. He just floated along, following his routine and going to his job."

Sullivan looked up in surprise. "He was working?"

"At a tree nursery, as part of our community partners program. He tended the plants. He was so proud of that job. I was surprised when one day he just didn't show up."

"Was there any trouble at work? Anything that could have triggered...?"

She shook her head. "No, they were very pleased with him. He didn't socialize with anyone, but he seemed...happy enough."

"Had he ever had suicidal thoughts in the past? Or any danger signs?"

133

She sighed and closed her eyes. "Sometimes, during his floridly psychotic episodes, he'd become extremely agitated. He'd think God was calling him home. Poor, poor lamb."

Sullivan perked up. "By home you mean the farm?"

"I mean heaven."

"What was his condition when he was first admitted?"

"His parents had delayed treatment and hadn't recognized how very ill he was. He was in a state of catatonic excitement. Wildly disorganized, agitated, almost panicked. He was lashing out in all directions. They had tied him up like a hog in the back of the truck to get him here." She shuddered as if at the memory. "Imagine."

"Are you saying he was violent?"

"Anyone in a panic can be violent if they think they're in danger. They would see it as protecting themselves or someone else from harm." She frowned and pursed her scarlet lips. "I don't think it matters what he was like back then. He was a very sick boy twenty years ago."

Remembering Green's theory that violence lay at the root of Lawrence's original committal, Sullivan forced himself to push the issue. "I understand he tried to kill himself. Do you know why?"

She began shaking her head.

"Was it some trouble at home? Someone mentioned a girl."

Her eyes widened. "A girl? Lawrence?"

"Was there any girl that he might have been interested in? Maybe a girlfriend of his brothers?"

Now she looked distinctly uncomfortable. "I can't imagine. His delusions were so full of evil and sinning, I can't imagine him actually wanting a girl. Or I should say letting himself want a girl. The home was very strict, and I gathered the boys' hands were strapped if they were ever caught masturbating.

134

Lawrence would have seen himself as evil if he'd even had thoughts like that."

*　　*　　*

"The circle's closing, Brian!" Green crowed once he'd listened to Sullivan's summary of the interview over the phone. "And I bet this Sophia is at the centre of it. If those notes are to be believed, she was screwing two brothers at the same time."

There was a pause, during which Green could almost feel Sullivan's weary skepticism through the wires. "Maybe, Mike, but I don't see how I added much hard evidence to your cockamamie theory. We need some independent corroboration from someone who was around back then. Like Tom or Sophia. Any luck finding either of them yet?"

"Not yet. Gibbs tracked Tom to a rehab centre in Toronto, but they say he went AWOL days ago."

"He's back on the streets for sure. A guy like that, been on the booze as long as he has? He's never going to make a go of it."

Green wasn't inclined to argue. They'd both known a lot of drunks in their years on the force, and Sullivan had much more personal experience with the ravages of drink than Green did. Green's father's idea of a bender was a thimbleful of sweet sacramental wine at Purim and the requisite four at Passover. Before Sullivan's father died of liver failure, he'd packed away whiskey by the truckload.

"Anyway, Toronto's keeping an eye out for us," Green replied without much optimism. In a city as overcrowded, fast-paced and ethnically diverse as Toronto, one misplaced derelict would not rank high in their priorities. Perhaps he should tell them Tom was a suspect in a possible murder

inquiry. "As for locating Sophia, nothing solid yet, but Gibbs has a few leads and we may get a break tomorrow."

That was a slight exaggeration, designed to stimulate Sullivan's flagging spirits, but if anyone could make something out of the slim lead he'd uncovered, it was Bob Gibbs. He'd unearthed the name of a distant cousin in a small village in Tuscany, who may or may not have a clue as to Sophia's whereabouts. The family had moved away from Richmond more than ten years earlier, following the bankruptcy of the father's landscape business. The last known address was somewhere in New Jersey, but the trail had petered out. However, neighbours of the family in Richmond recalled that Sophia had left town as a teenager under mysterious circumstances and was rumoured to have been whisked away to live with relatives back in Italy. Given her racy reputation as a teenager, pregnancy had been suspected.

Green had his own nagging fears about Sophia's disappearance which could be laid to rest only when he had irrefutable evidence of the woman alive and breathing in front of him. He'd had enough of magical disappearing acts. Gibbs had been all set to make the call to Italy when Green reminded him of the time difference. With Gibbs chafing at the delay, Green reminded him of the miracles of Canada411.com and suggested he run a few searches on Vincellis while he waited for the sun to rise on the other side of the world. Through his open office door, Green could see him hard at work on the internet.

"Okay," Sullivan said, breaking into his thoughts. "We're done down here, anyway."

"You're bringing Mrs. Hogencamp back with you to identify the body, right? Do you want me to set that up with the morgue tonight?"

"She's coming tomorrow. She wanted to drive herself, and

she didn't want to disrupt the routine of her patients. Peters and I are coming back up now, but I planned on calling it a day. Nothing else has come up that needs action today, right?"

Green was about to tell him to go straight home and enjoy his kids when Gibbs burst into the doorway, his Adam's apple bobbing with excitement.

"Sir? Sergeant Belowsky from Rural West is on the line, wants to talk to Sullivan. There's been a development at the Pettigrew farm!"

Eleven

Isabelle Boisvert had been walking along the path by the river, her head bent and her shoulders leaning into the sharp October wind. She had turned her collar up and balled her fists deep inside her pockets. Chouchou scurried at her side on a tight lead to stop him from chasing every squirrel and chipmunk in sight.

She had set off in high spirits, eager to scout her property for promising riding trails, but she quickly found her thoughts straying to the spooky discoveries of the past few days and to her husband's mounting resistance. She wasn't sure what she'd do if he dug in his heels and announced he was moving back to the city. This farm was her dream.

With her head bent and her attention turned inward, she would not have even noticed the boat if Chouchou hadn't started barking. He bounced at the end of his leash, yapping and straining towards the river. Isabelle knew all his barking cadences and readily recognized this one as a territorial bark.

Looking up, she saw that she was at the shoreline directly behind her house. The area was overgrown with neglected brush now, but she could still see the worn tracings of a path from the house through the trees to the riverbank. A small area had been cleared at the shore years ago, and the rotted remains of a wooden dock drooped into the water. She had been to the

river many times since they moved in, had even swum here earlier in the fall, and she knew there had been nothing but an old rowboat pulled deep into the bush and upturned. Its splintered hull hadn't been seaworthy in over a decade.

Yet today, once she'd threaded her way down to the river's edge, she saw a boat pulled up on the shore; a battered aluminum runabout with a tiny outboard motor on its stern and a pile of moth-eaten blankets on its floor. A hint of gasoline hung in the air. Chouchou was growling as he approached the boat, so Isabelle snapped the leash to quiet him as she peered around. Not a soul was in sight, but the boat was beached directly behind her house. *Sacré bleu,* was there another prowler on her land?

With a shiver, she scooped the dog into her arms and held him tight. He wasn't much use in a crisis, being barely five kilograms with all his fur, but at least he could serve as her early warning system. Wincing at the crackle of every leaf beneath her boots, she picked her way back towards the house. When she reached the edge of the tree line, she crouched in the tall grass and scanned the field ahead. The house sat about a hundred metres ahead, silent and undisturbed in the late afternoon sun. Wind tugged at the desiccated goldenrod that dotted the field, but she saw no other signs of movement.

Clutching Chouchou firmly under her arm, she ran low to the ground through the dry brush until she reached the back of the house. Still no signs of movement. She listened intently. Nothing. Crouching low and hugging the wall, she began to edge around the side of the house. A thud shattered the silence. Her heart leaped in her chest and a low rumble gathered in Chouchou's throat. She clutched him tight to silence him and peered cautiously around the corner of the house into the front yard. A man was walking across the yard

towards the house from the barn. He must have just come from there, slamming the rickety barn door behind him, she deduced. The man paused to look at the fresh bed of crushed stone where the burned shed had been, then with a shake of his head he continued toward the house.

From her distant vantage point, he looked past his prime but still attractive in a rugged, sinewy way, and he moved with a fluid lope. His khaki windbreaker and heavy work boots looked clean and new. Briefly she wondered if he was another of Jacques' workmen, hired to do some renovation Jacques had failed to mention. He had a purposeful stride rather than the uncertain, furtive scurry of a burglar. Her fears eased and she was about to call out to him when he reached the door, grasped the knob and thrust hard. No knock, no bell, just a hard shove as if he owned the place. The nerve of the guy.

The door was locked, and she hung back to watch him as he stepped back to survey the front of the house before heading around the side opposite where she was. Fear battled curiosity and outrage as she circled around the back to the other side. She peeked around the corner just as he lifted up the hatch to the root cellar and ducked down the steps into the basement. She slumped against the wall in disbelief. She'd never thought of locking that door, which opened into a dank, unused section of the basement where long ago the family would have stored their turnips, carrots, potatoes and other fruits of the fall harvest.

The man was in her basement now, and although she couldn't see him, she could hear thuds and scrapes as if he were shoving things around. Chouchou gave a low growl, and Isabelle clamped her hand around his muzzle. Holding him tight, she hurried across the yard to the tool shed. Once inside, she pulled the door carefully shut, pulled out her cell phone and dialled

911. Speaking barely above a whisper, she reported the break-in and was advised to stay out of sight until the police arrived.

She disconnected and peered out the shed door. Out here in the country, it might be a solid twenty minutes before the police arrived. She considered her options. She was alone in the country with no one even remotely within earshot, with a useless puffball of a dog and without even a shotgun or tiny .22 for protection. She had grown up with shotguns, but Jacques was adamantly opposed to all guns, so despite the advice of the real estate agent and the man at the general store, they had no guns. She could sit in this shed like a fool and wait to be rescued. Or she could check it out. The man had not looked dangerous, nor had he been carrying a weapon that she could see. He had looked like a typical blue-collar worker, a little gaunt and battered perhaps, as if he'd had a two-pack a day habit all his life.

She lifted her brand new axe from its peg on the shed wall and slipped back out the door. Chouchou was squirming under her arm, so she cast about for some way to contain him. Her eyes finally settled on the minivan parked in front of the house. Chouchou loved the car, because he thought he was being included in an adventure, so he might not bark if she put him inside. Praying that the man was making enough noise to mask hers, she slid open the van door, thrust the dog inside and pulled it quietly shut again. Ducking down behind the car, she held her breath while she listened. Nothing. The axe felt solid in her hand as she crossed the yard to the front door, slipped the key in and cautiously opened the door. Silence greeted her. She tiptoed down the hall to the head of the basement stairs. Still not a sound. Then a muffled scrape.

She eased her foot onto the top tread, held her breath and tiptoed down for a closer look. He had turned on the bare

light bulb which dangled from a cord in the centre of the ceiling, casting a harsh glare over the musty cellar. She and Jacques had cleared out much of the accumulated detritus of several generations and had taken van loads of old bicycles, broken lamps and chairs to the nearby dump. The cellar was still stacked with boxes, however; those waiting to be unpacked from their own move, and some full of Pettigrew junk that looked as if it had been sitting undisturbed in the dust for years.

The basement was divided into three rooms, one the old root cellar and pantry, the second a primitive storage and furnace area, and a third small section which the Pettigrews had obviously intended to finish as a den. Concrete had been poured over the earthen floor and two by four framing had been erected on the walls. Pine planking had been nailed on two of the walls, but the enthusiasm for the project must have died abruptly halfway through, leaving unfinished framing on the rest of the walls.

The intruder had already ransacked the storage area because the boxes were all upturned, leaving papers, dishes and old books strewn on the floor. He had moved on to the semi-finished room, where he now stood pressed against the wall, stock-still, his gaze slowly travelling around the room. Isabelle couldn't see his features clearly in the harsh shadows cast by the light bulb, but desperation was etched in his face.

As she took one last step to get a better look, her shadow slipped across the wall, catching his attention. He spun around, stared at her, stared at the axe she had hefted in her hand, and uttered a single, strangled moan before sagging against the wall in a dead faint.

*　*　*

Before Green had even turned off County Road 2 into the Boisvert's lane, he could see the three-ringed circus in the front yard of the farmhouse. Four cruisers and an ambulance sat at various angles to the house, red lights strobed the dusk, and clusters of dark figures dotted the yard. Green was gratified to note that despite the flashing lights, there was no sense of urgency in their movements. He'd been in communication with the sergeant en route, and once he'd determined that no one was seriously injured, and the scene was secure, he'd told Belowsky to hold all inquiries until he arrived.

He pulled his unmarked white Impala in behind the ambulance and had barely opened his door when Sergeant Belowsky detached himself from one of the groups and approached. The beefy man rolled as he walked, and his ill-fitting uniform looked about to split at the seams. But he was grinning as he swallowed Green's hand in a massive grip.

"Two incidents in one week," he said. "Gotta be some kind of record."

"What's the status?" Green asked.

"The suspect is in the kitchen, not giving any resistance. A bit stunned, is all."

Green raised a questioning eyebrow.

"Keeled over in the basement and whacked his head on the concrete floor, but the paramedics say he's okay."

"What about the homeowner?"

The sergeant's grin widened. "She's fine. Shook up, but spitting mad. I think the bad guy got the worst of the encounter."

"Has anyone taken a statement from him at all?"

Belowsky shook his head. "He's all yours. But the guy's not saying much anyway. Just that he wasn't breaking in, he used to live here."

Green nodded. The sergeant had told him this over the phone, and Green had already figured out this was either Tom or the long-lost Derek. If it was Derek, then the whole theory about Lawrence having killed him was out the window, and Sullivan's Brockville fishing expedition had been in vain. If it was Tom, then they finally had a real live witness to what had transpired in the family all those years ago. Green felt that addictive surge of adrenaline that always accompanied a break in the case.

Isabelle was knocking back a hefty brandy in the living room. After a reassuring word to her, he instructed Belowsky to take her statement while he himself headed to the kitchen. The intruder, he wanted to interview personally. As he passed through the archway, the scene before him reminded him of his own kitchen. Dismantled cabinets, mottled walls and the blackened remnants of several layers of linoleum flooring. Two uniformed officers were stationed in the doorways like brick walls, feet planted apart and arms folded. In the middle of the room was a large rectangular oak table surrounded by mismatched wooden chairs.

Slumped in one of them with his elbows on the table and an icepack pressed to his head was a lanky man with strings of sodden grey hair, deep pouches under his eyes, and at least three days' worth of salt and pepper stubble. As soon as he raised his head, Green knew it was Tom. The cocky confidence of the teenager in the photo was gone, but the defiant blue eyes were the same.

Before Green tipped his hand, however, he decided to see what story Tom had on offer, so without missing a beat he introduced himself and asked for a name and address. Tom apparently chose to play for time. He arched his eyebrows.

"An Inspector? Never met one of yous. Don't know why

you were called all the way out here for this. Like I told these other officers, I got nothing to hide. I ain't no burglar; I used to live here, and I didn't know anybody was home. I just came in to look for something I left here years ago."

"Your name, sir?" Green repeated patiently.

Tom hesitated briefly, and Green could see him weighing his options. Finally, he shrugged. "Tom Pettigrew. I live in Toronto."

"Street address in Toronto, sir?"

"I'm just moving."

Green kept his pen poised over his notebook. "So should I put 'no fixed address'?"

A scowl flitted across Tom's face. "Put Harmony House." Another shrug, this time with a hint of defiance. "I got a drinking problem. Hey, it's not a crime. When you run me through the Toronto police, you'll know I'm no saint, I been through the system lots of times. But that's in the past. I'm turning things around now, and this..." He gestured around him vaguely, as if to encompass the house. "This wasn't like that."

"So what was this about, Tom?"

"Facing some stuff." Tom seemed to perceive the skepticism on the faces around him, for he sat up straighter and thrust out his chin. "Look, I ain't proud of my life, okay? I know I ain't done one fucking worthwhile thing in the past twenty-five years. Last month, I woke up one morning in detox with bugs crawling all over me and a great fucking hole in my memory. Doctor said one more binge like that, and I might not wake up. Not that I really gave a shit at the time." He slumped again and shifted the ice pack gingerly.

Green was tempted to tell him to cut to the chase, but he sensed that the man had a story to tell. Who knows, maybe it was an interesting story. "So what happened?" he prompted.

Tom peered up at him dubiously through wet strings of hair.

145

"What happened is this woman from Harmony House comes to visit me. As tough and crapped over by life as me—raped by her brothers, beaten up by her pimp, carved up by johns, in jail half her life. She told me to stop feeling sorry for myself and get on with it. Either kill myself or clean up my act. I heard that a million times, but something about that broad... She was so ugly—tattoos, scars all over where she'd carved herself—she was like the end of the road. They got God at Harmony House, and I got no use for that shit. My old man whipped God out of me years ago. But just being at Harmony House..."

He paused to grope in his jacket pocket for a pack of cigarettes. He caressed one longingly, glanced around as if seeking permission to light up, but met stony, neutral stares. Finally, he jammed it unlit into the corner of his mouth. "I turned forty fucking years old last week. I heard Robbie was selling the place. I thought maybe if I came back and saw the old place. I didn't mean to scare the lady, I'm sorry about that."

"So what was it you had to face?"

"What?" Alarm flashed across Tom's face. Green waited him out, until gradually a sullen scowl replaced the alarm. "We didn't have a fairy tale upbringing here, officer. A lot goes on out here in the country that nobody sees or hears. I got a memory from every single one of these rooms, from the barn, and from the field out back. That root cellar where I come in, that was the old man's favourite place to lock me up. Maybe figured I was closer to the devil where I belonged. The room just over our head?" He jerked his thumb up to the ceiling. "Our mother strung herself up in that room. Dad didn't even cut her down, just went out and got tanked, left poor Robbie to find her. The kid just turned sixteen years old."

Green felt the bile of pity rise in his throat. He was no stranger to the tales of cruelty that scarred the souls of those

146

he met on the street, so he welcomed the emotion as a sign he was still human. To judge from the expressions of the patrol officers around him, so were they.

Yet even before the pity had receded, the seasoned police officer in him raised a flag of skepticism. Alcoholics were masters of melodrama, skilled at finding excuses for their failures and at mining the sympathy of others. Tom had spun a far longer, sadder tale than was needed to answer Green's question, and in the process had deflected attention from the one crucial fact he had let slip. Belatedly, Green retrieved it.

"What was it you came back to find?"

Tom had just removed the cigarette from his lips and held it longingly. It quivered slightly in his tobacco-stained fingers. Abruptly, he stopped to look at Green in bafflement.

Nice try, Green thought, not believing his confusion for a minute. "You mentioned you came to get something you'd left here years ago."

"My brother Derek's address," Tom replied. "He left home after university, and I ain't seen him since. But he used to drop my mother a postcard now and then, so I was hoping she packed them somewhere. Robbie said there were still some boxes of old junk in the house." He shrugged and placed the cigarette back in his mouth. "Like I said, I been trying to get my life back together, and he's almost all that's left of us. Except Robbie—who was just a kid when I left, and anyway he's written me off. Not that Derek and me got along all that great, but blood's blood, right?"

Green stifled the edge of excitement in his voice. Tom could be telling the truth, because Isabelle had said he seemed to be searching for something. "What was the last address you had for Derek?"

"How the fuck should I know?" Tom winced and pressed

his hand to his head. "I'm getting a fucking headache. Can we at least take this outside, where I can have a smoke?"

The paramedic intervened to perform a brief exam before allowing Green to continue. Green could see nothing to be lost by granting Tom's request and a lot to be gained from letting him relax and open up. Gesturing to a patrol officer to accompany them, he led the way outside onto the small front stoop. Dusk had deepened. To the west an eerie purple wash still cloaked the horizon but overhead the stars were emerging into the brittle black sky. Beside him, Tom cupped his hands against the chill night breeze as he lit his cigarette. Green waited in silence as he pulled the smoke greedily into his lungs.

"Derek's address?" Green prompted after several lungfulls.

"If I remembered that, why would I come all the way here to look for it?"

"The city? The state? You must remember that."

"Used to be Berkeley, I remember that part. Then I think it was one of them in-the-middle states. Mi-something? Never been good at geography."

"What was he doing there?"

"I don't know!" Tom flicked the ash onto the ground angrily. "Like I said, we weren't close. He just dropped Mom the occasional line, you know, so she wouldn't worry."

"But he was settled somewhere? Making a good living?"

"Oh, yeah. Derek was the smart one, always knew what he was going to get out of life." Tom jutted out his chin and cast Green a cunning look. "What the fuck's it to you anyway? That's what I was looking for, and I should've called on the lady properly, but I never was one for manners. So if you'll call off the goons—"

"Tom, there's no record of Derek being at Berkeley. No record of him ever living in the States."

Tom sat stock still, his cigarette halfway to his lips. He said nothing for a long moment, as if trying to assess the direction of the threat. Finally, he shifted his gaze from Green to the patrol officer, then to the circus of squad cars on the front lawn. His eyes grew hooded. "What the fuck's going on?"

He might be a career drunk, but he still had a decent share of brain cells, Green thought as he weighed his next move. He had no evidence to suggest foul play in Derek's disappearance, merely an uneasiness in his gut. He had even less evidence that Sophia had met a similar fate. A good investigator never played from a position of weakness. He needed leverage. Tom was almost certainly lying about Derek, but he was far too wily and experienced to roll over and confess just because Green accused him of lying. He'd simply clam up, claim memory loss, or say Derek must have lied to the whole family then.

Which was, of course, entirely possible. Derek and Sophia might have run off together, as the note suggested, and rather than risking the wrath of their strict, traditional families, they had opted to drop out of sight. If Derek had decided to sever all ties with his brothers and father but had retained a small soft spot for his long-suffering mother, he might well have sent home the occasional postcard containing a carefully constructed lie to reassure her. Green needed concrete evidence to the contrary before he confronted Tom. Evidence he hoped Sophia would be able to provide, assuming she was ever found.

In the meantime, Green did have concrete evidence of another tragedy that he could certainly challenge Tom on. Evidence that might rattle Tom sufficiently to shake loose some of the secrets he was storing inside. Green reached into his pocket, unfolded a paper and held it out to Tom in the porch light.

"Do you recognize this man?"

Tom didn't touch the photo, merely stared at it for a long time. In the silence, Green could hear the murmur of voices from the house. Out on the highway, a lone pair of headlights shot by.

Tom broke the silence, his voice like gravel. "You're thinking this is Derek?"

"Is it?"

Tom exhaled smoke in a rush and flicked his cigarette butt into the darkness. Before it had even hit the ground, he was reaching for another. He had to make three tries before he could light it. "Can't tell," he said finally. "Picture's all fucked up. Plus people always look different when they're dead, eh? Like something's missing." He spoke matter-of-factly, but his cigarette trembled, and a twitch had begun at the corner of his left eye. "What happened to him?"

Green explained briefly about the discovery of the body and asked if he'd mind coming downtown to look at the body.

"Rather not."

"If it is your brother, wouldn't you want to know?"

Tom rested his forehead in his hands. "Fuck, life always finds a way to kick you in the ass, eh?"

Green said nothing. Tom smoked. Shook his head. Then said "Fuck" and hauled himself to his feet. "Can I at least smoke in your car?"

Twelve

Viewing dead bodies had never been Green's favourite part of a case, albeit a necessary part when he'd been in the field. But months behind a desk had weakened his defences, and at the first hint of that peculiar morgue smell, composed of equal parts disinfectant, guts and putrefying flesh, he felt his stomach quail. He'd reached Sullivan en route from Brockville and arranged to meet him at the morgue, where he could have simply delivered Tom into Sullivan's capable hands without even passing through the lime green doors. But to judge from Sullivan's monosyllabic response, he was no more enthusiastic about an impromptu, after-hours visit with a three-day-old corpse than Green was. Besides, queasy stomach aside, Green was very curious to see how Tom would react.

Green made a second call from his cell phone as he, Tom and the unlucky constable from rural west district who'd drawn escort duty barrelled through the dark towards the city. It was to Dr. Alexander MacPhail. He reached the pathologist in the middle of a dinner party at which, from the sound of it, Scotch whiskey had been flowing freely for some time. Raucous laughter punctuated the background as MacPhail cursed into the phone.

"Goddamn it, lad! Check the man into the Y and go home to your wife and kiddies. The poor stiff will still be there in the morning, and so will I."

Green glanced over at Tom, who was staring stonily out the window in the back. He was on his third cigarette, and his hands were shaking, probably from need of booze. The stiff might still be there, Green thought, but my next-of-kin won't be. He'll be on the first bus out of town, as far from Ottawa as he can get. With profuse apologies and assurances that MacPhail would be back with his guests in no time, Green stuck to his guns.

When he and Tom arrived at the morgue, neither MacPhail nor Sullivan were anywhere in sight, but they'd only been waiting a minute before the elevator pinged. Green could hear MacPhail's angry stride all the way down the hall, and when the tall, rangy pathologist burst around the corner, his white mane defied gravity and vivid purple blotched his pock-marked face. He barely acknowledged Green's greeting as he unlocked the morgue door and pulled on his lab coat. But even in the throes of one of his famous whiskey-fuelled tempers, his professionalism took over when he turned to Tom.

"The body is in the cold room at the moment, sir. We have a few paperwork formalities, and then I'll have my assistant bring him into the viewing room next door. He'll be draped in a sheet, so you tell me when you're ready to take a look. His face has been badly damaged, so you'd best be prepared."

Tom acknowledged the doctor's tact with a curt nod. He was vibrating from head to toe, and his gaze flitted around the room, lighting restlessly on the stainless steel tubs and bowls, the rows of jars, and the three long, stainless steel slabs. Mercifully, there were no gurneys parked in the corners with telltale toes protruding. Green risked his first full breath of air.

The viewing room was small, airless and furnished in standard waiting room plastic. Tom barely glanced at the papers before scribbling a large, unpractised signature by the Xs that MacPhail had marked. Afterwards, Green settled into

one of the chairs, but Tom leaned against the wall with his hands shoved in his pockets, affecting a casual pose.

"I been through this before, you know," Tom said into the silence that had settled on the room. "AIDS, booze, freezing to death. It's all part of street life. I don't suppose Derek would ever look as bad as that. Always took fucking good care of himself, even the cowshit didn't smell on him."

Green had decided in the car that he would not mention Lawrence, for he wanted Tom off balance enough to shake loose a secret or two about his past. So far, the man wasn't giving away a thing. They'd been waiting five minutes when the door swung open and Sullivan came in, followed closely by Peters. Her eyes danced, and she looked as alert and animated as Sullivan did drained. Green barely had time for introductions before MacPhail cracked open the door again.

"Ready?" His assistant wheeled in a gurney that was discreetly draped in white, but even through the sheet, the contours of a tall, bulky man could be seen.

Tom thrust himself off the wall and strode to the centre of the room, his hands still in his pockets. MacPhail glanced over the paperwork, then nodded to Tom questioningly. Tom had begun to shake again.

"Take your time, sir."

"No," said Tom through gritted teeth. "Do it."

MacPhail reached up, and with a gentle, practised hand, he folded the sheet back from the face. Peters and Sullivan looked at the body, but Green watched Tom. Saw a faint twitch at the edge of his left eye, a flicker of raw horror that he fought to control. For a moment, he didn't even breathe.

"That's Derek," he managed finally. "Holy fuck, that's my brother Derek."

*   *   *

"Well, that throws your cockamamie theory out the window," Sullivan pronounced flatly as he jackknifed his bulk into the booth opposite Green at Nate's Deli. Nate's was a legend in Ottawa, having maintained its original menu and building on downtown Rideau Street since Green's boyhood. Until two years ago, Green had lived only blocks away and had become such a fixture in the corner booth that the waitress never bothered to bring him a menu. Montreal smoked meat platter with fries and a side of hot cherry peppers, all washed down by a pint of draught in a frosted mug. Green was nursing this pensively when Sullivan returned from dropping Tom off at the downtown Y. Sullivan was tired and cranky, but neither detective had thought it wise to abandon the poor man at a bus stop.

Green had been mulling over the same thought before Sullivan arrived. Tom's pronouncement that the body was Derek and not Lawrence threw his whole understanding of the case into disarray. He'd been so sure that Lawrence had murdered Derek, and that the family had locked him away to cover up the fact. He'd been so sure it was Lawrence who'd met his death in the churchyard, that he found himself at a loss. If Tom was telling the truth, they were looking at quite a different sequence of crimes.

"Do you think he's telling the truth?" he asked.

Sullivan picked up Green's mug and tossed back half of it in one grateful swig that left a foam mustache on his upper lip. He shrugged. "The guy was pretty much a basket case on the drive to the Y." He held up two fingers an inch apart. "This close to hitting the bottle again, I'd say. Besides, I don't see what he'd gain by lying."

"Well, for starters, it stops us asking questions about what

154

happened to Derek twenty years ago."

"Maybe nothing happened! Did that ever occur to you, Mike? Maybe Derek went off to the States like everyone says, and maybe Lawrence just flipped out and got committed. End of story."

Green leaned forward. "Then why did they all come back? Why was Lawrence rooting around in the farm yard that morning, looking for a treasure box he had buried twenty years ago?"

"We don't know for sure that was him. It could have been Derek."

Green shook his head. "Lawrence was there. The crucifix was found in the woods, and we know Lawrence had it. So he was there."

Sullivan groaned. He was reaching for Green's beer again when the waitress arrived with one of his own. She'd been serving there forever, still wearing a black mini skirt and a white blouse pulled tight across her breasts. The only sign of aging was the slow collection of wrinkles around her bright red lips and heavily shadowed eyes, which drank in Sullivan now with unconcealed lust.

"Hi, Sarge! Missed me, did you?"

Sullivan gave her the required grin. "Haven't been able to sleep a wink, Alice."

Her red lips drew back in a knowing smile. "Have to work on that. What'll you have, love?"

Sullivan pointed to Green. "Same as him, only skip the hot peppers."

She shook her head. "You gotta learn to live dangerously."

"Eating with him is dangerous enough."

Alice laughed, a throaty chuckle that made her cleavage quiver and her buttons strain, then she sashayed off towards the kitchen.

155

Sullivan's smile faded as soon as her back was turned, and he slumped back in the booth. "I really just want to go home, Mike. It's been a long day. Besides, Mary's out showing a house, and that means Lizzie has to take Sean to hockey."

"But we have to eat, right? And this way we can talk about the case too."

"I don't want to talk about the fucking case any more. Besides, don't you have a few family obligations of your own?"

"Our kitchen is still in chaos. My end of the deal is that I pick up smoked meat, a rye and poppyseed strudel on my way out." He grinned. "Sharon forgives a lot of sins for a fresh poppyseed strudel."

"Sharon forgives a lot, period. The woman's headed for sainthood."

Green laughed. "Fortunately, not in all areas. But the sooner we figure out what the hell is going on, the sooner we both get home to our saintly wives."

Sullivan took a deep slug of his beer and sighed. "Fine. I'm here anyway, so shoot."

"I had a brief interview with Tom out at the farm," Green began. "And he said the same thing Robbie told us. That Derek had sent postcards from some place in the States, but Tom's had no personal contact with him in years. In fact, Tom said he came back to the farm house to find Derek's address."

"And you believe that? That doesn't sound like you."

Green sipped his own beer while he brought his irritation in check. He needed Sullivan to participate, not begrudge every second he had to sit there.

"Well, let's assume it's true and see where it takes us." He began to tick off points on his fingers. "Let's say twenty years ago, Tom was in love with Sophia and wrote her that letter begging for a second chance. We know Sophia disappeared

shortly afterwards, and Derek never went to Berkeley as he was supposed to. That torn note suggests he had a secret lover he may have run off with. Maybe there was a huge fight over Sophia—remember that note had blood on it—and so Derek and Sophia dropped out of sight. Derek could have concealed his true whereabouts from his family and sent some postcards to reassure his mother, while he was living happily in the States with Sophia all these years."

Sullivan signalled Alice for another draught. "I'd say you just put Tom at the top of our list of murder suspects. He never got his life back together after his big brother stole his girl, and he's had plenty of time to build up a head of steam. So he dreams up a way to get Derek back up to the farm—probably told him about their father being sick—and he sets up the kill. Typical for a drunk. Blame everyone in the world for your failings except yourself."

Green nodded impatiently. "I agree he's up there. But some things don't fit. First of all, if Tom murdered Derek, why did he ID the body so readily? Why not lie?"

Sullivan snorted. "He's crafty. He's been in the system often enough to know about dental matching and DNA. He knows we'd ID Derek eventually, and then it would look even more suspicious for him."

"At the very least, why didn't he say he couldn't be sure after all these years? I watched his face, Brian. He was so shocked, there's no way he could have made up a credible lie. If he had killed Derek, he'd have had lots of time to figure out what to say."

"But if Tom didn't set this up, what made Derek suddenly decide to come home again?"

"Maybe his luck changed. MacPhail said the victim had fallen on hard times recently. Maybe his life fell apart, and he came back up here looking to reconnect."

"At exactly the same time Tom shows up looking for his address? Come on, Mike, the coincidence is preposterous. Tom's been playing us from the beginning, and you've been sitting on committees too long to recognize it."

Green held his temper with an effort. He knew it was preposterous, and it didn't help his mood to have Sullivan point it out. But at least Sullivan, as grumpy as he was, had begun to play the devil's advocate Green needed him to be.

Alice appeared, balancing their platters in one hand and Sullivan's second draught in the other. Green said nothing but watched uneasily as Sullivan downed a huge swig, for Sullivan's bloodshot eyes and the foul temper that morning still worried him. He knew Sullivan usually kept to a strict two-drink limit in order to avoid the risk of alcoholism that ran in his genes. Sullivan prided himself on the achievements and respect he'd earned as a cop, but a man can only take the stress and disappointment so long.

But Green knew Sullivan well enough to recognize this was not the time to broach the reason for his mood. He needed to rekindle Sullivan's enthusiasm and his passion for his work, so he searched for a way to draw him in. He gave Sullivan the time to douse his french fries in ketchup and shovel a fistful into his mouth before resuming.

"Of course the coincidence is preposterous," Green said. "But you're forgetting an even bigger coincidence. Lawrence was there too, and in my book he's at least as good a murder suspect as Tom."

Sullivan paused in the act of balancing succulent slices of smoked meat on his rye and looked at Green thoughtfully. "And what would be his motive after all these years?"

"Maybe revenge for locking him away all those years?"

Sullivan set down his precariously balanced sandwich and

sat back. Green was glad to see that he'd abandoned his beer and was deep in thought. "But I've just spent the day talking to the Brockville people about him. They describe him as gentle and kind of childlike most of the time. Maybe he'd lash out if he got desperate, but he wasn't really capable of that kind of long-term planning."

"But Angie Hogencamp also told me that after a month of being off his meds, he'd be getting delusional again, so anything is possible. He might have started thinking about how they all betrayed him, and all those years might have seemed like yesterday to him."

"We're still stuck with the same question though, Mike. What brought Derek back? It's just too big a coincidence to have three brothers show up in the same place twenty years later."

"I agree there are still a lot of things that don't fit." Green paused, feeling more relaxed now that he had aired all his ideas. "I don't know which brother killed Derek. But I do think if we're ever going to get to the bottom of it, we'd better start taking a closer look at what Derek's been up to all these years. And I think, just to verify Tom's story, we should still have Angie Hogencamp up to see the body."

* * *

At eight o'clock the next morning, Sullivan was scrolling through his emails, checking for urgent ones and half hoping he'd encounter one from HR that apologized for the mix-up and congratulated him on his promotion. It wasn't there, of course, and the heaviness of the day settled upon him like a wet shroud when he reached the end of the list. Preempting him, Green had called an eight o'clock team briefing to plan the next stage of the investigation, and Sullivan was going to

159

be late. With an effort he pulled out the Pettigrew file and picked up the phone to call Mrs. Hogencamp.

When she picked up, she sounded breathless and rushed.

"I'm so glad you called, Sergeant!" she exclaimed. "Your questions yesterday got me thinking. I don't know if there was a girl or not, but Lawrence was obsessed about something sexual when he was first admitted. He kept rambling to the nurses about sin and something being an abomination, about how God punished sinners, and he tried to save them. It made no sense, and the doctors just called it word salad. Gbberish. But if you listened carefully, he did seem to be trying to explain something. Trying to tell us something that had happened."

Sullivan flipped open his notebook, fully alert. Just when they thought they'd figured out what the case was all about, another ball came in from left field. Green was going to want every word. "Could you figure out what he was trying to say?"

"That he'd somehow failed. That Satan had taken control and had to be destroyed."

Sullivan groaned. Satan. There was a bad guy for you. "And did you figure out who this Satan figure was?"

"No, but he kept saying he had to go back home to get Satan."

"Did he mention any of his brothers in these ramblings?"

"He mentioned several names over and over, but I can't remember them all. It's been such a long time."

"Try, Mrs. Hogencamp. This is very important."

"Oh, dear." Sullivan listened to the sound of her muttering to herself. "Tommy? Derry, something like that."

"Derek?" Sullivan asked carefully.

"Derry, Lorrie—oh dear, I forget."

"What about girls? Anyone called Sophia?"

"Oh yes!" Mrs. Hogencamp's voice rose with excitement.

"That's when he'd get really agitated. That's when the Satan and sex and abomination would come in. His passion was actually quite scary."

"I'm not an expert in schizophrenia, Mrs. Hogencamp, so I need your help. Based on what you know of him, say he liked a girl and he surprised one of his brothers in bed with her. Would that trigger this Satan and abomination rant?"

"The boys had a very strict upbringing," she said. "Probably sex outside of marriage would be a very serious sin. If Lawrence had been aroused by a girl, he would have seen himself as dirty and evil. If he found his brother acting on those desires he loathed and repressed in himself...yes, he certainly would consider it an abomination."

Sullivan hesitated, searching for the most neutral phrase so he would not put words in her mouth. "What would he be likely to do? Kill himself?"

"It depends on how much self-loathing he had for his own sexual urges." She paused, her uncertainty returning. Sullivan could feel her retreating. "It's complicated to speculate. I hardly feel qualified..."

"Guess."

"He's a paranoid. Betrayal and revenge are central to their delusions. I think, if he were going to kill himself, he'd be much more likely to take one or both of them with him."

*   *   *

Back in the days when Green was in the field, his briefings had been one of the highlights of Sullivan's day. Green had a way of getting the big picture and seeing how the evidence fit together that was pure genius. Even his wild flights of fancy proved right more often than not. In his field days, he loved to pace in front

of the chalkboard, surrounded by crime scene photos and witness statements, scribbling points and drawing arrows back and forth until his case summary looked like a massive drunken spider's web. However, Bob Gibbs had long since demonstrated the power of computer software to project the case discussion onto a screen and to underline, highlight, and link ideas so that everyone could decipher them. Furthermore, at the end, the discussion and action plans were neatly summarized on a file in a disc, rather than erased with the next shift. So Green continued to pace, but he had replaced his chalk with a laser pointer and relinquished the recording role to Gibbs.

By the time Sullivan finally reached the briefing room after his phone call, Gibbs had a neat diagram projected onto the screen at the end of the room. In the centre of the web was a big circle marked "Derek?", and "murder/suicide" Around them like satellites were bubbles containing the names of witnesses and family members, with questions to be answered. Green was just pointing to Derek's bubble on the screen.

"Detective Peters, I want you to—" He broke off as he spotted Sullivan, and he raised a questioning brow. Whether the question was personal or professional, Sullivan wasn't sure. The man was far too astute not to have noticed his black mood.

"Any developments?" Green asked with careful ambiguity.

Briefly, Sullivan summarized his phone conversation with Angela Hogencamp. He caught the glint of triumph in Green's eyes, but this time it only served to depress him, for Green had said all along that Sophia was at the bottom of things. Why was the damn man right so much of the time?

"Bingo," Green said. "You've got a relationship with Mrs. Hogencamp, so I think you should pursue things at her end. Get her up here to view the body. I want you to show her Robbie's photo album too. It has pictures of all the brothers,

and maybe she can tell if any of them visited Lawrence in recent months. As for these other tasks," he waved his pointer across the screen. "Can you think of any avenues of investigation that I've missed?"

You know fucking well there aren't any, Sullivan thought. Since when do you miss anything? And since when does it matter what I think anyway? I'm only the officer of record on the goddamn case.

His scowl must have given him away, because before he could shake his head, Green walked over, laid a page of notes in front of him and headed out the door. "Okay. I got the briefing started while we were waiting for you, but I leave you to it. I was going to suggest Peters track down Derek's old college friends and Gibbs carry on looking for Sophia. But whatever you think is best."

Sullivan felt a prick of shame for his childish thoughts. He pushed back the bleakness with an effort as he studied the screen. "Any thoughts on the Pettigrew father? We don't have much on him. I can pop by the hospital after I pick up Robbie's album."

"No need," said Green cheerfully. "I thought I'd fit him in myself during my lunch hour. The hospital's not far from my house, so I can drop in on Bob the contractor." With a grin, he ducked out the door.

It took Sullivan fifteen minutes to complete the briefing. He had no qualms about sending Gibbs off with an Italian translator to phone all the Vincellis in the small Tuscany town where Sophia had supposedly been sent. But he wanted to talk Peters through every step of her inquiry before he unleashed her on the educated, well-spoken and politically correct crowd at Carleton University. No psychos, shrinks and the like, not a hint of cop bluster or arrogance. Ask politely, listen to the answers, and always thank them for their help.

He could tell from her pout that she was insulted by the tight leash, but he had no patience for egos. Let her prove him wrong by doing a first-rate job. After he'd dispatched her, he was heading back to his desk to call Mrs. Hogencamp again when he spotted Green watching him through his half open door. Green cocked his head to signal him to come in. Sullivan hesitated, bristling at the prospect of more Green meddling. But instead, when he finally entered the office, Green rose to shut the door behind him. He looked grave.

"Brian, I didn't want you to hear this from anyone else. Adam Jules is being transferred to East Division and Barbara Devine is taking over CID."

Sullivan groaned inwardly. They were going to have a conversation he didn't want to have. Not now. Not when he was still feeling crapped on and sold short. Adam Jules would be a loss; he was a cop's cop, who knew and respected every job under his command. Barbara Devine was a joke. Smart, tenacious and political, but nowhere near ready to run the most technically demanding and emotionally brutal division in the entire force. But today, none of that mattered. Nothing mattered, because for the first time in twenty years, his job didn't matter. And he was afraid that if Green made him talk about it, he'd tell him exactly that.

Green was watching him keenly, so Sullivan kept his expression as deadpan as he could. "Worse for you than for me," he said. "You're closer to the angels."

"And Gaetan Larocque is the new staff sergeant."

"I knew that," Sullivan said, to head off any expression of condolence.

"I was afraid you did. Tough break, Brian."

"Not your fault. Not anyone's fault, just the way the goddamn system works. A quota of this, a balance of that,

bilingualism always an asset. Whether the guy actually knows dick all about investigating major crimes doesn't matter."

"Larocque's a solid investigator. He'll learn. And you'll still be as indispensable around here as you always were. Probably more so."

"Yeah, training yet another rookie cop how to conduct a professional interview." Sullivan slumped in the chair and put his feet on the desk. Fuck it, they were going to have this conversation after all. "I've been thinking maybe I need to move on."

Green looked at the ceiling. Sighed and shook his head.

"I've been in this unit twelve of my twenty-one years on the force, Mike. Maybe that's the problem. Maybe they don't see me as diverse enough."

"Brian, this place can't run without you. Not with Devine at the helm and Larocque parading the troops."

Sullivan smiled wryly. "The place will learn to get along. They've got you."

"But there's nothing like Major Crimes. What are you going to do? High Tech? Auto Theft?"

"Maybe. I'll look around, see what I like. There are lots of ways of being a cop, Green, and a couple of short stints in other positions would bulk up my CV. So when another staff sergeant opening comes along..."

Green sank back in his chair. "Damnit, Brian," he muttered, "I know what you're saying, and you may be right. But promotions aren't everything, believe me. There are a hell of a lot of guys upstairs who'd rather be doing what you're doing. Nothing beats the satisfaction of liking your work and knowing you do a good job."

On that note, Sullivan hauled himself to his feet and paused at the door with a smile he only half meant. "Bullshit. Inspector," he said before he walked out.

Thirteen

At eleven-thirty, when Green could stand the claustrophobia of the station no longer, he escaped instead into the noontime traffic jam of downtown Ottawa. A blustery rain battered the city, compounding his black mood as he bullied his way across the Pretoria Bridge and up towards Main Street. All the way, he cursed his stupidity. Sullivan was struggling with a very real crisis of faith in himself and in the force and deserved the understanding and respect of the one man who was probably his oldest and closest friend on the force. Yet he, Green, had offered nothing but vacuous crap! He'd been so dismayed by the prospect of losing Sullivan that he'd thought only of himself and offered the man not hope nor affirmation but platitudes. And now there was little hope of rectifying it, for Sullivan was a proud man who would take his own counsel in the privacy of his own thoughts. He was too professional not to continue to do an exemplary job on this case and others, but Green knew he would be quietly looking.

So lost in thought was Green that he failed to notice his surroundings until he drove past Bank Street and saw Robbie Pettigrew's apartment building receding in his rainwashed rearview mirror. He did a loop back onto Bank Street and sat a few minutes in the front drive, contemplating the pouring rain. It depressed him even further to think of visiting a

crippled old man in a hospital bed to inform him of his son's death and to make him relive the tragedies of the past.

When Green finally mustered the courage to dash to the front door, a Muslim woman in traditional hijab was juggling several bags of groceries and a pair of overactive pre-schoolers while she searched her massive satchel for her key. Green's helping hand with the bags earned him a shy nod and entrance to the lobby. Hence, he knocked on Robbie's door unannounced and was surprised when a familiar, smoke-roughened snarl emanated from within.

"Who is it?"

Sullivan had dropped Tom off at the Y, but the man had obviously made his own arrangements. Recovering quickly, Green introduced himself.

The door opened just far enough for Green to plant his toe in it, and Tom's craggy, unshaven face filled the crack. "Well, if it ain't the fucking cavalry."

"Good morning, Tom. I'm here to see your brother Robert."

"Ain't here. Come back after five." Tom started to withdraw, then paused. "Better yet, I'll get him to call you."

"Well," Green continued blithely, "my main goal is to talk to your father, who I understand is very frail, so I wanted to know if Robbie would like to accompany me. But maybe you can come instead."

Tom recoiled. "Not on your life. What do you want to see him for?"

"I want to talk to him about Derek—about why he left, whether your father's heard from him recently, whether he knew why Derek came back?"

Green saw panic flare briefly in Tom's eyes before he wrestled his sullen disinterest back in place. "Waste of time. Derek wouldn't have contacted the old man in a million years.

167

They had a huge, knock-down, drag-out fist fight just before he left. And like always, Derek got the worst of it."

Green wedged his toe even further in the doorway and leaned against the doorframe, trying to hide his excitement. Unconsciously, Tom had let the door drift open a few inches, and Green was anxious to keep him talking. "What was the fight about?"

Suspicion flashed across Tom's face. "Ancient history, and none of your business."

Green sighed. "Look, Tom, I'm not here to hassle you. I'm sure you've taken plenty of crap from the Toronto cops over the years, but frankly, any guy who's trying to turn his life around no matter how fucked up it's been, gets my vote. I'm just trying to close this case. Your brother ended up dead in a village he swore he'd never return to, and I'm trying to find out why. It's all connected—why he left, why he came back, and what drove him to his death."

That was only half the story, of course, but Green hoped the half truth would be enough to put Tom off his guard. He didn't want Tom to know the police had any suspicion that Derek had been murdered or that Tom himself was a prime suspect. He kept his expression bland and expectant as Tom shifted from one foot to the other, running his hand through his stringy hair. Finally, Tom stepped back with a scowl. "Might as well come in, I'm due for a smoke anyway."

Green followed him into Robbie's little apartment, which was murky with cigarette smoke. A blanket lay neatly folded on the back of the couch, and the only sign of clutter was a pack of cigarettes and an overflowing ashtray on the coffee table. Tom pulled a cigarette from the pack and snapped open his lighter. As he sucked the smoke in deep, Green could almost see him uncoil.

"My little brother here's a good example why a man should

never get married. Two wives in six years, and both bled him dry." Tom gestured around the shabby room. "Wife number one got the leather couch and chair, wife number two the flashy home entertainment centre. Next wife'll probably take the bed right out from under him." He blew a series of smoke rings toward the ceiling. "Poor sucker. At least I never married my women."

Green eased himself onto the couch. "What about Derek?"

Tom froze, a smoke ring half formed.

"Was there a woman at the bottom of it all, Tom? Is that why he left?"

The smoke ring dissipated slowly upwards. "If there was, I didn't know about her. He was probably banging half a dozen co-eds up on campus, but he never brought them home. He wasn't that much of an idiot. Cow shit and a psycho brother would scare the crap out of any girl."

"You saw him actually leave home that day? To catch a four-thirty bus out of Ottawa?"

Surprise flashed across Tom's face. "How the hell did you know that?"

"We found some evidence at the farm."

The surprise changed to sheer shock. Tom's colour fled and his cigarette jerked in his hand. "What evidence?"

Green didn't reply. "He was arranging to meet someone called S. Was that Sophia Vincelli?"

Tom jammed his cigarette into the corner of his mouth and turned to the kitchen. "Want a drink? Coke?" He disappeared and Green could hear cupboards banging and glass tinkling. He moved so that he could see Tom's reaction.

"Was it Sophia Vincelli?"

Tom dropped ice cubes on the floor and groped around on his hands and knees to pick them up. Ash dripped from his cigarette onto the floor.

"I'll take that as a yes."

"Take it however the fuck you want. I don't know what Derek was doing, or who he was fucking. Only that he was getting the hell out."

"Along with the note, we found a love letter written by you to Sophia." The author of the letter was a guess, but the handwriting had been clumsy and unpractised, much more Tom's style than Derek's.

Tom stood up and tossed the ice cubes in the sink with a resounding crash. "It give you your jollies, Detective?"

"Sophia never saw it, you know. Lawrence stole it."

"He was a laugh a minute."

"Looked like you loved Sophia a lot."

Tom shrugged. "I hardly remember. My dick was permanently up in those days."

"I saw her picture. She was one hell of a beautiful girl."

"Ah-h, she's probably a fat bitch with ten kids by now."

"Still, it was no fun having your big brother steal your girl out from under your nose."

The tell-tale twitch had begun at the side of Tom's eye. "He wouldn't have lasted. He was too goody-goody for her tastes."

"What about Lawrence? Did he like Sophia too?"

"How the fuck should I know! He spooked her good, that much I know. Why all these questions about Sophia anyway? We're talking twenty years ago!"

"Because Sophia left town at the same time as Derek. Do you have any idea where she went?"

"You're thinking she went with Derek?"

"I don't know. Did she?"

Tom dropped new ice cubes into his coke and shook his head with disgust. "You must think I read minds or something. 'How did Lawrence feel?' 'Did Derek run off with Sophia?'

Looks like you know more than me. Lawrence stole my letter to Sophia and the note about her meeting Derek. Sounds like nobody got what they were supposed to, so who gives a fuck anyway?"

A key rattled in the lock, and the apartment door burst open, spilling Robbie into the room. He stopped abruptly at the sight of Green, a look of guilty fear crossing his face. Why do I always have that effect, Green wondered, before extending a hearty handshake. "Robbie, just the man I came to see."

"Your sergeant's already called. I'm just getting it."

"What?"

"The photo album. He called me at the store." Robbie scurried over to the bookcase and extracted the album. "He's meeting me at the store. I'm not sure why you need it now that Tom has identified Derek. Tom and I were talking...we'd like to take him back to the country to bury him with Benji and Mom as soon as possible."

"Have you told your father yet?"

Robbie had been heading back towards the door, and he stopped, clutching the album to his chest. "I'm not sure there's much point. It would just upset him."

"He needs to know, Robbie."

"Why? His health is so fragile. He can't talk or walk or feed himself. He just sits in his wheelchair and cries. It's awful."

"Can he understand what is said to him?"

"Simple things, I suppose. He can nod and shake his head, he can point to what he wants. But when he tries to talk, it's just a garbled mumble that I can't understand, and then he gets so frustrated he bangs his wheelchair and cries. I can't see the point of telling him."

Green thought about his own father, who was able to walk and talk but who was still so easily upset by the indignities of

171

old age. Sid Green would hate to be bypassed. "All the same, he's Derek's father—"

"For God's sake, Inspector!" Tom exclaimed, breaking the silence he'd maintained since Robbie's arrival. "Our father hasn't seen Derek in twenty years. He thinks he's happily settled some place in the States. Derek was the one success story in this fucked-up family. What goddamn good would it do to tell him his golden boy just took a dive off the church tower? Especially *that* church!"

Robbie gave Tom a puzzled look and Green jumped in to seize the valuable tidbit about the past. "Why especially that church?"

Tom settled onto the couch and lit another cigarette. Robbie's lips drew down in disapproval, which Tom pretended not to notice. "Reverend Taylor's church," he said with a snort. "We used to belong, before our old man decided it was too soft on sin. The old man likes his hellfire and brimstone, none of this turn the other cheek and the meek shall inherit the earth crap."

"So your family left the church?"

"Taylor was a half-senile old geezer who loved to take all the losers under his wing. Drunks, psychos, fags. One day Taylor did a sermon on how they were all God's children who just needed our help to return to the fold, and our old man walked out in the middle. Dragged us all straight across the street to the holy rollers. I remember, because I was toking a shitload of weed every week by then, and the old man told me he didn't care what that pinko faggot minister said, I was going straight to hell."

Green thought about Derek's body at the bottom of Taylor's church tower, and an idea began to take form. Whatever the reason for Derek's death, perhaps he had gone there to seek out an old refuge in his time of despair. "Did you all go to the new church then?"

Tom whipped his head back and forth. "The minister was

a mean old bible-thumper with a glass eye that looked right through you. One shot of that was enough for Derek and me."

"What about Lawrence?"

"That's when he really started to go off the rails. He'd listen to old glass-eye's bible thumping sermons, and he'd take it word for word. Taylor kind of accepted Lawrence, and it didn't matter if he started mumbling or wandering around in the middle of the service. Taylor took him under his wing, gave him little jobs like polishing the brass and putting out prayer books. Even taught him how to ring the bell. But our old man put a stop to that. Between him and the glass-eyed Nazi, they turned him into their own fucking warrior of God."

Robbie stared at him. "I barely remember any of that. So strange to think of Dad going every week to church. After Benji died, he never set foot in one again. Mum tried, but..." He trailed off, but Green knew exactly what he'd left unsaid. As Edna had said, Katherine Pettigrew had little energy for anything by the time her end drew near.

A strange spell of shared pain seemed to settle over the brothers, which Green was reluctant to break. But a second later, Robbie himself broke it by thrusting the album into Green's hands. "Anyway, now that you're here, you can take this to Sergeant Sullivan, and I'll get back to work." He cast Tom a wary glance as he headed back toward the door. Green suspected he didn't entirely trust his brother alone in his home.

"Actually, Robbie," Green said, "I'm headed to the hospital. I need to interview your father."

That stopped Robbie in his tracks. "What for?"

"Background on Derek. Perhaps your father has his address in the States."

"But I told you, he can't talk!" Robbie protested. "And the shock could bring on another stroke."

"Then one of you come with me."

Robbie glanced at his watch in dismay, but before he could object, Tom jumped in. "I'll come."

Robbie's eyebrows shot up in bewilderment. "You said you didn't ever want to see him."

"This is different," Tom muttered. "Can't have the cop crawling all over him."

I'd have thought you'd consider that a just punishment, Green thought, but kept silent. Left to bounce off each other, the brothers were providing a wealth of background material.

"But Tom..." A dubious look crept into Robbie's pale blue eyes.

"I'm not going to upset him, if that's what you're thinking." Tom held his hands up in surrender. "I'm sober, okay? The old man and I will have a grand old time. I'll be on my best behaviour, and he won't be able to say a fucking word. It'll be a first for both of us."

*   *   *

Throughout most of the car ride along Riverside Drive and up Bronson Avenue to Carling, Tom chain-smoked in short, jerky puffs that filled Green's car with clouds of smoke. The sprawling, multi-winged brick complex of the Civic Hospital had just come into view over the crest of the hill when he tossed the butt out the window and shrank down in his seat.

"This was a mistake."

Green flicked on his turning signal to enter the parking lot. "I thought you wanted to keep an eye on me."

"But I haven't seen the bastard in ten years. I hate his guts and he hates mine, and nothing's happened to make me change my mind."

"Tom, he's just a sick old man."

Tom fumbled in his pocket and pulled out another cigarette, this one bent and partially smoked. He lit it with shaky fingers. "You think. He's like old cowhide, just grows tougher the older he gets. The last time I actually talked to him was at my brother Benji's funeral. We were both so goddamn wasted, we could have killed each other. He never pulled any punches. Said it was my fault, because I let the kid down. After all that happened, all that fucking bastard made us do, he has the nerve to say I killed Benji!"

Green quickly rethought his plans. Benji was the son he knew almost nothing about, but who seemed to foreshadow the family's disintegration like a canary in a mine. Was there more to his death than a simple accident on a deserted stretch of road? Green navigated the car through the parking lot and drew up to the curb near the entrance. Slapping an official police card on the dash, he turned to Tom.

"How about we grab a fast coffee before we go up? Let you catch your breath."

Tom managed a twisted smile. "Got a shot of rye under that jacket?" He climbed out of the car, then eyed his half smoked butt. "I bet they don't even let you smoke in this hell hole."

Green steered him inside and along the broad corridor to the coffee shop. He bided his time as they purchased their coffees and selected a table. Tom was as twitchy as a cat, so Green chose his timing with care. Once both were settled back with their coffees, he picked up the topic as if it had never been dropped.

"I thought your brother Ben died in a car crash, so what could you have to do with it? Were you there?"

Tom stirred his coffee for the fourth time. Picked an invisible crumb off the table. "The road was straight, the night was clear, and Benji knew that stretch of highway like the back

of his hand. Plus there wasn't an inch of skid mark on the road. You judge."

"You're saying he ran into that tree deliberately?"

"Hey, it's a great family tradition."

"Why?"

Tom sipped his coffee in short gulps. "Why what?"

"Why would he kill himself?"

"Twenty-one years in that family not good enough?"

"You said 'after all your father made us do'. What did he make you do?"

Tom said nothing, merely continued to gulp at his coffee as if it were single malt whisky. Perhaps in his mind it was. In the background, the hospital PA system droned out the names of doctors. Finally, Tom shoved his chair back and stood.

"Well, let's get this circus over with. I got places to go."

Green wanted to ask where, but knew Tom wouldn't tell him. Besides, that really was none of his business. He was investigating a crime, and although he was not exactly sure what crime, he did know it did not entitle him to question every move his witnesses made. So he tossed out his coffee cup and followed Tom down the hall.

From all the descriptions he'd been given, Green pictured Norman Pettigrew as a tyrant with a ramrod back and a ferocious glare. But the man propped in a wheelchair by the window of room 512B was a frail, white-haired figure with a drooping head, a palsied right hand and drool down his chin. Unexpectedly, Tom hung back in the doorway, but Norman lifted his head marginally as Green walked in. His eyes followed Green's progress across the room, but otherwise he showed no interest. Why should he, Green realized. He'd probably been prodded and poked by thousands of medical personnel in the past three months.

Green placed a folding chair in front of Norman's wheelchair and sat facing him. He tried to catch the man's eyes and saw fleeting bewilderment in them before they drifted out of focus. Green reached out to shake the man's good left hand.

"Mr. Pettigrew, I'm Inspector Michael Green of the Ottawa Police. Can you hear me?"

Norman Pettigrew's hand jerked away, and Green heard his sharp intake of breath. Oh yes, he can hear me.

"Your son's name came up in an investigation, and I need to ask you a few questions. Do you mind?"

Norman's breathing eased and he struggled to lift his head, but Green sensed pride rather than fear or defiance. However, the man had five sons, and at least one was no stranger to police investigations. Green glanced back to see Tom still hovering in the shadows, seemingly robbed of speech himself.

"When was the last time you saw your son Derek?"

The old man recoiled as if slapped. His eyes bulged.

"Was it this year? Last year? Five years ago?"

Norman was shaking his head back and forth with each question, his breath coming in erratic gasps. A large tear pooled in his right eye and spilled down his withered cheek. His lips worked as he struggled to form words, but all that emerged were grunts.

"Gone," he finally managed, spittle flying.

"Yes, I know he's gone. Where?"

The man shook his head. "Gom!"

"You mean dead?"

More tears gathered and spilled, dripping unheeded onto his hospital robe. Norman twisted his head as if to escape Green's relentless presence, and his eyes caught Tom in the doorway. His breath spasmed, and his eyes flew wide with fright.

"No!" he gasped.

Tom detached himself from the shadows and walked across the room, his hands shoved in his pockets as if to contain them. "Yeah, Pop. Tell him. Is Derek dead?"

Norman whipped his head back and forth, his lips working frantically. Tom stood over him.

"Derek came to see you, didn't he?" he demanded.

Norman's eyes bulged, and his face turned purple.

"Didn't he! That's why he threw himself off the fucking tower!"

Norman began to choke, his wheelchair banging the wall. Green leaped to his feet and shoved Tom back towards the door.

"What the hell are you doing!" Green dragged Tom outside into the hall and slammed him against the wall. He pinned him with his arm while he shouted for help and scanned the hall urgently. A nurse with a meds cart hurried towards him.

"Norman Pettigrew in Room 512B—help him!"

Within seconds, a flurry of staff had descended on the room, and Green could hear them banging equipment around and speaking to Norm in soothing tones. Green turned his attention back to Tom, who stood with his head bowed and his anger drained. Green shook him and dragged him down the hall.

"What the hell was that about, eh? You could have given him a goddamn stroke!"

"Lost my cool," Tom muttered. "Sorry. Can't say I didn't warn you."

Swearing, Green fished some twoonies from his pocket and slapped them into Tom's hand. "Take the bus back to Robbie's and wait for me there! I've got to make sure we didn't do some serious damage back there. Although God knows, I'm beginning to think that's what you wanted!"

Fourteen

Green was delayed at the hospital almost an hour while he spoke to the medical staff in charge of Norman Pettigrew's care. By the end, he was satisfied that the old man had suffered no serious harm beyond a moment of fright. The doctor felt he had probably reacted more to his son's unexpected presence than to anything he said. Norman Pettigrew had very little remaining language function, particularly for more subtle and abstract language, and the doctor implied Green was wasting his time trying to question him about events that had occurred years ago.

The doctor did, however, believe Norman had the right to know of his son's death and to attend a memorial service at a later date when he was stronger. With stroke victims, he said, we can't really be certain to what extent recollections are left intact within consciousness, even though the patient can no longer communicate about them. He may remember everything about his son and feel quite strongly about honouring his memory.

Given the picture Green was beginning to form of this family, he questioned the accuracy of the word "honour", but the doctor's observations did give him pause. He left the hospital wondering if there was any way to reach into Norman's brain and tap those recollections that lay imprisoned there.

Green dropped in at home to discover that Bob and his crew, rather than being near completion, had removed the entire plaster wall between the kitchen and the dining room and were busy checking the studs. Electric saws howled and a fine layer of white powder coated everything.

"Dry rot, eh?" Bob announced dolefully. "Have to get it out, or your whole house will come down someday."

Green peered inside the remains of the wall, noting the chaotic tangle of wires and pipes that ran hidden between the framing. He prayed Bob knew what he was doing.

"Why didn't you call me?" Green shouted over the saw.

Bob signalled for his crewman to stop, bringing a stunning silence to the house. "You weren't in, eh? But your daughter said to go ahead."

"My daughter? When were you speaking to her?"

"She's upstairs. Came home for lunch." He grinned. "Likes her music loud, eh?"

Green bounded up the stairs two at a time and knocked on Hannah's door. Her latest punk rock offering clashed wills with the electric saw that had resumed downstairs, but Green wasn't sure which was worse.

She opened her door, her pixie smile quickly tossed under wraps when she saw who it was. Not the tanned, musclebound carpenter downstairs but her father, sporting a dubious look.

"What are you doing home?"

She shrugged. "No co-op today."

"Why not?"

"How should I know? It's no big deal, Mike. I'm home, aren't I, instead of out selling my body down on Dalhousie Street?

He wavered. She held the door open only a crack, preventing him from looking inside, and the police officer in

him imagined all sorts of ills. But it was her room, and her time, and if he was ever going to strengthen the fragile bond between them, he had to respect that. He cast about for neutral ground.

"You hungry?"

"Shouldn't you be at work?" she countered.

"Yeah, but I'm worried about Bob taking down the entire house while my back is turned." Sensing this conversation had lasted as long as it could, he moved to go. "Keep an eye on that for me, will you?"

As he climbed back into his car and fled the scene, Green's head filled with visions of dollar bills swirling down the drain. Like it or not, he'd have to ask Sullivan's advice about dry rot. Sullivan's aging split level in Alta Vista had been a do-it-yourself renovation project for him as long as Green could remember. While the mere idea drove Green mad, he suspected it had kept Sullivan sane through the more horrific crimes of their tenure.

Driving back past the Civic Hospital on his way to the station downtown, Green's thoughts drifted back to Norman Pettigrew. He couldn't get the man's face out of his mind. Before Tom's appearance, Norman had seemed confused and distressed, as if at the bewildering demands of the world around him. But at the sight of Tom, he'd become apoplectic. Not from confusion, but from what looked for all the world like sheer, raw panic.

Why would the sight of Tom have panicked him so much? And why had Tom confronted him? Did Tom really believe that his father was somehow responsible for Derek's death? Why would he think that, given that Norman had been confined to a hospital since well before Derek's death? Did Tom think Derek was still haunted by some past horror his

father had committed, or did he think Derek had visited his father just before he died and that something in the exchange between the two had driven Derek to his death?

On the other hand, perhaps Tom had an entirely different reason for staging the confrontation. He had claimed to be accompanying Green in the interests of protecting his father, an excuse that rang hollow considering the antipathy he'd expressed for the man. What if his real reason for tagging along was to control the information Green obtained, to steer the interviewalong certain lines and to prevent Green from getting answers to crucial questions about the past? Such as what had happened twenty years ago between Derek and his family?

Green thought back to the interview Tom had stepped into view at exactly the moment Green was asking about Derek's death. And also at exactly the moment when Norman was trying to say something. "Gone." He'd been adamant about that word, frustrated that Green couldn't understand it. Gone? Gom? Or...

Tom.

Was that what he was trying to say? And if so, why bring up Tom when Green was asking about Derek? One thing was clear, Tom had made sure he never got the chance to find out. But in that action, he had unwittingly tipped his hand. Something more was going on than just the death of a long-lost son, something that had its roots in an ancient feud. Something that implicated Tom.

Lying to Green was like waving a red flag before a bull; nothing made him more determined to uncover the truth. When he reached his office, he put in quick calls to all the troops in hopes that someone had made a useful discovery about the past. But Peters had been unable to find anyone who knew about Derek's old girlfriends, and Gibbs had hit dead ends all over Italy in his search for Sophia Vincelli. If she

had gone to stay with relatives over there, no one was admitting it to the cops. Green couldn't believe that an entire Italian family had no knowledge of Sophia's fate. It was more likely they were keeping that knowledge to themselves for some reason. Perhaps out of shame or loyalty to the family, perhaps out of simple mistrust of the police, or perhaps out of some deeper, more sinister motive. Gibbs had promised not to give up, but Green wasn't sure he had the necessary social cunning to take on a Mediterranean oath of silence.

Green was just radioing Sullivan when the squad room door opened and in strode the man himself, looking more energized than he had all week. He walked right into Green's office and tossed Robbie's photo album on his desk.

"We got an interesting new development, buddy," he announced, sprawling into Green's guest chair and stretching his long legs out.

"What's up?"

"Mrs. Hogencamp came up from Brockville to have a look at our dead man."

"And?"

"It's Lawrence."

They looked at each other for a long moment. Green felt a rush of mixed feelings. Triumph that his earlier instincts about the dead man's identity were correct. Dismay at the sinister implications it resurrected about Derek's disappearance, about Sophia, and about the twenty-year-old tragedy that had destroyed the family.

And most of all, bewilderment. What the hell was going on? "Did she recognize anybody in the photo album?"

"Well, that's the other interesting development." Sullivan's eyes had the old familiar gleam in them. Like a good storyteller, he liked to tease. "The photos are gone."

"What do you mean, gone?"

"I mean the photos of the brothers have been taken out of the album. Not all of them, just the close-ups of them when they're older."

"You mean the ones we saw just two days ago?" Green pulled the album across the desk and flipped through it. There were no empty spaces; other photos had been moved around to make the disappearance look less obvious. But Derek's grad photo and at least half a dozen other pictures were missing.

Green looked across at Sullivan, who was clearly waiting to see if Green's theory matched his own. "Robbie or Tom? They both had access to the album."

"No contest. Once a con, always a con."

"So he lied about the ID of the body and removed the photos so we wouldn't be able to disprove him."

"That's what I figure," Sullivan said. "Beats me why he'd lie, though. Just to throw us off the track?"

Absolutely, Green thought with that familiar rush of excitement when a suspect began to come into focus. Tom had been trying to sabotage the investigation all along, by misleading them on the identity of the dead man, by preventing Green from talking to the father, by claiming to have heard from Derek over the years, and now by removing the photos from the album. Why would he go to such lengths? Simply to cover up a murder that had occurred long ago?

Or one that had occurred less than a week ago.

"Maybe he lied because he killed Lawrence. And he thought if we were tracking down Derek's movements rather than Lawrence's, it wouldn't connect back to himself."

Sullivan snorted "That's pretty stupid. He must have known we'd catch the lie eventually, and that it would look more suspicious than ever."

"I'm not saying he's smart. Just desperate. Brian, I think we should bring him in."

"On what grounds? We don't have solid evidence that Lawrence was even murdered. And what's Tom's motive for killing him? Revenge for Derek's murder? We don't have proof that he was murdered either, for fuck's sake. This entire theory is a house of cards!"

Green knew it was, but he couldn't ignore all the dark hints of menace. "Maybe, maybe not," he said as mildly as he could. "We've got Gibbs and Peters tracking down the past, and if the proof is there, we'll get it eventually. But if we don't bring Tom in now, we'll lose him. If I'm right, he's got to know he's only one step ahead of us."

To Green's relief, Sullivan gave up the argument. He pulled out his notebook, flipped back a few pages and reached for Green's phone. "I'll check with Robbie to see if Tom's still there, and to make sure Robbie didn't take the photos himself for some reason."

Green held up a cautionary hand as Sullivan punched in the number. "Try to be subtle. I don't want to tip off Tom that we're suspicious."

As it turned out, Robbie was in no mood for subtlety. His voice was elevated an octave and shaking with rage. "I don't know anything about the pictures," he snapped. "All I know is, Tom's disappeared and so has the hundred dollars I had stashed in my desk drawer! Some things never change! Some people never fucking change."

*　　*　　*

Isabelle Boisvert sat at the kitchen table, her phone in her hand and her address book open to the Fs. Outside, a sodden

gray had descended, matching her mood. Rain lashed the windows and wind swept across the field, ripping through the bushes and swirling dead leaves across the yard. The damp seeped into every corner of the old house.

Jacques had roared off that morning in a cloud of rage. He had arrived home last night to find the last of the police units leaving, and so fortunately had been spared the full details of Tom Pettigrew's visit, including Isabelle's escapade with the axe. Nonetheless, Tom's uninvited visit had been the last straw, and Jacques was now insisting that the farm be sold. Isabelle had refused, prompting him to demand that she choose between him and the house. She had tried to calm him, but to no avail. Gentle and mild-mannered though he was, when he reached his limit he could be more intransigent and irrational than anyone she knew. She had tried to buy them both time by suggesting she call the real estate agent to see how much money they would lose. Jacques had countered with the announcement that while she was playing nice with the real estate agent, he would consult a lawyer about nullifying the sale.

The truth was, she was ambivalent. Sitting in the damp, drafty house, battered by rain and facing a long bleak winter, she wasn't sure she wanted the cursed place either. But the prospect of spring, with ponies in the paddock and green shoots of corn in the field, renewed her hope. She was damned if his stubborn fear would make her give up her dreams.

Finally, she took a deep breath and dialled Sandy Fitzpatrick's number. She was hoping he'd be out so she could delay any decision, but he picked up cheerfully on the second ring. When she explained her request, there was a long pause.

"But you've only lived in it a month," he said, his cheer dying abruptly.

"My husband finds it very long to drive," she said. "We

didn't realize how bad the traffic was along Prince of Wales Drive into town."

"It's a very bad time of year to sell country property. Buyers look in the spring, sometimes in early fall. But we're getting towards November. Nothing looks appealing in November."

She sighed. "I know. Just give me some idea how much we'd get for it, so I can discuss it with my husband."

"You'd have to take a huge loss on it."

"How huge?"

"Twenty or thirty thousand. If you can even find a buyer, which I doubt."

Twenty or thirty thousand... She glared out into the gloom.

He must have sensed her dismay. "You know what I suggest you do? Spend the winter fixing it up like you planned. Get as much done as you can by spring, and then if you still want to sell it, you can put it on the market then. It'll be much more likely to sell and if it's fixed up, it'll go faster at a better price."

Her spirits lifted slightly. This was a possible compromise that made enough business sense that she might be able to persuade Jacques. Yet the renovation project seemed endless. "Seems like we'd just throw good money after bad. Where would we even begin? The basement is damp and smells. It's even still full of the Pettigrew junk!"

"Oh, dear!"

"From a legal point of view, can I throw it out? I don't want to deal with that family any more." She meant that Jacques would have her head if she even spoke to them, but she settled for some personal whining.

Sandy countered by offering to come out with his pick-up truck and take it off her hands. Gratefully, she acquiesced and hung up, glad to have made one small dent in the mountain of work to be done. She flicked on the basement lights and

went down to begin clearing up the mess Tom had made. She'd only just finished stuffing the last of the papers back in the boxes when she heard the roar of an engine outside, which triggered a ferocious volley of yapping. By the time she returned upstairs, Sandy was standing on the doorstep, dripping in the rain.

"You were fast," she said, shoving Chouchou under her arm as she let him in.

"Like I said, business is dead this time of year. Besides, my mother just dropped in for one of her advice sessions—" He gave her a rueful half smile. "Sometimes it's my love life, sometimes my business. So any excuse in a storm."

He peeled off his yellow slicker and shook it outside before hanging it on a peg. She turned to lead him towards the basement but found he'd stopped at the entrance to the living room and was looking inside with rapture. Isabelle had been stripping the old paint, and now much of the woodwork around the walls and fireplace mantle glowed a dark oak.

"Wow!" Sandy exclaimed. "I forgot how beautiful the old wood was before they painted it over. You've increased the market value already."

"It was pretty badly damaged in places. I had to sand off huge scratches, and I'll have to do the same with the window sills upstairs. Someone really carved them!"

"Well, don't forget five generations of rugged country brats grew up in this house. It was lived in, the scratches are part of its charm."

He ducked his head and followed her down the steep rickety stairs to the cellar. He frowned when he reached the bottom and saw the boxes cluttering the floor. "Robbie should have taken all this before you moved in."

Isabelle recalled the frazzled, dejected young man she and

Jacques had met the day before closing. "He was going to, but the one time we did meet him he was very distracted by his father's illness. I also think he hated having the sole responsibility for this place. Of course, now that his brother has come, maybe—"

"What!" Sandy whirled on her, his eyes wide.

"Tom. We had some excitement—"

"Oh, Tom." The shock faded from Sandy's eyes, and his lip curled with disdain. "What the hell did Tom want?"

"This stuff. Apparently he was looking for another brother's address."

Sandy had bent to pick up the nearest box, and he paused to scrutinize her curiously. "Did he say why?"

Isabelle shrugged. "Maybe something to do with the dead man they found at the church."

Sandy propped the box on the bannister. "I heard that was Lawrence, so I guess Tom was trying to contact Derek."

"Ah, yes. DP—the one with the bad love affair."

Sandy looked startled. "What?"

She smiled. "Just some initials he scratched on the window sill upstairs. It feels like the family is still here, and this place is haunted by all the tragedies and deaths that occurred in it. Like even the house is weeping. Look at this." She swept her hand to encompass the beautiful natural pine planks that panelled half the walls. "Even this room is sad, like they started with such enthusiasm that just died."

Sandy had busied himself dragging boxes across to the stairs. Now he straightened, flushed and breathing hard. "They did. This was the middle son's project. Benji was a natural carpenter, loved woodwork, could build anything. He worked construction around here in the summers while he went to school. He was finishing it for himself as a place to get

189

away from his parents' moods. But then he died..." Sandy shrugged. "A real shame. He'd had a rough few years, but he was trying to get his life together."

Isabelle pulled her sweater around her tightly, sensing the damp and despair in the room. She didn't want to know any more about the history of this house. She wanted to rip it all down, at least symbolically, so that it could start from scratch. As Sandy began to carry boxes upstairs, she pitched in gratefully, and within half an hour the boxes were all piled in the front hall by the door. Although the rain had tamed to a melancholy drizzle, Sandy backed his truck right up to the steps to minimize the trek across the yard, which had become a muddy swamp.

Ten minutes later, Sandy tossed a tarp over the boxes, declined her offer of a hot cup of coffee and headed through the mud to his cab. He nodded at the pile of gravel in the hole.

"Sorry I jumped the gun on that, Isabelle."

"It's okay," she replied. "It was giving me the creeps anyway, with the fire, the axe and the bones—"

Sandy swung around. "The what?"

His astonishment amused her, as she realized how her words must have sounded. "Just an old cow bone. But I'm glad it's all gone. Your friend was very nice about it and promised to help me build a pond."

Sandy climbed into his truck, revved his engine and leaned out the window. "Yeah, Scottie will do right by you. Don't let the snake tattoos scare you; he's got the heart of an elephant."

With that, he waved and bumped off down the rutted lane, spewing mud in his wake. Feeling better about the country and its people, Isabelle returned to the basement, which now echoed emptily, and began to examine the half-finished walls. The framing was still solid but in places the pine planking had

190

curled and cracked beyond salvation. She peered behind the panelling, where unidentifiable little creatures had taken up residence in the darkness, spinning thick clouds of web and collecting bits of dust and debris into cozy nests. God knows what was living back there. It would all have to be ripped down, cleaned out and fumigated. More money.

As she peered behind, a small dust-covered bundle caught her eye, jammed in behind the pine planks near the base and almost hidden from view. Curiosity battled revulsion as she reached around the plank and groped in the darkness, trying not to think about spiders and mice nipping at her fingers. Her hand closed on the bundle, which crackled beneath her grip. After some wiggling, she fished out a filthy object covered with cobwebs and chewed by mice. When she'd brushed off the dirt, she discovered the shredded remains of a small paper bag. The bag flaked as she opened it to reveal a collection of papers bound by a rubber band. Curious, she sat down on the bottom stair beneath the light and slid out a pack of papers. Lined foolscap, frayed and water stained at the edges, covered in a large, barely legible scrawl.

Upstairs, Chouchou barked a vigorous greeting that stopped abruptly. Isabelle heard the door open above her and a soft, cautious tread crossed the hall. Since Chouchou had stopped, it was probably Jacques back unexpectedly from work. Or perhaps Sandy, who had met Chouchou and who might have decided to give her more help. She rose to look up the stairs, preparing to call out. In the next instant the basement door opened, silhouetting a lean figure in the light from the top of the stairs. Not Jacques or Sandy. Not nearly big enough for Sandy. She thought of hiding, but knew she was clearly visible in the light hanging over her head. She backed up into the room and summoned all the bluster she could manage.

"What do you want!"

The figure began to descend the steps. Halfway down, he came into the light, and she recognized the man from last night. Anger surged through her fear.

"Tom Pettigrew! What are you doing here!"

Tom's eyes were locked on the package in her hands. He'd reached the bottom step and stood facing her. In the yellowish glare, he looked sickly pale except for the purple bruise above his left eye. He reached out a soothing hand.

"Sorry, don't mean to frighten you. Those letters are mine. I—I thought they got lost in the move."

She backed up still further. "And you were just going to waltz in here and make off with them?"

He shifted his gaze from the package to her face. "No, I was coming to ask you for them. I rang the bell, but I guess..." He held out his hand. "Please. They're all I got left of my kid brother Benji."

She was going to hand them over to him then, but something in his desperation struck her as odd. She wanted to be upstairs, where she could see better and where she had escape routes readily at hand.

"Fine," she said. "But let's go upstairs where we can talk about this stuff in more comfort."

He stepped away from the stairs to encourage her to go first, but she shook her head. Clutching the sheaf of papers firmly, she clumped up the narrow stairs behind him and watched as he disappeared through the door into the brightness of the kitchen. Just as she was stepping through into the light herself, she sensed a movement behind her. She spun around, alarm surging, saw his arm sweep down. She had no time to scream before pain exploded in her head.

Fifteen

Robbie slammed the phone down so hard that Green heard it from four feet away. Belatedly, Sullivan jerked the phone away from his ear and dropped it back into its cradle. There was no need to repeat a word.

"He's long gone," Sullivan observed grimly. "A hundred bucks buys him a bus ticket back to Toronto, where he'll go underground for sure."

Green leaned his elbows on the desk, his mind racing to try to figure out Tom's next move. The man's behaviour was looking more suspicious every moment, yet there was something about it that didn't make sense. If his theory about Derek's death was true, Green could understand why Tom and the family had covered it up. He could understand Tom's descent into a life of drink and the festering hatred he'd held for the psychotic brother who'd ruined his life. He could even understand that hatred erupting ultimately into murder. But Green saw Tom as a man who ricocheted from crisis to crisis, never planning his next move or foreseeing the consequences. If Tom killed Lawrence, it would have been on impulse, when the sight of his brother resurrected memories and emotions too intense to deny.

But why had Tom turned up in Ashford Landing in the first place? How could he possibly have known Lawrence was

there? And what had he been doing at the old family homestead? Tom had claimed he was looking for Derek's address, but that was almost certainly a lie. Yet he was obviously looking for something, for he was tearing the basement apart. Robbie had said Tom was adamant about retrieving some important things from the house. And so far, he hadn't succeeded.

"No," Green said quietly, breaking the silence of minutes. "I don't think he's dropped out of sight yet. Because he hasn't accomplished what he came back here for."

He was about to explain when there was a sharp rap on his door and a young constable stuck his head in. "Sorry to disturb you," he said diffidently. "But Rural West is calling. Seems there's trouble again at Ashford Landing."

Green's heart leaped into his throat. "The Boisvert farm?"

"No, sir. Some woman called McMartin. She wants you there right away."

* * *

Edna McMartin was visible even from the highway, clothed in a bright yellow rain slicker and massive Wellingtons. She was planted outside the front door of her house with her arms folded across her chest and her grey hair frizzing in the icy mist. As Sullivan drew the car to a stop, she stomped over, her face crimson and her eyes blazing.

"He took the truck, the bastard! Bold as you please, comes out of the woods, gets in the truck, and takes off!"

The two detectives climbed out and Sullivan took her elbow to steer her towards the house. A light rain had begun again, turning the ground slick.

"Were the keys in the truck?" he asked gently.

194

She shook off his hand and stalked ahead towards the door. "I told you cops that! I'd just come back from town, and I leave them in sometimes when I'm going to go out again. I don't expect anybody to steal it right off my front doorstep!"

Sullivan followed her inside. "You're sure it was Tom Pettigrew?"

"I was right there at the kitchen sink." She led the way through to the kitchen, which smelled of spices. Six small pumpkins sat on the counter, surrounded by an array of cookware. She gestured through the window which overlooked the front yard and the outbuildings. "Saw him plain as day."

"But you haven't see him since he was a young man."

"Tom Pettigrew doesn't change! Same shifty-eyed weasel that used to lead all the boys into trouble. Dropped out of school, good for nothing but bush parties, drugs and fornication." She pursed her lips. "Norm should have sent him to the army like he planned. And Katherine! See no evil, hear no evil. Not from her angelic boys!" She paused, as if realizing she'd gone too far. Sullivan had seated himself at the table with his notebook, while Green remained by the window, content to let Sullivan take the lead. Green was looking out, not at the spot where the truck had been, but at the woods where Edna said Tom had come from. The woods that ran along by the river. A faint alarm bell went off in his head.

"We've notified our uniform patrol and the Ontario Provincial Police," Sullivan was saying. "Did you see which way he turned on the highway?"

She pointed south. Toward Toronto, Green noted. Quickly, Sullivan relayed the truck's description and plate number to the OPP Comm Centre so that they could issue a region-wide alert to watch all the highways leading to the 401.

"If he has half a brain, he won't take the 401," Green

interrupted. "He'll stick to the back country roads." Which he probably knows inside out, he thought but didn't say. No point rousing Edna's ire even further. Her crimson colour had not abated one bit.

"He better not wreck that truck," she retorted. "Else I'll hold you boys up in Ottawa responsible. You had him yesterday, why the dickens did you let him go!"

Green was saved from having to explain about writs of Habeas Corpus by a commotion in the back room. An instant later, Jeb McMartin appeared in the kitchen doorway, dressed in mud-caked work boots and a sodden flannel hunting vest. Leaves and twigs clung to his vest and hair. Edna opened her mouth to scold him, but his worried frown stopped her short.

"I can't find Kyle," he said. "I've looked all over. Chicken coup, barn, even the path down to the river."

"His rabbit hutch?" she demanded.

He nodded. "All the hiding places I could think of."

Husband and wife looked at each other in silent, shared panic. It was Edna who finally gave word to their fear. "The truck!"

"Wait a minute," Green said. "Are you saying Kyle might have been in the truck Tom stole?"

She turned on him. "This is your fault! You and that daughter of yours. Dressing like a whore, giving him ideas. She never should have been allowed in the classroom looking like that. It was a disgrace—"

"Just a minute!" Once Green recovered from his surprise, his temper flared. "My daughter has nothing to do with this. Kyle was at home when he disappeared."

"But I couldn't send him to school, could I? Not with her getting him all hot and bothered. A boy like that, with the mind of a child. I told the teacher—"

196

Green was about to leap into the fray again, but Sullivan cut him off with a soothing hand. "Let's concentrate on the boy," he said to Edna. "What makes you think he was in the truck?"

She shot one last glance at Green before reining herself in. Privately, Green thanked Sullivan for his wisdom. The woman's son was missing, and he doubted he would be any calmer in her shoes.

The husband stepped into the breach, wringing his hands. "Kyle was angry at us for keeping him home from school. When he's angry, he...he hides. He likes the back of the truck because it's covered, and I keep my hunting and fishing gear there. Fishing tackle, ammunition—"

Sullivan glanced at him sharply. "Firearms?"

Jeb swallowed. "No, but I have knives for gutting game." He sank down into a chair at the table as if his legs would no longer hold him. "He'll be frightened. He doesn't know his way around the countryside, and if Tom spots him—"

"We don't believe Tom is dangerous, sir," Green lied, hoping to hell he was right. Even if Tom had actually killed Lawrence, surely to God he wouldn't harm an innocent kid.

"You don't know Tom. He'll try to outrun the police. And if he's been drinking..." The man began to rock.

Sullivan spoke calmly, calling them both back to task. "How much gas was in the tank?"

"Maybe half a tank? He can get almost all the way to Toronto without a stop. And Kyle—" Jeb's eyes filled with tears. "Oh, my God, my boy will freeze to death in the back."

Sullivan leaned forward. "Let's not get ahead of ourselves, Mr. and Mrs. McMartin. We'll find him long before that. As Inspector Green said, we have no reason to believe Tom is dangerous. He's not fleeing apprehension, or anything like that. Probably he just wanted the quickest way home." He

reached for the phone. "We'll get the OPP on it right away. They have the full range of emergency response capability."

Even to Green, Sullivan's reassurance sounded hollow. They had no idea how dangerous or desperate Tom was, nor what he was up to. He couldn't possibly know they had suspicions about Lawrence's death, so this reckless flight in a stolen truck made no sense! The alarm bells began to ring louder in Green's head, for the McMartin farm was right next to the Boisvert farm by a path through the woods.

Sullivan had moved out onto the porch out of earshot while he talked to the OPP, but now he returned. "Two officers from regional headquarters in Smith Falls are on their way over here to get some information on Kyle and Tom, and they'll keep you informed at all times. They'll also be collecting an item of Kyle's clothing for the canine unit, in case that's needed."

Sullivan's tone was the essence of calm authority, and Green watched the McMartins gradually uncoil. While they went in search of clothing, Green put in a quick call to the Boisvert house. There was no response. He told himself it was early yet, barely four o'clock, but by now the alarm bells were deafening. He asked Sullivan for the keys to the Impala.

"Stay here until the OPP has things under control," he said, grabbing his raincoat. "Then meet me over at the Boisvert house. I've got a bad feeling about this."

*   *   *

The Boisvert farm looked deserted as Green raced down the muddy lane. The minivan was parked out front, and there was no sign of trouble, but when Green climbed out of his car and crunched up the gravel, he heard frantic yapping from inside.

There was no answer to his ring, nor to his knock. The door was unlocked, but when he tried to step in, he was confronted by a snarling, snapping flurry of fur. Quickly he withdrew, but not before he'd glimpsed the torso and lower limbs of a body sprawled in the hall. Slamming the door shut against the dog, he dialled 911 and snapped out orders for police and ambulance assistance.

Afterwards he dashed around the exterior of the house, checking for intruders and peeping in windows until he was able to see the entire scene. Daylight was already fading under the iron gray sky, but he could just make out the body of Isabelle face down on the floor with a dark pool spreading across the floor beneath her head. With a curse, he ran back to the door.

"Chouchou, it's okay," he soothed, holding out his hand, but the dog launched itself at his fingers. Steeling himself, he burst through the door and rushed at it with a menacing roar. It scrambled backwards into the kitchen, its tiny nails clicking on the tile. He slammed the kitchen door shut, flicked on the hall light and turned to Isabelle. Quickly, he checked her pulse and breathing. She was warm, her pulse strong and steady. He allowed himself to breathe again. Softly, he called to her. No response. Louder. Still nothing.

The hair at the back of her head was matted with crimson blood which had pooled beneath her in a glistening stain, but he could see no active bleeding nor any fragments of broken bone. Her colour was bleached, but her breathing was steady. She'll be all right, he thought to reassure himself as he removed a knitted throw from the couch in the living room to spread over her. Then he dialled 911 again to update her condition before doing a quick check of the rest of the house. It was standard procedure, but he knew it was pointless. The person who'd done this was long gone.

When he returned to await the ambulance, the rest of his detective instincts belatedly took over. He phoned for a forensics team and a quick survey of the scene. The door to the basement was open and the light was on at the base of the stairs. Isabelle lay in the kitchen, near the basement door. She had been struck from behind, probably when she was emerging from the basement, and had pitched forward into the room. Tom had either hidden in the kitchen behind the open basement door, or he had followed her up from the basement.

Green fished some nitryl gloves from his pocket, slipped them on and ducked down the basement stairs. The boxes from yesterday were gone, but otherwise the basement looked undisturbed. No signs of a struggle except for a heavy cast-iron pan lying at the base of the stairs. Leaving it in place, he climbed back upstairs and knelt to check on Isabelle again. She was still out cold, but this time her eyelids flickered slightly. He felt his spirits lift further, but as his worry dissipated, a fresh anger took hold.

He should never have let the bastard go! Tom Pettigrew had played them all for fools, and in the brief time he had been in town, he'd cut a swath of destruction and deception a mile wide through the lives of relatives and innocent strangers alike. A swath of destruction that had not ended yet, not as long as a bewildered, mentally disabled boy was hurtling through the darkness in the back of a stolen pick-up truck.

As Green sat on the floor at Isabelle's side, he sifted the silence for the sound of approaching sirens and cursed the delay of the long country drive. Then he glimpsed a small white corner of something peeking out from under the door next to the kitchen. It looked like a piece of paper. Curious, he opened the door to discover a closet packed with boxes, brooms and a vacuum cleaner. On the floor lay a folded piece

of paper which had apparently slid under the door and lodged against a box. He retrieved it and brought it into the hall light.

Unfolding it, Green discovered it was a sheet of grimy foolscap, covered in a large, untidy scrawl and creased as if it had been folded and unfolded countless times. There was a date at the top. June 17, 1990. Green's heart leaped. A voice from the past!

Dear Benji,

Happy B-day! Congratulashuns! You're a big man now, twenty-one, hansum as the devil and you even bought your self a set of wheels! How about driving down to the big TO and taking your old brother out for a nite on the town? I no Im not much to brag about but the truth is I miss you man. People yused to call me the tuff one and Derek the sensitive one but the truth is I loved him more than anything. He was my big brother and he was sposed to be ar shining egsample. Hell, Dad tried to drive that into me offen enuff. I hope hes eased up some, at least on Robbie. I died when Derek did, thats the truth. Mabee its keeping the secret all these years. Mabee if we had it out in the open and had a proper buriel for him, mabee I coude get over it. But I found the body, man. And I was the one that had to catch that fucking lunatic and lock him up. I no you dont like to think about it all. Us setting the fire and making sure every goddamn bit of blood and brains was burned. but I keep thinking hes not at peace. Ar eny of us? Im sorry, I was just going to wish you an happy birthday, not tell you my sad sack life. Ill get by, I always do. So—

Green's heart hammered as he deciphered the page. The note was unsigned, but he knew it had to be from Tom; it was written in the same illiterate scrawl as the letter to Sophia. He

re-read it, turned it over, searched for more pages, but there were none.

The paper shook in his hand, and bile rose in his throat as he absorbed the enormity of the horror laid out on the page. If ever there had been a doubt that Derek was murdered, this piece of paper shot that doubt to hell. Here was the confirmation of what he'd feared, yet it was ten times worse. Not only had Lawrence murdered Derek, not only had the parents covered it up by committing Lawrence to a mental hospital and fabricating Derek's departure to the States, but they had co-opted their remaining sons to dispose of the body and help in the cover-up. Sons who were little more than boys themselves, forced to set a fire that would obliterate all traces of their brother.

Green thrust himself to his feet, forced his shaking hands to slip the note into a plastic evidence bag. He wanted to scream his outrage, beat someone, hold his own children tight and promise them he would never, ever, do this to them. Pity blurred into the anger he felt at Tom. No wonder the man had never recovered. No wonder he had confronted his father as he did, seeing not a frail cripple in the wheelchair but a tyrant who had not understood how trauma and secrecy could shatter a young mind.

Green turned to look out the kitchen window. In the distance, he saw red flashing lights streaking towards the scene, and he felt a wash of gratitude. At least the living would be taken care of. Daylight was fading, but he knew immediately that something was wrong. Where the shed had been, where two days earlier he had groped around in the tangle of raspberry canes and burnt timber, there was only a pale patch of gravel filling the hole. The hole where Derek's bones had almost certainly been buried.

A normal house or barn fire would never burn hot enough to incinerate a body, no matter how hard poor Tom and Benji

tried. Derek's bones would still have been there, scorched and jumbled by the elements, but now they were scattered God knows where. Who the hell had ordered that? Tomorrow he would have to find out where the fill had been taken. Every last little trace of debris would have to be painstakingly excavated and each nugget of material brushed clean, all under the watchful eye of the coroner and a forensic anthropologist.

Green knew just the person he had to call. If there was anything left of Derek down there, Dr. Peter Cole from the Museum of Civilization would find it.

*　　*　　*

Darkness had settled and a cold, relentless rain drenched the last of the emergency vehicles as they drove up the lane to the highway. Green stood in the kitchen window watching the blurry red line of tail lights wobble into the distance. Behind him, he heard the monotone voice of Lyle Cunningham making his preliminary videotape of the crime scene. Cunny insisted on utter silence during the taping so that some officer's black humour would not end up broadcast all over the courtroom, and he was already incensed enough about the mess of blood, muddy footprints and puddles of rain water created by the emergency workers attending to Isabelle. Now she was safely on her way to hospital, still semi-conscious but stable, and all that remained was for Ident to piece together what had happened.

That was not going to be a surprise, Green thought. Without even bothering to be careful, Tom had simply tossed the cast-iron pan he had used to hit Isabelle down the basement stairs before he fled the house.

The last of the vehicles had just turned onto the highway when a bright pair of halogen beams streaked into view and

swung into the lane. As it drew near, Green recognized Sandy's red truck. Green grabbed his raincoat and ducked out into the rain to intercept him before he added further chaos to Cunny's scene. He held up his hand just as Sandy opened his cab door to leap out. In the passenger seat, the interior light illuminated a big man with a bull neck and a John Deere baseball cap, whom Green recognized as Sandy's fishing companion in his office photo. Both men looked tense and angry.

"What the hell happened!" Sandy demanded. "Someone in town said Isabelle was attacked!"

"She's been taken to hospital, but she'll be all right."

Sandy strained to see around Green towards the house. "Was it Tom?"

"I prefer not to speculate," Green replied.

"What the hell does he want! The bastard's kidnapped Kyle, and I know he broke in here yesterday."

Rain traced icy streaks down Green's back, and he clutched his collar closed. "Again, we're still investigating, but we have no evidence that your stepbrother was abducted deliberately. He just happened to be there." He squinted at Sandy thoughtfully in the glare of the cab light. "Tell me, Sandy. Your mother and stepfather were pretty upset to think clearly. What do you think Kyle would do once he realized he'd gone from home?"

Sandy glanced at the other man questioningly. "Probably stay put, don't you think?"

Green took the opportunity to reach across Sandy to offer his hand to the stranger. "Inspector Mike Green."

"Phil Scott." The man crushed Green's hand in a massive, calloused grip.

Green addressed both men. "So you figure he'd stay with the truck?"

Sandy nodded. "It would be familiar. Everything else

204

around him would be strange, and when Kyle is scared, he hides. So he'd probably try to stay out of Tom's sight."

"That means he wouldn't try to seek help, say from a gas station attendant?"

"Not unless he knew the guy." Sandy sighed. "My mother's been so paranoid about strangers taking advantage of him that she's put the fear of God into him. He's quite a good-looking kid, and so sweet natured..." He paused, an awkward shame creeping over his face. "Jeb told me what my mother said about your daughter. I'm sorry, that was a cheap shot. I know how crazy Kyle was about her. Living out here on the farm with all his spare time spent on chores, he doesn't have many friends, and he just lit up when she started working in his class. I think it was good for him. I mean, he may be disabled, but whether Mom likes it or not, someday he's going to want a sexual relationship."

To his own surprise, Green was appalled. He knew Hannah was far from virginal herself, but now that she was not just an abstraction, he found himself reacting as all fathers did. As he'd seen Sullivan react a hundred times when the boys came sniffing around Lizzie. Over my dead body.

No doubt that was Edna McMartin's reaction, but Green cast about for a more palatable phrase with which to voice his disapproval. "A natural parental concern, I think."

Sandy shrugged. "I suspect she's more worried about losing control of him."

"And about what the church yaps would say," Scott chimed in. "Don't underestimate that. All the tight-assed bitches in the communion line and all."

Even though Edna was not the warm and cuddling type, Green thought the commentaries unduly harsh. Life had not been gentle with her. "But he does have the mind of a child," he said. "And it's normal she'd worry that someone would use him."

Sandy ceded the point reluctantly. "Still, she's got years of trouble ahead if she doesn't take her head out of the sand. Why do you think he was hiding in the truck? He's been giving her a hell of a hard time over missing school. Crying, temper tantrums... So she's been pretty tough on him."

A stance that no doubt is tearing her apart now that he's gone, Green thought. How easy it was to do the wrong thing as a parent, and how quickly that misjudgment can come back to haunt you. In the hopes of sparing Hannah confusion, he'd stayed out of her life when her mother moved across the country and married another man, but now she was making them all pay in spades. Sometimes he wondered if the debt could ever be paid. Probably not.

* * *

The Shabbat candles flickered cozily across the white table cloth Sharon had laid on the table in the dining room, and the extended Green family was gathered together for the first time all week. But try as he might, Green could not get into the spirit. His thoughts were still trapped in the horror the day had revealed and in his unresolved fear for those involved— for Isabelle, Kyle, even desperate, battle-scarred Tom. He'd left instructions that he was to be notified the instant Kyle and Tom were found, and he found himself straining for the sound of the telephone.

The kitchen was still in pieces, so that night the take-out fare was cheese blintzes from Vince's Bagel Shop nearby. The rest of the family was digging in with noisy alacrity. Tony was gleefully spreading sour cream all over his high chair and Modo had positioned herself strategically underfoot, ready to lick any overflow that came within reach. Sharon was

celebrating the prospect of two days off with an unaccustomed second glass of white wine.

Green's father Sid was seated across from Hannah, his pale watery eyes fixed on her as if he wanted to drink in every nuance. She was the spitting image of her dead grandmother, Sid's wife, and even after four months, the very sight of her made him clap his hands in ecstasy. Now, every Friday evening when Green picked him up at his seniors' residence to bring him to dinner, Sid was waiting at the front door, with a light in his eyes and a lift in his step that belied his frailty and age.

For Hannah's part, Sid was the only family member besides Tony who could make her smile. But not tonight. Tonight she was picking at her food, pushing her salad around her plate and nibbling at the edge of a blintz. She said nothing, and not even the antics of her brother and the dog raised a laugh. Green noticed that she'd taken out half her earrings, and her eyelids were devoid of glitter. He remembered her unexpected presence at home that day and Edna McMartin's allusions to her clothing, and his detective mind clicked into action.

He eyed her thoughtfully. "Hannah," he began, testing the waters with a careful toe, "has Kyle been away all week?"

She shrugged. "So?"

"I had occasion to speak to his mother today. In connection with my case," he added quickly when he saw her mouth open in protest. "Has she been keeping him home?"

Hannah didn't rally a smart retort, merely pushed a lettuce leaf across her plate.

"She seems a bit overprotective," he ventured.

Still Hannah said nothing. Sharon glanced at Green quizzically but had the wisdom to keep quiet. He tried again. "Old-fashioned too, like many rural people. I suspect she'd be pretty formidable if she decided to tear a strip off the school."

"Spit it out, Mike," Hannah said without looking up from her lettuce. "You want to ask if I've been kicked out of my placement."

"No, I…" He paused. Detective instincts seemed to run in the family. "Yes."

She lifted her thin shoulders in a small, disinterested shrug. "Well, fuck it. Fuck her. The kids liked me, and Kyle was happy in school for the first time ever. The parents have a leash on him so tight, he's afraid to do anything. It's their problem, Mike. They don't see he's a normal kid who wants to do normal things."

He deftly avoided defending the parental point of view. To Hannah, the freedom to be was a sacred right. "Have they taught him any street smarts? Would he know what to do if he was lost?"

"What kind of question is that?"

She had finally looked up from her plate, and her eyes were shrewd. Detective instincts certainly do run in the family, he thought, as he debated how much to tell her. Finally, he explained that the McMartin truck had been stolen with Kyle hiding in the back. She lost all defiance and looked for the first time like a frightened sixteen-year-old.

"This is all your fault! I knew taking that crucifix back was a bad idea! They've been really mad at him about it, and really mad that he tried to lie about it. It's like they don't trust him any more. I bet he was just trying to get away from her eagle eye. And now—oh my God, he won't know what to do! Is this asshole dangerous?"

He didn't tell her what he really thought, that he had no idea what Tom was up to or capable of. He shook his head and risked giving her hand a quick squeeze. Hannah hated to be touched, but in this instance, she seemed too pre-occupied to object.

"The man just wants to get home to Toronto," he said. "Anyway, we've got police on all the highways. The OPP is sure to catch him any minute."

She searched his face for a moment with an appraising gaze. "I did tell him once, when we were doing a life skills activity in class, that if he was ever lost, he should look for someone in uniform. I hope he remembers that."

She didn't seem to appreciate the full meaning of her words, but Green felt an unexpected swell of emotion that robbed him of speech. Regardless of how jaded and anti-authority this little bundle of rebellion was, deep inside she too knew that the police were the good guys.

Sixteen

After a fitful night's sleep, Green arrived at the police station the next morning before the weakening autumn sun had even struggled over the horizon. By ten o'clock he had briefed the duty inspector to arrange for equipment, staff and the return of the mobile command post to the village. He'd also apprised MacPhail and Ident of his suspicions and set Sullivan to work applying for a coroner's warrant. Officially, the excavation would be under the supervision of the coroner, but Green also put in a call to his old friend Dr. Peter Cole. Bones were the physical anthropologist's speciality, but he spent most of his days researching them from his lab at the Museum of Civilization, so he was delighted to escape into the fresh country air to help the police, even on a Saturday.

Tom's letter was turned over to the Ident Unit, and the OPP was harassed numerous times for updates on their search. Nothing. Tom, Kyle and the truck had vanished into the countryside. Although Green had tried to sound reassuring in his reports to the McMartins, he expected them to go straight to the Chief to report his gross negligence in releasing Tom in the first place.

However, if the McMartins didn't complain, Green was certain Jacques Boisvert would. Tom had broken into their home just the day before and had a dangerous confrontation with his

wife. The poor man had arrived home last night to find his front yard full of emergency vehicles and his wife lying in a pool of blood, surrounded by paramedics. He had spent a frantic night at the Civic Hospital ER, pacing the halls and hounding doctors until his wife was pronounced out of danger. She had undergone surgery to relieve a subdural haematoma and was now settled in a private room. Jacques had been joined in his outrage by a large, vocal contingent of her relatives who'd driven in that morning from her little hometown of Bourget.

Despite Green's best efforts, the media were soon crawling all over Ashford Landing and feeding every minuscule lack of progress into living rooms across the city. Jacques Boisvert and Edna McMartin were both centre stage, threatening dire consequences for the entire force if Tom was not behind bars by the end of the day. Jeb McMartin delivered his plea with tears in his eyes and a quaver in his voice. "Don't hurt my boy," he said simply. "Take the truck, keep the truck, but let my boy off at a safe place on your way."

Superintendent-to-be Barbara Devine was fit to be tied. She was set to assume command of CID on Monday, and she did not want the resolution of this bungled mess to be the first task she had to face when she walked into her new office. "Find the kid, Green," she snapped into his phone. "Dig up the body, solve the murder, and deliver it all to me on a neat little platter in time for my ten o'clock press conference Monday morning."

Green knew all about her preference for neat little platters, and her desire to win at all cost, from a double homicide he'd worked on a few months earlier. He considered this latest threat an ominous beginning to her tenure as his boss. How the hell was he going to work with the woman? He had just hung up on her when his phone rang again. He hesitated only an instant before picking it up, hoping it was good news from the OPP.

"Mike?" came a very young, uncertain voice.

"Hannah?" He did a quick calculation. On Saturdays, this was still the middle of the night for Hannah in the best of times. On top of that, he knew she'd had a restless night because he'd heard her prowling around the kitchen at four in the morning, when he himself had been miles from sleep. "Where are you?"

"Down the street at the Elgin Street Diner."

"What are you..." He checked himself just in time. In the four months she'd been with them, she'd never once called him at work. "Be there in five," he said before she could change her mind.

She didn't even try to protest, simply hung up, which was another first. She was normally fond of the last word.

He grabbed his jacket off his chair and ducked out of his office with only the briefest twinge of guilt about the case he was abandoning. Even he was entitled to a coffee break once or twice a year. If ever there was a time to work on that fragile bond between his daughter and him, this was it.

She was perched at the counter on a stool so high her tiny feet did not touch the ground, sipping a huge frothy cappuccino and flirting with the young man cleaning the coffee pot. She cast Green a desultory glance.

"I could have told you on the phone, you know."

"I felt like a coffee." He glanced at the young man. "I'll have the same as her, and toss in two cinnamon buns."

Out of years of habit, he took the table in the back corner, and she joined him with lagging feet. Gazed into her coffee, twirled her spoon.

Eventually, "Any word on Kyle?"

He shook his head. "But it's early yet."

"I saw the news. The village is really pissed at you."

"I think Kyle is pretty special to them. As he is to a lot of people."

She shrugged, as if to count herself out. "He was scared, you know. That afternoon that we went out to his place? When you left us alone in the barn? I don't know if it's important, if maybe..." She licked foam off her spoon, concentrating on every speck. Green restrained himself with an effort. "Maybe if I'd said something then, this wouldn't have happened."

"Hannah, it was an accident that he was in the truck."

"No, it's because he was hiding. Because he was scared his parents would be mad. He knew he shouldn't have been where he was, so he was afraid to say what he saw."

In spite of himself, he stiffened. The young waiter set his cappuccino and plate of buns on the table with a clatter, which Green barely heard. "Maybe you'd better start at the beginning, honey. Tell me everything that you and Kyle talked about that afternoon."

A faint scowl of resistance creased her brow, as if she hated being forced to part with secrets. "At first nothing. He was upset, scared like, that his mom would see him not working. I even took up a pitchfork and cleaned up some cow crap." She wrinkled up her pert nose. "So be grateful. Anyway, I asked him where he got the crucifix for real, and he said he just found it on the ground. In his special place."

"What special place?"

"He said it was a secret, and I shouldn't tell anyone, because some bad man might come after him."

Green sucked in his breath. "What did he mean by bad man?"

She shrugged. "He said he saw a bad man running in the woods. Kyle was scared, so he hid from him. Sometimes it's hard to understand what he's trying to say, but later I got to thinking—what if he saw this man who died in the church yard? What if he saw something he shouldn't have? He acted really

scared, Mike. Like he'd seen something that freaked him out."

Green mulled this fragment of evidence over carefully. To a child, Lawrence would have looked like a bad man, dressed in ragged clothing, covered in grime like a wild mountain man. The sight of such a figure running would have been scary. The question was—where and when had Kyle seen him? It could have been right after Isabelle chased him away, in which case he would have been running out of confusion and panic at the disappearance of all he'd come back for. Or it could have been right before he reached the village, in which case Kyle might have been the last person to see him alive.

"Did Kyle say where he saw this man running?" he asked casually. "Near his house?"

She shook her head, reaching over to steal a small corner of cinnamon bun. "It didn't sound like that. But Kyle always tells things in a jumble, and you have to connect it together. He was talking about these kids playing hockey and some church bell ringing and the bad man running in the graves, and how he had to hide so they wouldn't see him. But when I asked who wouldn't see him, he just shrugged."

"But he definitely said the bad man was running away?"

She nodded. Raised anxious eyes to face him. "Kyle's such a bad liar, Mike. Something was bothering him. Not just the crucifix he knew he shouldn't have had, but something he saw. What if he knows something about that man who died? What if he saw something he doesn't even know he saw, and now he's in danger—"

He resisted the urge to take her hands. "But honey, the man is dead. Even if Kyle saw him running away, he's not a threat any more."

She rolled her eyes as if in exasperation at his lack of imagination. "But what if there's more, Mike? That's the

214

feeling Kyle gave me—that the bad guy was running away from someone. And that's the person Kyle was scared of."

Green was so astonished that he was barely aware of reassuring Hannah and setting off back down Elgin Street toward the station. His mind was racing. Isabelle had spotted Lawrence around eleven and had chased him into the woods behind her property. He could have covered the two kilometres to town in half an hour, less if he'd kept running full tilt. Yet Kyle had been walking in the woods in the late afternoon just before dinner. He had gone towards town and perhaps caught sight of some village boys playing. If he had seen Lawrence running away at that time, long after his earlier fright, then something else must have frightened him.

It wasn't much, but put together with the other tiny pieces of evidence—the torn jacket, the odd position of the body and the unlocked church door—it was enough to banish his last lingering doubts. Lawrence had not jumped to his death of his own volition. Someone had chased him into the church and up the tower. Someone had either pushed him or frightened him into jumping. Not just someone, Green thought grimly as he reached the station. Tom. Hannah's story merely confirmed his fears. Only worse, because not only was Tom probably a killer, but now he was off in the wilderness with the fragile, confused youngster who had witnessed it all.

As soon as Green reached his office, he picked up his phone. He needed more than the vague, jumbled impressions that Kyle had reported to Hannah. He needed to know exactly what Kyle had seen that afternoon. Since he couldn't ask Kyle or Lawrence, that left only two other people he could ask. As unwelcome as the intrusion would be.

Jeb McMartin snatched up the phone before the second ring, a tremor of hope ringing through the fear in his voice.

"Sorry, Mr. McMartin, I've had no word as yet. Have you?"

"No." Green could almost see the man's shoulders droop. "We had a hope earlier on, someone spotted a old black Ford on the highway near Napanee, but it was the wrong truck."

"I have a question about Kyle," Green said. "Did he tell you anything about the afternoon he went for his walk?"

"What do you mean? The day the fella died?"

"Yes. Did he mention seeing anyone? In the woods or near the church?"

There was a pause. "Are you saying Kyle saw something? About Lawrence Pettigrew?"

"I don't know." Green cursed his need to alarm the man further. "He said something about a bad man who was running away. I was hoping he'd told you more."

"He never..." The man's voice dropped warily. "He never said he was in the woods. Or that he went to town."

Green backtracked quickly. "Sorry, false lead. When I—"

"Just a minute!" Panic snagged Jeb's voice. "Are you saying my son could have seen something? That he's in danger?"

"We have no reason—"

"Bull! Why else would you ask? We know Tom Pettigrew beat that poor Boisvert woman half to death. What the hell else is he up to?"

I wish to God I knew, Green thought, extricating himself as hastily as he could so as not to have to lie any further. When he hung up, he wondered how the McMartins would feel when the first of the Ident vans arrived to turn the Boisvert front yard into an archeological dig.

He sat at his desk a few minutes, calming his nerves and trying to sort out his next move. All the bases were covered. Sullivan was handling the warrant and coordinating the excavation. Sue Peters was acting as liaison with the OPP—a

straight-forward, one-of-the-boys job which shouldn't tax her diplomacy skills. Gibbs had been dispatched to snap at the heels of the RCMP forensics lab to see what they could glean from Lawrence's tin can and from Tom's letter to Benji. There was nothing else to do. He could sit by the phone, working on budget projections and chewing his nails.

Or he could go back out to the village and see for himself what Kyle McMartin might have seen.

*   *   *

In the true spirit of a Canadian October, the torrential bluster of the day before had given way to a cold, brittle sun which sliced through the denuded trees and streaked the forest floor in red and gold. Green parked at the edge of the village square and paused to get his bearings. On the far corner of the square nearest the river sat the deserted church. Beside the church was a modest cemetery filled with lichen-covered stones and surrounded by a wrought-iron fence. Behind the cemetery and the church lay the woods, which stretched in a broad swath along the river's edge all the way north past the McMartin and Boisvert farms.

Three boys were playing street hockey in the parking lot of St. James Church across the road, and they watched him through oblique eyes. He headed down to the river, which curved into a natural bay, where a small marina had been erected long ago to serve the commercial boats travelling the Rideau Canal system. A boarded-up bait shop and ice cream stand gave testimony to the changing fortunes of river life, but the shoreline and docks were still lined with boats that had been pulled up and covered with blue tarpaulins for the winter. Wind gusted across the clearing, snapping the tarpaulins and swirling leaves about. Green shivered and

balled his hands into the pockets of his thin jacket.

To his left, he spotted the entrance to the footpath through an opening in the underbrush, and he picked his way across the sodden leaves and discarded wrappers that littered the marina. Once inside the woods, the wind died down, and the faded grays and browns of the waterfront gave way to the golds and reds of the forest floor. The path spooled out ahead of him, dipping and weaving around trees and over rocks into the distance. He could see nothing that looked like the special hiding place Kyle might have meant. But Green was a city boy; his secret lairs had been the crawlspaces of back porches and old bridges, or the recesses of abandoned garden sheds. What did he know of country hiding places?

He retreated into the open and called to the boys playing by the church. They sauntered over, hitching their pants and tugging their caps down low. One wore a Sens cap, another a Maple Leafs cap. The third, a small, wiry boy with dirt an inch thick on his face, wore a plain black one. Green took out his badge and introduced himself, enjoying their efforts to maintain their casual air.

"Do any of you boys know Kyle McMartin?"

They bobbed their heads as one. "Yeah, we all used to go to school with him."

"You know he's missing, eh?"

Again the heads bobbed. "I saw him the day before," the Leafs fan said.

"Me too," echoed the Sens fan.

"Did you ever see him walking in these woods?"

"He wasn't allowed," said Maple Leaf.

"But sometimes he did," countered the small boy darkly.

"Did you see him Sunday afternoon? Just before dinner?"

The boys exchanged baffled looks followed by shrugs of

disappointment. "But he hides if people come," the small one said.

"I'm told he has a special place where he hides in the woods," Green said. "Do you know where it is?"

The two taller boys looked chagrined that they could shed no light, but the small one brightened. "I bet it's Bear Rock."

Bears, Green thought with a wary glance at the woods. "Can you show me?"

In unison, they volunteered and scrambled down the path at such a pace that Green found himself leaping over rocks and ducking boughs to keep up. Fortunately, it gave him little chance to think about bears. A hundred yards along the path, the boys veered away from the river and followed a thin, barely discernible trail that threaded through the undergrowth. Up ahead, the path climbed a small knoll dominated by a massive rock covered in lichen and dead vines. Near the top of it, an overhang created a sheltered, mossy niche trampled flat by many visitors. The boys clambered up the rock excitedly, using small cracks and knobs to gain a foothold, and once they'd reached the top they looked down on him with triumph.

"Kyle's mom thinks he'll fall, so he's not supposed to come here. But I've see him here."

Green approached the slick rock with caution and tested his footing on the first toehold. The niche was just above his head, hardly high enough to present much danger in a fall. He pulled himself up to the first toehold, cursing his stupid city pants and his leather shoes. Overhead, the boys danced and gave him climbing advice. After a few precarious moments and a string of silent curses, he reached the niche, clambered gratefully on all fours over the damp moss and sat down. To his left, down the knoll through the trees, he could see anyone who passed by on the path. About a hundred yards directly

ahead, just as he'd thought, was a clear view of the graveyard and the back door of Ashford Methodist Church.

He glanced up at the grinning boys who commanded the top of the rock. "Were any of you boys playing in the square last Sunday afternoon when the man died?"

All their heads bobbed.

"Did you see anything? Hear anything?"

"Well, we were playing a game, eh?" Maple Leaf began. "So—"

"I heard yelling!" the wiry boy blurted.

"You did not," Maple Leaf countered.

"I did! From that old church!"

Green looked at the little boy, whose eyes glowed big and excited in his dirty face, and put on his most authoritative stare. The last thing he needed was to have the facts in this case further muddied by a small boy with an active imagination and a burning desire to impress. "What exactly did you hear?"

The boy stared back, undaunted. "A man. Screaming."

"What did he say?"

The boy broke his gaze. Dropped his head. "I only heard a bit."

"What?"

"Sounded like 'Get away, get away'." He shrugged. "He was bawling."

"That's bullshit," the Leafs fan said. "You never told us that."

Green kept his gaze locked on the boy. "Did you look to see if anyone was there?"

"Well, no, 'cause I was in goal, eh? And anyway, the church bell rang, and I didn't hear no more."

"Good job. You'll make a good detective someday." Green gave the boy a solemn nod, which brought a proud smile to his dirty face. Once they'd all clambered down from the rock,

he took all the boys' names, gave them his card and thanked them for their help. He returned to his car, furious that none of the street canvasses had turned up this boy's story. Back inside the car, he turned the heater on full blast, warmed his hands and scrubbed the muddy patches on his knees. As he slowly thawed, he pondered what he'd learned. Late in the afternoon of that Sunday, Kyle had been sitting on his special rock, watching the village square in perfect view of the back of the church. He had seen Lawrence running. Not creeping up with the furtive tiptoe of someone afraid to be seen, nor the tentative step of someone unsure of what he'd find, nor the purposeful stride of someone seeking a way in.

Now more than ever, Green was convinced that Kyle had been an unsuspecting witness to Lawrence's last panicked flight to his death. Perhaps he had even seen the assailant, heard Lawrence begging him to leave him alone. Had Kyle actually seen Lawrence fall to his death? Somewhere in the confused jumble of the boy's mind, did he actually know whether Lawrence had been pushed or jumped to escape? See who he was running from? It had to be Tom, for who else would be desperate enough and stupid enough to risk exposure in the middle of a Sunday afternoon, with boys playing in the square and church bells calling the faithful to service?

Green was convinced he had the whole picture, but he didn't have one damn bit of solid physical evidence to nail the bastard down. Yet. Maybe in the love notes, the bloody fingerprint, or the fingerprints on the tower ladder, Ident would get lucky.

Green was just reaching for his cell phone to call Cunningham when it rang, and Gibbs' voice crackled through the interference.

"Anything from the lab or the RCMP?" Green yelled.

"Yes sir!" Gibbs' voice burst with excitement. He'd had to stand over them to get some preliminary reports, but all the media attention on the missing boy had proved useful in mobilizing the interests of the brass. The documents expert had determined that the letter to Benji and the love note to Sophia were in the same hand. Obviously Tom's, Green thought without the slightest surprise. The short note about the bus appeared to be a more educated hand.

"What about the blood type on the note?"

"The RCMP's not done that yet, sir."

"Cunningham's fingerprint report?"

"No hits on that so far, sir. Cunningham said to tell you Tom Pettigrew's prints don't match anything."

"Not even the bloody note?" Green felt his excitement fade. He'd been counting on that fingerprint to give him some concrete evidence that his theory was on the right track. Now, not only didn't he have that confirmation, but he had the added complication of a print which was likely connected to the murder scene but didn't match any known witnesses. A defence lawyer's dream. Mentally, he flipped through the list of players, wondering who else he should print.

"Uh...sir?" Gibbs interjected cautiously, and Green sensed him searching for words. "Superintendent Jules has left a few messages, sir. He asked me to pass them on. Something about needing an update?"

I'll bet he does, with the media banging at the doors. "That's fine. I'm heading to the command post, and I'll update him from there."

"Well, sir..." Gibbs hesitated, and Green could hear a quiver of excitement in his voice. "There is something else. I'm on my way out there, with someone I thought you'd want to see right away."

Seventeen

Sullivan's Saturday morning found him at the police station at the crack of dawn as well, labouring over the paperwork needed to obtain the coroner's warrant for the Boisverts' front yard and for Scott's landfill site, where the debris from the yard had been moved. Then the regional coroner had to be roused from his morning coffee to sign the warrant, which proved to be a cakewalk. With all Gibbs' failed efforts to locate Derek and with Tom's letter to Benji as the crowning touch, the doctor barely had to set down his coffee while he scribbled out his signature to set the excavation in motion.

The Boisverts had no objection to the execution of the warrant. From his place at Isabelle's hospital bedside, Jacques waved his hands as if nothing could shock him anymore.

"Go ahead!" he exclaimed. "Dig! Dig the whole damn place! *Je m'en fous!* I'm not living there ever again!"

Isabelle, lying pale and weak against the pillows, did not even lift her groggy head to protest.

Upon leaving the hospital, Sullivan headed out of the city towards Scott's dump site, which was located just north of Merrickville, another of the historic towns dotting the Rideau River. Unlike Ashford Landing, however, this one had remained prosperous by trading its original identity as a canal lock station for a modern one as a quaint heritage village for tourists and artists.

As he cruised south along the highway, Sullivan reflected on the number of people who, like the Boisverts, had left the congestion and high prices of the city for a little spread of green space and fresh air. It had an undeniable appeal. He owned a modest split-level on a city lot shoehorned into the suburb of Alta Vista. Every morning he backed out of his drive to join his neighbours in line for the red light on to Smythe Road. Every night he returned home to his barbeque on the back deck, the sound of his neighbours' TV, and the frantic juggling of Sean's hockey practices and Lizzie's jazz lessons. All while Mary was out showing yet another house in the hope that this time she'd make a sale so they could pay for the goalie camp Sean needed.

Maybe it was time to make a change not just in his career but in his home as well. Maybe he could stand to live in the country again, if he didn't have to farm the land. If he could just skidoo on it, hike and fish, teach his boys to hunt rabbits and listen to the hoot of the owls at night.

Scott's business came upon him while he was still caught up in reverie, nearly causing him to miss the turn. He banked sharply and squealed the tires as he swung up the driveway to the massive chain link gate. In the distance, he could see a brick bungalow and a corrugated metal warehouse. Much to his annoyance, a heavy padlock held the gate locked, so he tried the old-fashioned country remedy; he leaned on his horn until the front door of the bungalow opened, and a large muscular man stuck his head out. He was wearing nothing but jeans and an undershirt, but reluctantly threw a flannel jacket on top before stomping down the slope to open the gate. His initial scowl turned to alarm at the sight of Sullivan's badge.

"What's this about, officer?" he asked as he hauled back the gate.

Sullivan handed him the warrant, which Scott peered at

with a puzzled frown. He looked as if he'd just woken up two minutes earlier and couldn't get his brain in gear. "All the contents from the Boisvert excavation? What in hell's name do you want that stuff for?"

Sullivan pointed to the fine print.

Scott squinted. "Looking for bones, clothing, personal effects... What the fuck?"

"A team will be arriving shortly to sift through the stuff, sir. It shouldn't take long, then we'll be out of your hair. Now if you'll just show me where it is."

Sullivan had passed through the gate and gestured to the man to lead the way. Scott, now finally waking up, shook his head in disbelief. "The Boisvert woman was digging out there, but she never said anything about this! Holy fuck! I was just supposed to dig a foundation for the garage!"

Scott stopped by the house and pointed to a vast pile of bulldozed branches, dirt and rocks which extended into the gully behind his house. "It's out in the corner over there. I haven't had time to bulldoze it over, so it should be... Holy fuck! What happens if you find something? I mean, am I in trouble because...?"

"Not unless you're knowingly concealing something," Sullivan replied.

While Scott gaped, Sullivan set off across the property to the pile of debris that Scott had pointed out. The man lagged behind, fumbling in his pocket for his cell phone. He stabbed a button and cursed under his breath as he waited. Sullivan paused, tuning a sharp ear while pretending to examine the soil. In his line of work, it never paid to assume anyone was above suspicion.

"Sandy!" the man exclaimed. "Call me ASAP. Holy fuck, man! What the hell did you get me into?"

*   *   *

225

Green stood at the door of the command post and watched the pair climb out of the car onto the grassy shoulder. Gibbs headed straight for the truck with the eagerness of a puppy on the scent, but the woman hung back, shielding her eyes with a gloved hand as her gaze swept the village square. She tottered an instant on her spike-heeled boots and tugged her fur collar tighter around her neck before turning resolutely towards him.

Green held the door open for her as she clambered awkwardly up the steps. Inside, she paused and flicked her wary gaze around the gleaming chrome interior. She was all sinews and angles, with brassy tips on her black cropped hair and a harsh red slash of lipstick across her sallow face. She looked nothing like the lush, seductive teenager of twenty years ago, yet Green would have known her anywhere.

He extended his hand. "I'm Inspector Green. Thank you for coming, Ms. Vincelli."

"Albert. Got married. Divorced." She sized him up with tired, pouchy eyes. "I heard you were looking for me. What's this about?"

He glanced at the work stations sandwiched along the walls. The truck was a marvel of high-tech efficiency, but hardly a place to put a skittish witness at ease. "Let's go across to the church where we'll be more comfortable. Gibbs, if that stuff is drinkable," he said, nodding towards a coffee pot hissing on the counter, "bring us some coffees and then join us, okay?"

Gibbs' eyes were dancing with triumph, although by his own admission, he had played only a minor role in her surprise appearance. The Mediterranean grape vine must have been buzzing, for she had walked into the downtown headquarters on her own, asking to see him. Now she followed Green obediently across the square to the Anglican church, pausing only briefly on the alien threshold before joining Green in the small ante-room. She sank into the padded vinyl chair he offered her and crossed

one lean, stocking-clad leg over the other, affecting a casual, slightly bored air. But her fingers betrayed her. Laden with rings and topped by inch-long crimson nails, they tapped a restless rhythm on the arm of the chair.

Green sat down in an adjacent chair, affecting a chatty mood that was nearly impossible in the watchful eye of a stained glass Jesus. "You're a difficult person to track down," he began amiably. "Where are you living now?"

Her fingers stopped. "Am I in trouble here?"

"Not at all. We're hoping you can help us with an incident that occurred out here twenty years ago."

"So this doesn't have to do with Rocky? My ex?"

Green shook his head. "We need your address for our report, that's all. Routine."

"I was out west, but I'm back in Ottawa now." She paused, like a woman who'd learned to choose her words carefully, then dictated her address. "I've been kinda keeping out of Rocky's way. So what's this incident you're talking about?" Abruptly her eyes widened. "Twenty years... Jeeze, Tommy Pettigrew! The same Tom Pettigrew that abducted that kid on the news?"

"I understand you and he were close back then?"

She was still caught in the revelation. "I should have made the connection. That's totally something Tommy would do. Jump in, do something wild, and then find himself in a mess. But what's this got to do with twenty years ago?"

Briefly Green described Lawrence's death, the discovery of the love letters, and the possibility that Derek had been murdered. Sophia reacted with pure, deathly pale, mouth-dropping horror, betraying no sign that she had any foreknowledge. Beneath the brassy style and the prickly façade, Green sensed a woman who cared. When Gibbs burst in with the coffee, she busied herself with cream and sugar for several minutes to regain control.

227

Once she'd had three unsteady sips, she shook her head in dismay. "So you think Lawrence killed Derek?"

"That's the way the evidence is leaning," Green replied. "Knowing the family as you did, what do you think?"

"Lorrie was a very sick puppy, but he was always a gentle kid. Sensitive and sweet. He couldn't stand meanness, and I never saw him fight back, even when kids picked on him."

The use of the diminutive name startled Green, for no one, not even Sandy or Tom, had referred to the dead man as Lorrie. It occurred to Green that the nicknames of the Pettigrew children implied a family warmth that belied the bitterness of their later lives. "But people in the village seemed afraid of him," he said. "Some parents wouldn't let their children go to the Pettigrew farm because of him."

"That's just because they didn't know him. And anyway, he worshipped Derek! Derek was the only one in the family who was nice to him. Now if Lorrie was going to kill anyone, I would have bet Tommy."

"Why?"

"Tommy was so mean to him. And..." She flushed, giving him yet another glimpse of the softer woman inside.

"And?"

"And Lorrie believed in being good. He wanted people to be pure."

"Which Tom wasn't?"

She chuckled. "Hardly. Poor Lorrie worried so much about Tommy's soul. Tommy didn't give a damn about his soul."

"Yet you went out with him?"

"Yeah. I sure pick 'em." She began to swing her leg up and down, and a wistful smile curved her lips. "Tommy was like riding a roller coaster; the lows were scary, but the highs were really, really amazing."

Green told her about the love letter Tom had written her. "Why did you break up with him?"

She looked surprised to hear about the letter. "Tommy wrote something? Boy, he must have been more desperate than I thought. Poor Tommy. All he ever wanted was to be a somebody, but he couldn't read worth a damn, so he flunked out of high school and then got fired from all his jobs because of his temper."

Green thought of Isabelle Boisvert and the boy in the back of Tom's truck. Deftly he changed gears. "Tell me about his temper."

"He wouldn't learn to take crap, you know? Life is full of crap, from the Grade Two teacher who sticks you in the corner to the boss who yells because you ordered the wrong screw. Tommy's gotta make an argument out of everything. And when we'd go out, any guy that looked at me sideways, Tommy would take him on."

"Was he ever violent?"

"Sometimes, if the other guy wanted to push it too. Lots of times, Tommy would go home at night with a bloody nose."

A vivid picture was beginning to emerge in Green's mind of family life at the Pettigrew farm. Of wild, headstrong Tom and gentle, timid Lawrence, of parents struggling to cope with the clashing spirits of their many sons. "What about Derek? Was he more like Lawrence or Tom?"

The mention of Derek erased the wistful smile from her lips. She dropped her eyes sadly. "I can't believe he's dead. What a waste! Everybody thought Derek would be a somebody. He was so smart. Like Lorrie, he'd never fight, kept everything in. But he was strong inside himself, you know? Like he knew where he was going and could leave all this family stuff behind."

"Was Tom jealous of him?"

"Oh, totally!"

"Did he have reason? Over you, I mean?"

She shook her head, but alarm flashed across her face. "There was nothing there! Derek and me talked a bit. One day, especially, I was going out to the farm and—" She clamped her hand to her mouth in dismay. "Mamma mia," she murmured.

"What?"

"Nothing. I just thought what if... No." She whipped her head back and forth, as if to chase the thought away.

Green leaned forward sharply. "What if what?"

She chewed her lower lip and splayed her fingers to rearrange each ring in turn. Green waited until she finally made up her own mind. "One day I was going out to see Tommy, and I took the river path because it was dry enough."

"When was this?"

"Just before I broke up with Tommy and left town."

"When was that? Spring of '84?"

She nodded. "May. Derek was just back from the university, maybe a couple of weeks. He was getting ready to go to the States." She looked up in horror. "Jeez, you mean... he never even left?"

"Looks that way." Green curbed his impatience with an effort, sensing the case was about to break open before his eyes. "Please go on, Sophia. You were going out to meet Tom."

She nodded. Absently, her crimson nails carved deep indentations into the vinyl arms of the chair. "I heard yelling in the distance from the farm. Men's voices, really loud. It made me nervous, because I knew Tommy and his father argued a lot, and it always put Tommy in a rotten mood. I didn't really want to see him if he was so mad. So I waited in the woods, and suddenly I saw Derek coming down the path. He was kind of running, kind of limping, but his head was down so he didn't see me. When he reached this big tree—the old maple with the tree fort in it—he leaned against it and started bawling. He had a big bruise on his

cheek and kinda cradled himself like every sob hurt. I never seen a guy so upset, so I asked him what was wrong. That was the main time we really talked. He said he didn't know what to do with his life, 'cause everything he wanted was against what his family believed, and he had to get out of here if he was going to survive."

"Did he say who beat him up?"

She shook her head, but the crimson nails dug deeper, as if to suppress her unvoiced fear. "He talked about wanting to help people, maybe be a minister, but the kind that preached the true message that Jesus gave. Not the tight-ass, unforgiving types his family liked. But he didn't know where he could go. We'd had a couple of talks before about how his parents wanted him to be an engineer, but he wanted to help people. Build spiritual bridges, he said. Not physical ones." She blushed at the unfamiliar sound of the words from her lips. "Derek always had his head in the clouds."

"Doesn't sound like enough reason for a beating, or for tears."

"Well, I think there was a woman too. That he loved, but couldn't have."

Green perked up. Maybe the mysterious "S" Derek was supposed to run away with. "Any name?"

"No, I just got the feeling it couldn't work out."

Green eyed her thoughtfully. She had relaxed slightly and was trying to smooth out the dents she'd made in the vinyl, but she still seemed spooked. Something about Derek's beating and Tom's jealousy troubled her. Because Lawrence had intercepted the note about catching the bus, perhaps she had never learned the full depth of Derek's feeling. Could it be that she was just now putting the signals together?

"Do you think that woman might have been you?" he asked. "And that Tom suspected it?"

She looked shocked. "Oh Jeez, no! I mean...if Derek liked me, he never let on."

Despite her pretense at shock, Green wasn't convinced. "But you thought Tom gave him the beating because of you, right? Is that why you broke up with him?"

She looked up from her fingers to give him a reproachful frown, as if he was making her face possibilities she preferred to avoid. "Tommy saw us talking in the woods," she muttered. "He saw me put my arm around Derek. He freaked out. I don't know if he beat up Derek, but his freak-out scared me enough that I thought 'I need to get out of here'. So I told Tommy it was over and then I asked my parents to put me on the first plane over to Italy." She smiled. "Believe me, they were only too happy. Nona Vincelli was already fixing up the bedroom in Orvieto."

Green's instincts were screaming. Whatever the true extent of Sophia's and Derek's relationship, the final fateful days before the tragedy were slowly coming to light and the mystery of the stolen notes was falling into place. Tom—wild, dangerous Tom—had been in love with Sophia and insanely jealous of his older brother's friendship with her. Then Derek was beaten up, Sophia suspected Tom was responsible, therefore she broke up with him. Lawrence stole Tom's letter begging for a second chance, and Sophia left town, leaving a desperate, vengeful Tom blaming...who? Derek, who had stolen her affections? Or Lawrence, who had thwarted Tom's attempt to win her back?

A number of questions remained unanswered. Namely, had Tom known that Lawrence stole his letter? Who had actually beaten up Derek, and who was the real object of his love? But one thing was becoming increasing clear, Green realized with a shiver of foreboding. Of all the members of the family, Lawrence was not the one with the most rage and the most compelling reason to murder Derek. Tom was.

Eighteen

In the bright autumn sun, the Riverview Seniors' Home looked less desolate, and even the stench of manure from the field across the road had dissipated in the crisp, dry air. Green swung the car into the parking spot next to the main entrance, marked Nursing Supervisor, and leaped out before the engine had even shuddered to a stop. As he sailed through the front door, he prayed that, like his own father's, Reverend Taylor's memory for what had happened twenty years ago was better than for what he'd said five minutes ago.

During the drive over, which had taken ten minutes even at his record-breaking speeds, he had tried to refute his new theory, but the more he considered it, the more horribly plausible it became. According to the letter he'd written Benji, Tom had been the one to discover the body. How simple it would have been to kill Derek himself and lay the blame on crazy, defenceless Lawrence?

Knowing Tom, it was probably not a premeditated killing but an explosion of the rage he was famous for. But when he'd found himself covered in blood and Derek dead, he'd thought up the perfect way to conceal his crime. Why should he ruin the rest of his life for one brief moment of blind madness, when Lawrence was already beyond the hope of a normal, fulfilling life? Treatment in a mental hospital was no less than he needed and deserved anyway.

Green could almost hear Tom's infamous, self-justifying excuses rushing to his aid. No wonder he had been so quick to identify Lawrence's body as Derek, thereby heading off any further inquiry into Derek's disappearance twenty years ago. No wonder he had been desperate to find the letters he'd written to Benji and to prevent Green from talking to his father. "Gom", the father had said. Did the old man know something? Suspect something?

And most telling of all, the theory also gave a much more compelling motive for Tom to murder Lawrence. Not to avenge the death of Derek and the ruination of all their lives, but quite simply to shut him up. Which showed just how deadly Tom really was, and the lengths to which he would go to protect himself.

Green's pulse hammered with excitement. The theory was all circumstantial, based on hints and suppositions, and there were few people still around who might know what had happened back then. His instincts told him Taylor was one, if he could ever get at the memories Taylor had jumbled inside.

As it turned out, that was not as difficult as Green had feared. Taylor had just finished his afternoon rest period and was freshly dressed in preparation for his daily walk. Green caught him just putting on his old fashioned brimmed hat. His blue eyes were bright, and he actually remembered who Green was.

"Nice day," he remarked, swinging his cane. "You fancy a turn outside, boy? Hate to miss one of the last fine days of fall."

Taylor walked with the gait of an old military man, shoulders squared and eyes straight ahead, but his stride was short and his progress slow. Green was able to stroll comfortably at his side and concentrate on a wise choice of words.

"I need your recollection of events twenty years ago, Reverend."

"That should be no problem, my son. Twenty years ago is clear as crystal."

"The Pettigrew family. If you recall my visit last Monday, one of the sons—turned out to be Lawrence—died in your church yard."

"Lawrence, eh? Pity. Always wondered what happened to the poor lad. He was ill, you know, hearing voices and seeing angels all over the place."

"I'm told you helped him. Gave him chores and even let him have a key to the church. Is that correct?"

"Lawrence only wanted to help. Poor boy got so confused when they took him over to that other church. I promised him he'd always have a place in my church too. Although I never expected him to—" Taylor blinked. "Oh, dear."

"To do what?"

"To jump to his death. I thought I was helping."

"I'm sure you were. But I have more bad news, sir. It seems highly likely that twenty years ago, instead of leaving for California, the oldest son, Derek, was murdered and his body concealed by the family."

Taylor made an odd sound, half-moan and half-grunt. He lurched forward, forcing Green to dive for his arm. Holding him steady, Green gestured to some nearby Muskoka chairs sitting in a cluster around an empty fish pond.

"Perhaps we'd better sit for a moment, Reverend."

"Eh?" Taylor straightened and shrugged off Green's hand. "Nope, have to finish my walk. Have to keep the legs strong and the mind sharp. Derek dead? Dear, oh dear."

"I understand he'd been going through a bit of a personal crisis the last year or two. Thinking about his future, not sure what path he should follow. Did he confide in you?"

Taylor swivelled his head carefully to study Green, his eyes shrewd beneath his bushy white brows. "Who you been talking to, boy?"

Green was surprised at the accusation in the man's tone. His sixth sense stirred. There was something more to this story, and he hated having no idea what it was or how to get at it. He decided to take a wild guess.

"The Pettigrews were an extremely traditional family. I know they disapproved of your liberal views and moved over to a stricter—" He groped for words in the unfamiliar landscape of Christian allegiances.

"Narrow-minded. Un-Christian," Taylor snapped.

"Yes. You said you continued to help Lawrence, and I'm assuming you continued to help Derek too. I think he used you as a sounding board to help him sort out what he was going to do. I'm not criticizing you for that, believe me."

"Plenty did. Norm Pettigrew did. Told the whole town I was leading his boys down the path to perdition. People are what God made them, Detective. The only sin is in condemning them for that."

Taylor had become dangerously red, and he tottered on his spindly legs. This time when Green took his elbow to steer him to a chair, he did not protest. He sank into the wooden chair as if his legs had given out, and Green was surprised to see tears in his eyes. His intuition that there was more to this story grew stronger.

"You're not just talking about Derek's change of career choice, are you, Reverend?"

"It was a big dilemma for the lad," Taylor continued as if Green hadn't spoken. "He'd been raised on the Bible, felt its teachings deep in his soul."

"What teachings?" Green persisted.

"Eh? Oh, the straight and narrow and all that—"

Taylor placed a peculiar emphasis on the word "straight", and with that hint, out of the blue an idea came to Green. It was novel and unexpected, yet brilliantly apt. "Are you saying Derek was gay?"

236

Taylor didn't reply, but he flinched as if retreating from the bald truth, and in that retreat Green had his answer. "That's it, isn't it? He confided that to you, and you didn't condemn him. Is that what the father couldn't stand? Is that why he took the family from the church?"

Taylor shut his eyes and leaned back in the chair, suddenly shrivelled and old. "How could I condemn it, son? That would be to condemn..." He stopped short of what Green suspected he was about to confess. Instead he opened his eyes to study Green helplessly. "Yes, I helped him. I listened, I interpreted the gospel to him, I tried to help him reconcile his two great loves—his love of God and his love of his fellow men. He tried to fight it, you know. As so many do. He met a young man at the university, but it took him a long time to admit what they felt for each other. After that broke up, he didn't come back to talk to me for a long time. He tried women, he tried celibacy, but you can't deny your nature."

"Do you know if he was involved with anyone at the end?"

Taylor nodded. "He came to see me. He looked like he'd been in a bar brawl. Said his father had caught them together and beat him up. Norm is a big man and had about fifty pounds on him, but Derek was very, very angry when I last saw him. He told me that was the last time, and if his Dad ever came at him again, he was going to give it back."

Taylor's anger energized him, and he sat up straight, his brows quivering. "By the love of Jove, if that boy's been murdered, I wouldn't look past Norm Pettigrew if I were you!"

*　*　*

When Green climbed back into his car outside the seniors' home, it was past two o'clock, and his mind was reeling from

mental overload and physical starvation. There was yet another message on his voice mail from Superintendent Jules requesting—no, demanding—his update. Green punched the delete button with a curse. Before he briefed Jules, he had to figure out what he himself thought.

Was it possible that Norm Pettigrew had killed his own son? A man who strapped his boys' hands when they masturbated, a man who invoked the wrath of God and the threat of hell to keep his boys in line? It was Norm who had beaten up Derek on the day Sophia met him in the woods. In Norm's world view, Derek's homosexuality would have constituted a mortal sin, an affront against his own authority as moral leader of his household and a threat to his vaunted stature in the community. To Norm, the sight of his son in the arms of another man would have been an abomination.

How much greater would his outrage have been if a few days later he'd discovered Derek was running away with his lover in open defiance of his orders? Had he intercepted the note and known what 'our place' meant? The shed, of course! Where all the boys went to get away, where perhaps Derek had been waiting for his lover that day, only to come face to face with his father instead. And where, in the argument that erupted, this time Norm had found a weapon more lethal than his fists.

Green raced over the scenario in his mind, probing it for flaws. He felt he was getting close. The concrete details of the crime were filling in, the niggling inconsistencies ironing out. The theory explained Tom's hatred of his father and his comment "after all he made us do". If Norm had made Tom clean up the bloodbath he himself had caused, and forced him to support the lie that Lawrence was to blame, no wonder Tom could barely stand the sight of him.

As exciting as this new theory was, however, there was one

large, gaping flaw in it. Lawrence's death. For while Norman would have been sufficiently strong twenty years ago to overpower Derek, there was no way that the frail old man Green had met in the hospital was capable of chasing Lawrence up the tower to his death. A major flaw, for sure. But it was not essential that the same person killed both Derek and Lawrence. Perhaps Tom hadn't known his father killed Derek and had lived all these years with the belief that Lawrence had ruined all their lives. It still fit his character to go off the deep end at the sight of Lawrence.

Two plausible scenarios for Derek's death, two possible killers. Twenty years of deception, anguish or wilful amnesia. But even if the excavation uncovered Derek's bones, even if the OPP caught Tom and brought him in for questioning, how would they ever get at the truth? After twenty years, any physical evidence that had actually survived the fire would have been degraded by the elements.

Except Lawrence's airtight tin can and the unidentified bloody fingerprint. That pesky little piece of evidence that refused to fit anywhere.

Green reached for the phone excitedly. Lyle Cunningham and his partner would be out at the excavation site, but with any luck, someone else in the Ident Unit would be slaving over samples in the lab. Sure enough, Sergeant Lou Paquette's booze-ravaged voice growled through the wires after the third ring. His first reaction upon hearing Green's request was a flat no, but Green was ready for him.

"This is shaping up to be a major kidnapping-double homicide, Lou, with both us and the OPP in on the search. Before I call Superintendent Jules to update him on our progress, I want to have all our bases covered. We can't wait till Cunningham's free; I need to know ASAP if the guy we're pursuing is a killer as well as

a kidnapper. I need to assess degree of risk and advise the OPP if they should call in their Tactical boys."

The mention of all the high-powered interest did the trick. With dark references to Cunningham's displeasure, Paquette agreed to take Norman Pettigrew's fingerprints at the hospital and compare them to the bloody print on the note.

"But you break the news to Cunny," he added as a parting shot. "You know what a control freak he is."

I will, Green promised as he hung up. Later. He had to eat, but even more crucially he had to brief Jules. The man had scattered enough messages around that he could no longer be ignored. And to judge from his tone when Green reached him at home, his patience had already been well exceeded.

"Thank you for your promptness," Jules said, deadpan. "I am still technically in charge of this division, Mike, at least until Monday. And you'll find Barbara Devine is keen to be kept informed."

More than keen, Green thought grimly. As he outlined the current state of the case, he eased the Impala into gear and backed out of the Nursing Supervisor's parking spot. A man of normally few words, Jules didn't say a thing while Green summarized his quandary about the lack of evidence and witnesses to differentiate the two possible suspects.

"What about the boy?" he asked when Green finished.

"Kyle?"

"No. The youngest son."

"Robbie?" Green was taken aback, for Jules must have retained every word he'd uttered. The man still had a mind like a surgical scalpel. "He was only eight when the first homicide occurred."

"Eight-year-olds can remember," Jules said. "Besides, I understand he's been calling all around downstairs demanding to know what's going on."

Green winced in dismay. Events had unfolded so fast over the past twenty-four hours that he'd forgotten all about Robbie Pettigrew. He left the man sputtering over the telephone about Tom absconding with his money, but that infraction was trivial compared to the ensuing cascade of catastrophes Tom had wrought. Robbie would have seen the news of Isabelle's assault, Kyle's abduction and the massive manhunt in the country side. The poor man deserved an explanation before he also learned about the search for Derek's body in the front yard of his childhood home.

"I'll phone him right away," Green said. He had to pull off the road to look up Robbie's number, but was lucky enough to catch the man on his first try. It proved already too late to cushion the shock.

"What in the name of God is going on, Inspector!" Robbie cried at a voice level to shatter glass. Green jerked the phone away several inches. "I just got a call from Jacques Boisvert! He wants to annul the sale, he's threatening to sue. What's this about my brother being buried in the yard? I've been standing by the phone waiting for your call for hours. I'm going crazy, Green!"

Green suppressed a weary groan. This was a complication he didn't need, and a phone call wasn't going to suffice; the man deserved better than that. Besides, as Jules had pointed out, eight-year-olds sometimes remembered things. Even if they didn't know it.

"Are you up to driving, Robbie? I'm near Manotick, so why don't I meet you there for a sandwich?"

"I can't eat, for God's sake!"

Who's talking about you, Green thought, but behaved himself. "Coffee then. At the pub on—"

"I want to go out to the farm."

Oh, fuck. "Not a good idea, Robbie. It's a restricted area

right now. Let's sit down someplace relaxing, and I'll bring you up to date."

Green had tried to sound soothing, but even so, Robbie peeled into the pub parking lot half an hour later, suggesting he must have virtually sprouted wings. He was wide-eyed and flying on adrenaline. Green sketched as brief and understated a picture of the case as he could manage, but Robbie grew whiter with every detail. By the end, tears brimmed in his eyes, and he clutched his head in his hands.

"Ohmigod, ohmigod," he whispered over and over, beginning to hyperventilate.

Green glanced around the little pub. He had chosen a booth tucked around the corner near the kitchen, and fortunately the mid-afternoon crowd was thin, so no one was paying them any heed. He searched in vain for a paper bag, but finally had to improvise.

"Take it easy. Cup your hands around your mouth and breathe. Don't talk, just breathe."

Robbie raised shaking hands to his face and tried to breathe. A lone tear spilled over and travelled down his cheek.

"We don't know anything for sure," Green said. "We haven't even found a body yet, let alone identified it as Derek."

"But it's going to be there," Robbie said. "You know that. Tom's letter, the fire, the axes—it all fits! Ohmigod! To think this happened, and the whole fucking family just buried it!" He pressed his hands to his eyes, fighting emotion. Rage or grief, Green wasn't sure. Probably a little of both. "I thought it was all my fault! All my fault that my father drank, that my mother killed herself, that no one would play with me and there were no flowers in the garden and no tree fort in the woods. I thought they didn't care! I was the extra son, the accident that nobody really wanted. I used to look at those

pictures in the album, and I saw how happy they used to be, but never with me." Tears poured down now, mingling unnoticed with the torrent of words. "And all along it was this fucking...!"

He groped at the air in a futile search for a word monstrous enough to describe the event. For a moment he was struck dumb, then he dropped his hands and took a deep breath. "You may not know the body is there, but I do. I even know how he was killed. We never had axes at the farm after that, not even when I insisted. When I bought an axe once to split wood, Dad threw it in the river and went on a two-day bender. I wanted to rebuild the shed instead of leaving that eyesore, but Mum nearly flipped her lid." He raised ravaged eyes to Green. "I've lived with this for twenty years, Inspector. I know it's true. I've never known why, but this... Mum, Benji..." His voice snagged. "This explains it all."

Green steeled himself to insert his first cautious probe. He was no expert in trauma cases nor in the recovery of childhood memory, but he'd seen enough trauma victims in his time to venture a try. At all costs, he had to avoid suggestive or leading questions.

"Do you remember anything at all about it, Robbie? Anything about that day?"

Robbie nodded. "I remember the fire. I had nightmares about fires for years. I was locked in my room—I guess Mom and Dad wanted me safe and out of the way—but I remember the noise of the flames. They roared and crackled like thunder. I'd never heard a fire so loud. I remember being scared my parents would get hurt. And it stank. A horrible stink I'll never forget. Sweet, putrid, so sharp it clung to your nose and stayed in the air for days, even after they put the fire out."

Burnt flesh does have a stink all its own, Green thought grimly. "Do you remember them putting it out?"

"I couldn't see, because my bedroom was at the back, but I

remember people screaming. Ohmigod, everyone was screaming. And there was a..." He stopped, his eyes narrowing as if he were casting his thoughts deep into forgotten corners of his mind. "There was one sound coming from a bedroom nearby. A high-pitched wailing, like someone keening, that went on all night. Nobody came. Not to get me, not to stop the keening. I was so scared I curled up under my bed. It was very hot in the house, and I was afraid it was burning up too. Ohmigod, I haven't thought about this in years!"

"It might help us if you can remember how the fire started."

Robbie was shaking his head. "That's all that sticks in my mind. The fire raging."

"Was it day or night?"

Robbie picked up his cup in both hands, tried to take a sip but couldn't steady the cup. With a grimace, he cradled it as if to warm his hands. "It must have been day when it started because I remember it gradually getting darker in my room. And all I could see was this spooky orange glow on the trees."

Knowing that the crime had occurred in May and that Derek was supposed to be at the bus station in Ottawa at 4:30, Green took an educated guess as to the time of the murder. Maybe he could use it to dislodge a few more memories.

"Did you take the school bus home?"

Robbie nodded.

"And it stopped at the end of your lane?"

Again a nod.

"I want you to try something. Make yourself comfortable. Lean back in the booth, stretch your legs out and let your hands rest in your lap. Good. Now shut your eyes."

Robbie, red-eyed and shell-shocked, leaned back, and after a moment's hesitation, his eyelids flickered shut. A flash of fear

crossed his brow. Green didn't blame him, for Robbie knew that something horrible lurked in his mind, and he had no wish to shine too bright a light on it.

"Relax," Green dropped his voice to a soothing murmur. "This is nothing fancy; it just eliminates distractions. Now I want you to take a deep breath. In slowly, slowly." He watched the man take a shallow, jerky breath. "Now let it out, slowly, all the way. Let yourself relax, sink into your chair. Now again, deep breath."

It took Robbie five deep breaths to relax enough to inhale evenly. Green crossed his fingers as he took the next step. He forced his voice to sound mellow, but inside he was quaking. He had used this focussing technique often to help witnesses remember the colour of a bank robber's eyes or the model of the get-away car, but he'd never tried to recover such a horrific memory from a long-forgotten childhood. He didn't know whether it would succeed, or whether Robbie would shatter in the process. And if he did shatter, would he, Green, be able to patch him back together again? Would anyone?

Green took his own deep breath. "I want you to picture yourself climbing off the school bus. You're standing at the end of the long lane beside the mailbox, looking at your house. You can see the barn with its square log sides and its rusty tin roof. Behind it the tall, red brick house..."

Green tried to remember the photo he'd seen in the album. "There's a clump of yellow daffodils out front, and a big tree beside the house with your tire swing on it. Its limbs are still bare. This is all far away, because you're still standing on the highway. Can you picture this?"

Robbie nodded.

"Now I want you to start walking down the long lane towards the house. Slowly. You're tired from the long day, your backpack is heavy, and it bumps against your back."

Robbie squirmed a little.

"The shed comes into view. What colour is it?"

Robbie wet his lips. Didn't answer.

"Tell me what you see, Robbie."

Robbie's eyes flew open.

"Is it on fire?"

A whispered "No."

"Do you see people?"

Robbie stared at the tabletop, trembling. Green debated asking him to shut his eyes again, but dared not push further. Whatever Robbie had now, it would have to be enough. Green leaned forward.

"You've remembered something, haven't you?"

"Not the killing," Robbie replied breathlessly. "But that awful keening while I'm coming down the lane. And...Tom." Robbie clutched his head. "Tom screaming. Chasing someone. They were both slipping and falling. Tom tackled the other man and grabbed his throat."

Green reminded himself not to be leading. "Who's the other person?"

"I...I don't remember Lawrence very well, so..."

"Then what happened?"

Robbie shook his head. "I don't know. I don't remember. I think a car came along the lane behind me, because I remember someone holding me down on the floor of the back seat. Nothing else."

Green uttered a silent prayer of thanks. Robbie was in one piece. Pale, stunned, and likely to be revisited by the nightmares of his youth, but intact. He didn't seem to have witnessed the murder nor seen the bloody aftermath. He had only a disconnected picture of Tom and a vivid image of fire. Yet in those few fragments of memory, two salient facts stood out. First,

the father was nowhere to be seen in the scenario Robbie had described. He had seen only Tom and someone who was almost certainly Lawrence. Secondly, Tom had tried to strangle Lawrence, and probably would have succeeded had the car not arrived in the nick of time. On balance, the Tom-as-killer scenario had not fared well in this latest series of revelations.

As if to drive the point home, Robbie grabbed his arm just as Green was getting up to pay the bill. "Does this mean it was Tom? Did that bastard kill our brother and ruin all our lives?"

"I don't know," Green replied. Without much conviction.

Nineteen

It was well into the afternoon by the time Green pulled his unmarked Impala up behind the long line of official vehicles in the Boisvert lane. Although technically in charge of the scene, MacPhail had been and gone, leaving instructions that he be called if any human remains turned up. Peter Cole and Lyle Cunningham had cordoned off the entire front yard between the barn and the farmhouse and had already removed most of the gravel fill to a pile at the side of the house. Following standard archeological procedure, the area had been staked and divided with thick twine into grids one metre square to aid in systematizing and recording the search.

A crew of uniformed and Ident officers was fanned out over the grid on their hands and knees, painstakingly lifting the soil with trowels. One of Cunningham's assistants roamed the scene with cameras draped around his neck, shooting video and still recordings of each section. Cunningham himself was working with Cole in the hole, sifting through the dregs of the gravel. Both men wore overalls and thick gardening gloves, and their cheeks glowed red, whether from exertion or the bitter wind Green wasn't sure, but they waved cheerfully. Amazing how some people found digging up bones an exhilarating adventure.

The yard was cluttered with tools for digging and cleaning

any artifacts they located, but fortunately there was no sign of Jacques Boisvert. Probably still out holding press conferences about police incompetence, Green thought. Spotting him, Sullivan detached himself from a small cluster of officers sitting on the front stoop. As he approached, he looked intense, focussed and on top of his game. Either he'd put his personal disappointment behind him, or he was so caught up in the case that his detective instincts had taken over. Green felt a rush of relief, for he was bursting to discuss the information he'd gathered that morning, and he needed Sullivan at his most pragmatic and astute.

"Any news?" Green left the question as wide open as possible.

"Nothing from the OPP. We've got Toronto in on the search too, because by now Tom has probably reached there. He must have filled up on gas in some backwater town and paid cash. Remember, he's got Robbie's hundred bucks."

Green pictured Tom pulling up at some old-fashioned, one-man gas station—the kind where the attendant actually fills the tank—and wondered if he was still unaware of Kyle's presence in the back. Despite what Sandy had predicted, perhaps the boy had hopped out, or spoken to the attendant, or at least been spotted as he huddled half-frozen in the back.

Sullivan seemed to read his mind. "OPP's got a region-wide 'Be on the look-out' and orders to check every gas station in the target area. If Kyle's still in the truck, maybe we'll at least get a sighting as to his condition."

Green grimaced. And if he isn't still in the truck, Green thought, where is he? Murdered and dumped in a roadside ditch? Tossed out into the bush to cope for himself? Or fleeing on foot through a rugged countryside of lakes, beaver swamps and forest broken only by vacant cottages and the occasional

farm? Fending off the frigid night that had been taken over by dogs, bears, coyotes and maybe even wolves, all on the prowl for food?

Sullivan nodded, worry tightening his own features. "One good thing. At least, he's a country boy."

Yeah, Green thought grimly. A country boy whose parents have sheltered him so much that he won't know even the basics of keeping himself warm. "Have his parents been told that he may have reached Toronto?"

"Oh, yeah. His parents—" Sullivan broke off as they both spotted twin plumes of dust racing down the lane. Sunlight glinted off the bright red truck in the lead, and a moment later Sandy Fitzpatrick skidded to a gravel-spraying stop six feet away. In his wake lumbered a dusty black dump truck with "Scott Construction" stencilled on its cab door. Four people piled out and slammed doors. The McMartins, Sandy and his friend Scott. The four gaped at the digging crews, then stomped over to face down the two detectives. To Green's surprise, Sandy took up the fight before his mother could get a word in.

"What the hell's going on, Green! Jeb says you think Kyle's in danger, and this morning a bunch of cops show up at Scottie here's dump site with a warrant to search all the fill he took from the yard. And now I see... What the hell are they doing!"

"Searching for something," Green replied.

"I can see that," Sandy snapped. "What?"

"Till we have all the facts, I won't speculate," Green said. "But we will keep you informed of all developments that relate to Kyle. That I promise."

Sandy was still staring at the hole in disbelief. "You're wasting your time. Everything in that shed burned to a cinder years ago."

Edna shouldered him aside and folded her arms across her

chest. "That's right. Saw it go up myself from over at my place. You should be putting your energies to finding our Kyle, not pawing through some old dirt!"

A shout from one of the workers caught their attention. They all looked up to see an Ident van lurching down the lane. It moved cautiously, as if protecting a precious cargo, but as soon as it stopped, a uniformed officer flung open the rear door and leaped out with an excited cry.

"We found something over at Scott's place!"

Green snapped an order to the four to stay put, although he knew he was probably wasting his breath. He and Sullivan hurried across the yard, ducked into the rear of the van and slammed it shut. Inside, as their eyes adjusted to the gloom, they made out a large cardboard box, in which lay four objects encased in plastic evidence bags. Green bent closer. Through the rust and the dirt, he was able to make out the head of an axe, a rusty belt buckle, a long brown bone...and half a skull, cracked down the middle.

"Derek!" Green exclaimed, and despite all his advance warning, he felt the strength seep from his legs. "My God, it's true. They fucking burned him up."

The rear door of the van cracked open and Sandy peered in, his face the colour of ash. "What!" he gasped. His eyes fixed on the contents of the crate. "What the hell did you find!"

He started to scramble into the van, clawing at the men blocking his way. His mother stepped forward swiftly to grab his arm. "Sandy!" she snapped. "Stay out of it! We have to help Kyle!" She pulled him out, and he thudded against the side of the van, red-faced and panting as if he'd run a marathon. Green signalled Peter Cole over to the van, then jumped out and shut the door firmly behind him. Edna turned to unleash her emotions on him.

251

"What the dickens is going on! You said Tom wasn't dangerous! Just wanted to get back home, you said! Now you're thinking he killed his own brother?"

Privately, Green noted with interest that she had automatically thought Tom the most likely murderer in the family, despite her antipathy for Lawrence. But aloud, he hastened to curb the speculations he had unleashed. "No, Mrs. McMartin, I didn't say that. Until the experts examine them, we don't even know what these things are. They could be animal bones and some old junk that was thrown out in that shed long before the fire."

"You're digging up the whole yard just for animal bones?" She shook her head, tight-lipped. "I don't think so, mister."

Sullivan's call sign crackled faintly on his radio, and he reached to turn it up. Edna froze in mid-rant and all eyes locked on him. Quickly he unhooked his radio and responded as he walked out of earshot. He kept his face deadpan as he listened, but Green could tell by his rigid focus that the news was important. Green turned back to the group and held up his hands, hoping to defuse one crisis before another was upon them.

"My advice is to go home and let the experts here do their job," he said. "If and when we have solid information, we will decide our next course of action. Obviously, before we release any information, our first priority will be to ascertain what happened here and to speak with the Pettigrew family."

Sandy was pacing by the van, his head bowed and his skin now the colour of putty. Phil Scott was whispering to him in a low voice in an attempt to calm him, but Sandy merely wagged his head back and forth. There was an intimacy between the two that suddenly struck Green full force. Holy fuck, he thought. "S"! Of course! It was Sandy whom Derek had been planning to run off with. Sandy whom Norm

Pettigrew had found in the shed with him. Sandy who had no pictures of girlfriends or family on his walls, just him and his sports buddy Phil Scott.

For her part, Edna seemed so focussed on Kyle that she didn't even notice her elder son's distress as she turned to her husband. "You can go home if you want, Jeb, but if these city cops think I'm taking my eyes off them for one second, they got a thing or two to learn."

Green was just choosing the right blend of sympathy and authority to order them off the property when Sullivan strode back across the yard. He was rubbing his hand through his bristly blonde hair in a gesture Green knew well. Sullivan was worried. Unfortunately, the others seemed to read his mood as well, for they all looked at him expectantly. Even Sandy stopped pacing and swung on him with burning eyes.

"That was Detective Peters, who's been liaising with the OPP," Sullivan said. "They found the truck near Madoc, this side of Peterborough."

"And?" Edna shot.

"It was abandoned. Out of gas. Unfortunately there is no sign of either Kyle or Tom."

"Nothing? No sign Kyle was even still with him?"

Sullivan shook his head. "But Madoc's on the way to Toronto, which is likely where Tom is still trying to go. The OPP are organizing a massive search and—"

"I know that part of the country," Scott exclaimed. "It's full of little lakes and cottages, all vacant at this time of year. There's a thousand places to hole up!"

"Madoc?" Jeb began. "Didn't Norm used to have—"

"Forget it!" Sandy snapped, heading for his truck. "Scottie, let's get going. We've got to be there for Kyle when they find him." Sandy revved his truck to life.

"I'm going with you!" Edna pushed Scott aside and jumped into the passenger seat.

"But Mom—"

"No argument! Poor Kyle will be terrified. Drive!"

"What about me?" Jeb sputtered.

Scott was already climbing into his own truck. "Come on with me, Jeb."

Jeb eyed the massive dump truck with dismay, but Scott leaned over to push open the passenger door. "We'll pick up my Blazer on the way."

Both trucks began to reverse in the yard to turn around. Sullivan stepped forward to block the path of Sandy's truck.

"Get out of my way!" Sandy yelled.

Sullivan folded his arms. His voice, surprisingly calm, boomed over the revving of the engines. "Sir, this man is desperate. For your brother's safety as well as your own, you must stay out of it."

Sandy leaned out the cab window to stare him down. He was quivering with rage, but after a few rigid seconds, he sucked in a deep breath to calm himself. "We will. But Mom's right. Kyle will need to see us when you find him. We'll just go to the Madoc station to wait."

When Sullivan didn't budge, Sandy leaned back with his hands open in surrender. "Listen, I've sold a few properties around there, so I know that country. I might even have a tip or two the police can use."

Edna stuck her head out the passenger window. Desperation was written all over her face. "I've tried all my life to protect that boy like he was my own, and he's not going to know what the dickens hit him. Please let me be there."

Sullivan stared at her for a moment, then flicked his gaze towards Green with a questioning look. My call, thought

254

Green. He studied the pair carefully. Sandy sat quietly, but his hands were locked on the steering wheel, and his eyes stared over Sullivan's shoulder at the lane ahead. Edna, however, was ashen; her eyes were huge and dark with fear. Green gave a slight nod for Sullivan to step aside.

Edna mouthed a silent thank you, but Sandy said nothing as he gunned the engine. Together the detectives watched the two trucks roar up the lane, the pick-up skidding as it accelerated and the dump truck slowly grinding through its gears. When they turned south onto the highway, Sullivan swore and kicked at a rock they had churned up onto the road.

"Can't say I blame them for wanting to be close to the search," Green said. "I'd do the same in their place."

Sullivan looked at him grimly. "They're going off half-cocked, Green. They're going to be a menace."

"We'll alert the OPP highway patrols to keep them in sight. And when they check in with the Madoc detachment—"

"They aren't going to check in!" Sullivan snapped. "These are country men. Hunters. They know the meaning of every sound, every plant, every mark on the ground. They're going home to get their shotguns, and then they're going after Tom."

Sullivan's face was grim and his gaze far away, as if he were back in the landscape of his youth.

"Well, then," said Green, trying to sound matter-of-fact, "we'd better get our asses on up there."

Twenty

Sullivan stopped to retrieve a road map from his own car, then gestured to one of the brand new squad cars sitting in the grass. "We'll take one of these fully loaded beauties. You drive, I'll navigate."

After a quick exchange with his friend Belowsky, Sullivan ran to a squad car and jumped into the passenger seat. Green did a rapid U-turn and peeled off up the lane while Sullivan unfolded the map and pored over it, cursing the small print.

"Turn left on the highway," he said before flipping on the radio speaker to try to raise Peters. He grabbed the door strap as Green accelerated onto the highway, then wrestled the map back into position. When Peters came on the radio, he asked her to put him through to the OPP incident commander. After some shouting and scuffling, a clipped voice came through.

"Inspector Riordan here. Nothing to report as yet, but we're getting our teams mobilized."

Sullivan gave him a terse account of the latest complication. "They'll likely be travelling south on two, then west on 43 over to Highway 7. It's a bright red Dodge Ram, registered to—" Sullivan glanced at Green questioningly.

"Sandy—maybe Alexander—Fitzpatrick."

"Sorry to do this to you guys when you've got enough on your plate," Sullivan added. "He's not dangerous, just a loose

cannon, but check the firearms he has registered anyway."

"Yeah, right," Riordan replied with heavy sarcasm. Both officers knew there was a good chance the weapons weren't registered yet, and even if they were, the new firearms registry was in such a bungle, nobody would be able to find the file anyway.

Sullivan signed off then perched his reading glasses on his nose to peer at the map. "Might be slow going for them, what with all these little towns. If we go fast enough, we should be able to catch them ourselves."

As they crested the hill, the village of Ashford Landing came into view, dotted with cars and pedestrians ambling about their business. Green hit the emergency lights, and they sailed through the town at twice the posted speed limit. Green flashed Sullivan a quick grin. "Haven't done that in a long time!"

Sullivan hung on to the strap as they slewed around a curve. "Yeah, just remember you haven't driven high speed in a long time either, so don't get us killed. The OPP's been notified, and they'll have everything under control up there."

But Green could feel the adrenaline coursing through his blood. The urge to join the chase and get the fugitives in his own sights, to take Tom down and deliver everyone to safety, was irresistible. In a crunch, on a high, he could never believe other people wouldn't screw up, miss a crucial clue or misread the bad guy's intent. It was a character flaw he'd learned to keep under wraps so as to appear to believe in teamwork, but Sullivan knew him too well.

To calm himself and regain some distance, Green slowed his speed marginally and began to fill Sullivan in on his discoveries of the day. As they talked, the countryside flew by, mostly fields dotted with farm fields and clumps of proud old trees. Straight ahead, the sun slowly sank towards the west, casting long shadows down the road.

"Gay?" Sullivan remarked as Green told him about Derek. "Not an easy label out here, I can tell you. This is pretty conservative country; anti-gun control, anti-government, anti-gays, anti-abortion."

"Surely not everyone."

"Enough. Especially twenty years ago. United Empire Loyalists hammered a life out of this bush, and it's still God, the Queen and their own bare hands." Sullivan ruffled his bristly hair. "Puts a different spin on the romantic triangle, that's for sure. Wonder who the lover was?"

Green gave a Cheshire cat smile. "I know exactly who the lover was. Our buddy in the bright red truck."

"Fitzpatrick?" Sullivan's eyebrows shot up, and Green could almost see him replaying the scene at the Boisvert farm moments earlier. Reinterpreting the burning rage in Sandy's eyes. Not a distraught man out to protect his brother but a much deadlier man out for revenge.

"He'd have been awfully young," Sullivan observed dubiously.

"About seventeen. But sometimes, the first love is the strongest."

Sullivan watched the passing scenery thoughtfully. Occasionally, through the barren trees, they could catch glimpses of the river blazing in the late afternoon sun. "You think this construction guy Scott is his current partner?"

"Looks that way. I suspect they keep a pretty low profile, although Scott's tattoos are a bit over-the-top."

A large town came into view ahead, spreading its industrial tentacles into the surrounding farms. Green hit the emergency lights again.

"Better put the siren on," Sullivan said. "Smith Falls has some of the craziest traffic for its size, and we have to go right through the main drag."

Green hit the siren with glee and watched the vehicles inch

resentfully towards the curbs to let him pass. Sullivan talked him through the complex sequence of turns that led through the town and once they were safely back on the open road, he pulled the visor down against the setting sun and picked up the thread of their conversation.

"But you'd think if Sandy was the lover Derek was supposed to meet," Sullivan said, "wouldn't he have known something about the murder? Or at least raised the alarm about Derek's disappearance? I mean, if he was going to meet him that afternoon, he might have witnessed the whole thing, for God's sake. Would he have kept quiet all these years just 'cause he was scared to reveal he was gay?"

Green searched his memory for the fragments of information Sandy had dropped about Derek. It was possible that as a seventeen-year-old he'd been too frightened to admit the whole story and expose himself to the public censure and scrutiny that would follow. As the years passed, any confidence he might have gained in his sexual orientation would have been overshadowed by his fear that his own innocence would be suspect because he had kept quiet for so long. By the time Green had come asking questions about Derek, Sandy'd had twenty years to rehearse his story, until his reaction of shock and bewilderment became second nature.

Yet his story had an odd ring of truth. The pallor and dilated pupils he'd exhibited in the yard earlier were signs of genuine shock that were difficult to fake. When questioned about the shed a few days ago, he had nonchalantly remarked that he'd seen the fire through the trees from his house. From his house! Not while en route to a clandestine rendezvous nor while fleeing from the discovery of his lover's bludgeoned body.

Perhaps most compelling of all, when Green had first asked him about the Pettigrew sons, Sandy had not missed a beat

over Derek. He hadn't painted him as the saint others had but rather churlishly implied that Derek considered himself above the common country folk he'd grown up with. If anything, Green thought with a twinge of excitement, he had sounded a little bitter. Like a lover left behind?

He voiced his thoughts aloud. "Perhaps he never got the note, and that's why he never showed up at the meeting. Remember the note was in Lawrence's treasure can. Maybe Lawrence intercepted it before Sandy even saw it. So Sandy didn't know he'd been invited, therefore he assumed Derek had left him behind. All these years he'd assumed, just as the town did, that Derek was living the high life down south. That would explain his meltdown today when he discovered Derek never got off the farm."

Sullivan peered at his map with his reading glasses perched on his nose, then squinted over them at the empty road ahead. He adjusted the visor against the sun's blinding glare. "Funny we haven't caught up with him, unless he's driving like a bat out of hell." He flicked on the radio to call Peters, who reported that the OPP had had no sightings of the red truck at any of their surveillance points along Highways 43 or 7. Sullivan frowned at the map. Once the truck got past the town of Perth, Highway 7 was virtually the only route west toward Madoc through the rolling bush country riddled with lakes.

"He's trying to avoid being seen," Green said once Sullivan had signed off and turned the radio down low, so that the routine chatter washed over them unheard. "He wants to get to Tom without having to answer to the police. What about back country roads?"

Sullivan traced his finger across the map and shook his head. "Nothing direct, and those roads twist and turn, impossible to make good time. I think he went down to the 401."

Green cast him a startled glance. "It's way south, and he'd have to go all the way north again when he got off."

"But he can make much better time. More than fifty clicks an hour faster than back country. He knows we wouldn't be looking for him there, and even if we tried, it's much easier to slip through our nets in that huge volume of traffic." Sullivan turned the radio back up to tell Peters to get the OPP to look for Sandy on the throughway. He glanced at his watch. "He'd be nearing Kingston by now. Put a cruiser at the exit just past Belleville. I'm betting he takes that road back up north again."

The incident commander himself came on the radio to brusquely inform them that the OPP traffic patrol would do its best, no thanks to the Ottawa Police, but that most of their available units in that area were needed for the manhunt. Green glanced at the sun, which now sliced the horizon with its dying rays, and stomped harder on the gas pedal.

"They're going to run out of daylight to conduct a proper search," he said once Sullivan signed off. "Do you think Sandy can get there ahead of us?"

Sullivan braced himself as they hit a curve. "Not at this rate. But it looks like it's going to be a long night."

Green's cell phone rang, startling them both. He fumbled to find it on his belt, jerking the wheel as the car drifted off track. Scowling at him, Sullivan snatched the phone. Lou Paquette's gravel voice came through loud enough for even Green to heard.

"Where the fuck are you boys? You sound a hundred miles away."

"Good guess," Sullivan said. "What's up?"

"Green wanted some answers on this mystery print he's got. Tell him it's still a mystery. The old man's a no match, and damn near had another stroke when I showed up to print him."

"We owe ya, Lou. Any other news back there?"

261

"The place is humming. Biggest excitement we've had all year. The brass is crawling all over the case. Our bigwigs talking to the OPP bigwigs. Tell Green he's going to have to check in before his new boss puts his balls in her sights."

Sullivan chuckled. "I'd like to be around for that one. Any news from the dig?"

"Yeah, Cunningham called, so excited he forgot to be pissed. The bone guy says it's definitely a human skull, probably a large male. Looks like it was cracked open, maybe with that axe. They're going to try to test the axe for blood, which would be the icing on the cake."

After Sullivan disconnected, he took the opportunity to phone his staff sergeant. Green let the discussion wash over him unheard as he mulled over the latest developments. The damn fingerprint didn't fit anywhere! But it had to mean something. Someone else had been present at the murder scene that day. Not Tom, not Lawrence, not Norman. That person had touched the note with Derek's blood on their hands. Yet the note had been stuffed in Lawrence's tin can and buried under the planking in the corner of the shed, while Lawrence had ended up with Derek's crucifix around his neck. Furthermore, Robbie had seen only Tom and Lawrence, glimpsed Tom chasing Lawrence in order to kill him. That memory had been abruptly broken by the arrival of a car down the lane. Who? Almost certainly one or both parents, who would have therefore witnessed the same scene Robbie did. And drawn whatever conclusions Tom had pointed them towards.

In his letter to Benji, Tom described having to "catch the fucking maniac" and lock him up. What if that was the truth? Green could think of only one way that all these disparate pieces of the story fit together. Someone had met Derek in the shed earlier, killed him and left the body. Lawrence had either

witnessed the killing or stumbled upon the body afterwards, along with the fragment of the note. Following his own peculiar logic, Lawrence had put the note in his can with his other articles of sin, and buried it in its usual spot. Perhaps he had even stayed with the body, and at some later point Tom found his brother bludgeoned to death, Lawrence covered in blood, and jumped to the horrified conclusion that Lawrence had killed him. A conclusion which seemed all too credible to the rest of the family, who had watched Lawrence's descent into madness.

In his rage, Tom had attacked Lawrence and was probably prevented from strangling him only by the arrival of the parents in the car. That even explained the so-called suicide marks found on Lawrence's throat when he was admitted to St. Lawrence. The family's cover-up was thorough indeed!

The scenario was impeccable. There was only one major missing link; the identity of the actual killer. Green approached his dawning answer carefully, examining it from all angles. Reverend Taylor claimed Derek was distraught after the fight with his father and decided his new love affair could not work out. Sophia had implied much the same thing. According to both, Derek had been planning to give up and leave his lover behind. The note about the bus seemed to imply otherwise, but it was only a fragment. What if he, Green, had been reading it backwards all along? What if the note was not from Derek, but to Derek, telling him to meet him at three p.m. at "our place".

The shed. Green held his breath as he considered the beauty of the idea. The logistics of how the notes were passed remained a question mark, but not an insurmountable one. Perhaps they had a secret mail drop on the path between their two houses, by which they could arrange their trysts. Sandy, defying Derek's order to stay home, or perhaps unaware he was about to be dumped, left the note to meet Derek in their

special place. Once there, Derek told him it was over and Sandy flew into a rage, grabbed the first instrument he could lay his hands on and crashed it down onto Derek's skull. Then in a frantic effort to erase all traces of his presence, he seized the note which might still have been in Derek's hand, unknowingly tearing it as he pulled it free.

Pure speculation, with only the barest of bones to hang it on, but it fit all the facts! Now it was time to see if it could withstand the sober second thought of Brian Sullivan.

As they raced through the deepening dusk, past lakes and rocky outcrops and acres of skeletal trees, Green put his theory into words. Sullivan listened as he always did, quietly, intently and without interruption. At the end, his thoughtful expression had creased with worry.

"You're not objecting, Brian."

"I was remembering. This morning when I took the warrant to Scott, first thing he did was call Sandy. Said what the hell did you get me into? Like it was Sandy's idea to cement over that shed."

"Right! Because now that the house had passed to new owners, they were starting to dig things up!"

"Gives Sandy a motive for bumping off Lawrence too." Sullivan was warming to the idea. "Lawrence might have witnessed the murder or seen him leaving. Sandy couldn't be sure he'd stay crazy enough not to say something. When Lawrence showed up back in town, Sandy must have been shitting bricks!"

All of a sudden the solution to one of the enduring puzzles leaped into focus. The church door! Not only could Sandy have spotted Lawrence and lured him to the church, but as a realtor he even had access to the key to open the door. Perhaps he had begun with a reassuring talk about their old days together, only to turn deadly when Lawrence showed his fear.

But Green's euphoria at his sudden insight died abruptly as the next question hit him. "But if Sandy's the killer, why is he going after Tom? Why put himself in the limelight and risk his connection to Derek being exposed?"

Even as he uttered the question, he felt his blood run cold. Kyle had seen something that afternoon in the woods, and Green, through sheer stupidity, had passed that information on to Jeb.

"Maybe he's not going after Tom," he said. "It's Kyle."

Twenty-One

As the two detectives pulled into the brand new OPP station in Madoc, night was already stealing into the shadows at the edge of the road. Two cruisers were parked out front and a couple of officers were talking by the front door, but there was no sign of the mobile command truck nor the specialty teams the incident commander had mentioned. Let's hope all the officers are out in the field, Green thought, covering every inch of dirt from here to Peterborough.

Sullivan must have seen the scowl on his face, for he shot him a warning glance. "Just remember we have no jurisdiction here, Green. We're here as a courtesy, but it's their show. Their call."

"Their turf, but our suspect. Our victims. All I want is to be kept in the loop." Green jerked open the cruiser door, but before he could even get out, one of the officers came down to greet him.

"You here on the abduction case?"

Green introduced himself and Sullivan. "Where the hell is everyone?"

"Over setting up Mobile Command, sir, near the location of the stolen vehicle. That's where the search is starting from."

Green's annoyance flared further, but he held his tongue and snatched the map from Sullivan. "Show me," he said, spreading the map on the hood. In the dimming light, the

officer traced a route deep into the back country north of Highway 7. The map showed little but lakes and bush. It's going to be a long night, Green thought with a sinking feeling.

"Any sighting of the red Dodge Ram?" he asked.

"No, sir. So far he hasn't been spotted on the 401 or the 7, but he should be pulling in here any moment. We've been instructed to detain him, to keep him out of the way."

"Whatever you do, hang onto him. Don't let the guy anywhere near the search, he may be implicated." Green folded up the map and circled the cruiser to yank open the passenger door. He signalled Sullivan out with a jerk of his head. "This time you drive, and I'll navigate."

Using the map light in the cruiser, Green guided them through a series of obscure turns in the deepening twilight until distant pinpoints of red and white light lit up the trees ahead. As the detectives drew closer, the massive mobile command truck became visible on a grassy knoll beside the road, surrounded by half a dozen cruisers, SUVs and pick-up trucks, all sporting official OPP insignia.

Sullivan pulled onto the grass next to a pick-up, and both men climbed out. The wind had died down, but darkness had already chilled the air. Green took a deep breath, smelled the crispness of cedar and the faint decay of fallen leaves. The mobile command post was a fifth wheel trailer positioned at the highest point of the knoll, probably to facilitate communications in this remote, rocky terrain, Green surmised. No one was outside, but the murmur of voices emanated from within.

As Green and Sullivan approached, the side door opened and a slim, impossibly fit-looking man emerged. He had a brush cut, pencil-thin mustache and shoulders so square Green expected him to click his heels and salute. The man

instinctively headed towards Sullivan with his hand outstretched.

"Inspector Green? I'm Mark Riordan."

Green bristled. "I'm Green. Any sign of them?"

The man didn't miss a beat, pivoting smoothly to give Green's hand a sharp tug. "Not yet. Come on inside, and I'll bring you up to speed."

Inside the trailer, Green's attention was immediately drawn to a brightly lit table in the centre of the room, on which lay a huge topographical map. More maps and white boards covered most of the walls, and the other tables were cluttered with technical equipment. An officer in a dark windbreaker was hunched over a phone at the front of the trailer, and several others milled about in the cramped space, checking equipment and jotting notes. Radio chatter crackled in the background, providing status reports.

Green headed over to the map on the table. A plastic overlay was marked with indecipherable lines and squiggles. "Where are we?" he asked.

Riordan circled his long, calloused finger to encompass the entire surface. "This map details the immediate area within a twenty mile radius. The maps on the wall are to a smaller scale and show all the roads and navigable paths between here and Peterborough." He tapped a spot marked in red. "Mobile Command." He drew his finger along the road to another mark nearby. "The suspect's truck was located here, about five hundred metres further up this road. Canine unit started at the truck a little over an hour ago, picked up a trail heading north towards this lake area."

"But he's had a hell of a head start," Green said. "Probably twenty-four hours."

Riordan inclined his head and spun on his heel towards a

map on the wall. "Based on your man being on foot and being encumbered by a child who may not be able to travel very fast—"

Green thought of the muscles rippling across Kyle's chest. "He's a well-developed teenager who can probably outrun all of us."

Riordan barely registered a reaction. "By our calculations, on a path or road they could have covered thirty K by now, so we've set up patrol units on each of the roads at that perimeter." He pointed to some faint lines on the map. "Old logging roads and rail lines. We've got our ERT people on ATVs checking the outlying parts for signs of activity." His finger hovered over a tract of land unscarred by either road or trail. "If they're bushwhacking—and preliminary indications are that's the case—then the dog's our best bet."

"One dog?" Green said incredulously. Beside him, he felt Sullivan fidget uneasily, but all Green could picture was one dog against this vast acreage of bush.

Riordan stiffened almost imperceptibly. "Plus an experienced search team. There are four Emergency Response Team members out on foot with the dog, providing back-up."

"What about helicopters? Boats on the lakes?"

"That's the next step if it comes to that. But a careful grid search from the last known position is still the best approach."

One of the officers approached to draw Riordan aside. "That was Spencer, sir. K-9 lost the trail near a stream. The dog's going in circles."

A scowl rippled across Riordan's tight control. "Your fella must've done something to throw the dog off. Does he know dogs? "

"He probably hunted with them as a kid," Sullivan said. Green suspected the wily Tom had learned a lot of other tricks

during his misspent youth, and whatever gaps remained had been easily filled during his jail stints. Trust Tom to spoil this man's perfect search plan.

"Well, the dog's good," Riordan said as if reading his mind. "She might figure it out yet."

"It's practically dark, though," Green said.

"Not a problem. The weather's clear, and our ERT teams have good gear. My information is your suspect is not armed?"

"Not likely," Sullivan said. More officers wandered in to study the map. Sullivan glanced around the room. "Anything we can do?"

Pointedly Riordan's gaze took in their city suits and a faint smile twitched across his military features. "You'd be most help finding out eve rything you can about our suspect—his knowledge of the terrain, any contacts in the area, his survival skills, his habits—and feeding it to Detective Logan over there." He nodded to the plain clothes officer on the phone. "We've already got your Detective Peters out with one of the patrol units."

A chuckle ran through the knot of officers jotting notes on the white board nearby. Green didn't even want to speculate what the chuckle meant. His gaze was drawn again to the topographical map on the table. To the endless acres of uninhabited wilderness and the tiny back lane on which the truck had been found. It didn't make any sense! It was miles from anywhere.

He turned to Sullivan. "Would you get Bob Gibbs on that right away and hook him up with Logan here?" He looked back at Riordan. "While we're out here, I'd like a look at the truck and the surrounding area. It might give us some ideas."

Riordan's mustache twitched in disapproval. "Don't disturb the scene."

Green was already striding to the door and the only response he allowed himself was the slamming of the truck door on his way out.

"Disturb the scene," he muttered to Sullivan as he swung the cruiser back onto the road. "Who the fuck does he think we are, the Keystone Kops?"

"He's just a control freak," Sullivan replied. "Funny thing about inspectors."

Green ignored the bait. He had already turned his attention to the road ahead, where presently a patch of light came into view As they drew near, they saw a police van positioned in the road so that its headlights shone into the bush, illuminating a black pick-up tucked into a laneway off the road. It was almost completely obscured by overhanging brush, and Green realized they were damn lucky anyone had spotted it at all.

Yellow crime scene tape draped the trees and spanned the road, blocking passage. One scene-of-crime officer in white overalls was prowling around the outskirts of the truck, shooting video and still photos, while his partner crouched over a patch of dirt at the back. Green's breath caught. Had they found out something about Kyle?

He called and introduced himself. "Find anything useful?"

"Lots of dirt and leaves," said the one by the back, straightening up. "We'll be loading it onto a truck to take it back to our indoor facility. We're just checking the vicinity now. There seems to be a patch of urine by the back here."

"Any sign of a struggle in the truck? Blood?"

"Not that we can see."

Green felt a wave of relief. It didn't mean much, for there were half a dozen ways Tom could have disposed of Kyle, but at least he hadn't killed him in the truck. "What's the closest village they could have gone to?"

"Nearest town is Marmora, about fifteen K back down on 7. There's also Brady's Country Store at the junction of Cordova Road about three K up this way. But our guys checked there, and no one's seen the subjects."

Green thanked him and headed back down to the cruiser. Inside, he consulted the map and located the junction of Cordova Road. It was even further into the boonies. He stared thoughtfully through the windshield at the surrounding bush, combing his recollections of the argument with the McMartins at the Boisvert farm that afternoon. Something niggled at the edges of his memory.

Sullivan started the engine. "What next, navigator? A bite to eat, maybe?"

Green ignored him. "Look at this goddamn place! It's not on the road to anywhere. If Tom was going to Toronto, why the hell would he come up here?"

"Maybe he got lost."

The memory came loose. "No, he didn't! I think he knew exactly where he was going." Green's mouth went dry as another memory fell into place. "Fuck! So does Sandy!"

Sullivan frowned. "What are you talking about?"

Green swung on him, excitement fighting fear in his thoughts. "Do you remember back at the Boisvert farm, Jeb McMartin started to say 'Madoc, isn't that where Norm used to have—"

Sullivan's frown cleared. "And Sandy cut him off."

"That's right! I'm betting the Pettigrew family used to come up here, maybe even owned a place. And I bet Sandy knows where, and that's why Madoc OPP hasn't seen a trace of him. Remember Sandy said he knew this area because he sold cottages up here? We've got to move our asses if we want to find the Pettigrew place before he gets there."

They drove back to the command trailer. Riordan took down the details and excitedly looked up township records on his computer. Their brief moment of triumph died when the search turned up no properties listed in the name of Norman Pettigrew, or any other Pettigrew.

"We'll have to do a title search down at the County Registry office in Belleville," he said. "And on a Saturday night, everything is closed up tight. It may take a while to find someone to open it up and go through the files."

"I'd go straight to the Mayor and Chief of Police," Green said and was pleased to see Riordan's poker face break into a smile. Maybe the two were more alike than Green had thought. He paused as he headed for the door and matched the other man's smile. "Brian and I will be on the road double-checking the homes in the area, but we'll keep you informed. Tom Pettigrew is still a danger, but right now I think our biggest threat may be Fitzpatrick. So let us know—"

Riordan nodded. "You'll be the first."

When Green returned to the car, Sullivan revved the engine and guided it back onto the road. He drove effortlessly through the darkness, one hand on the wheel and the other rubbing his chin. "Do you really think Sandy would hurt Kyle? He's his brother, after all."

"Stepbrother, actually, which may make a difference. And as for whether he'd hurt him, well, he bludgeoned his own lover, didn't he? Besides, after all the bad calls I've made, I'm not taking any chances with this one."

"So what's our next move?"

"You're the country boy, Brian. Tell me how we find out where the Pettigrew place was. It may take them a long time to track down the title in the registry office. It might have been thirty years ago."

"That won't matter around here," Sullivan grinned. "At least, not with the local folk. They'll remember who owned a store fifty years ago, probably still call it by that name."

"Okay, so we find some local folk." Green glanced out at the empty bush. "Somewhere."

"Brady's Country Store is our best bet. Probably been in the family for generations, and Brady will know everyone's business for miles around."

Brady's store turned out to be a dilapidated two-storey frontier home of faded white clapboard. The sign across the front proclaimed in old-fashioned red lettering that it was Brady's General Store and Tackle Shop. Assorted signs had been taped in the window beneath. "Hunting and fishing licences available", "Live worms", "Propane for Sale", "Videos for rent". All the lights were out on the main floor, however, and a large "Closed" sign hung in the window.

Green sat in the car and looked up at the building dejectedly. He was conscious of time ticking away, and of Kyle being held captive by one erratic, volatile man and stalked by an even more desperate one. All because of Green. Kyle was with Tom because Green had not detained the man after he'd first broken into the Boisverts' house. He was being stalked by Sandy because Green had told the McMartins he might have witnessed something on the day Lawrence died.

To his surprise, Sullivan climbed out of the car and headed around the back towards an even more dilapidated wing at the rear of the store. Inside, Green could see the faint glow of a light upstairs.

Sullivan hammered on the door. "Brady!"

A dog barked, followed by a man's gruff bellow as a series of windows lit up downstairs. A moment later the porch light came on and the door opened to reveal a wizened old man

with no teeth and a stringy white beard that hadn't seen a razor in ten years.

"What the name of Jesus do you want! He's closed! Gone down to Belleville."

Sullivan grinned. "You Brady?"

"Yeah. But it's my son owns the place."

"Brian Sullivan, with the Ottawa Police." He stuck out his hand cheerfully.

"Eh?" The man shouted, ignoring Sullivan's hand.

Sullivan raised the decibel level and repeated himself. "Beautiful country," he added. "You from around here?"

"Never could make enough money off that place to get out," Brady retorted, eyeing Sullivan's hand warily before deciding it was safe.

Sullivan pumped his hand heartily. "I know that feeling. Most of my folks are still up in the Valley. Further north, though, Renfrew County."

"Where?"

"Renfrew," Sullivan shouted. "Madawaska Valley."

"Oh, yeah?" The man thawed. "Pretty up there, ain't got the lakes, but lots of good rivers for trout. Not so many cottages up there either, eh?"

"Oh, it's getting there. Ottawa's taking over everything."

Green shifted impatiently, resisting the urge to sound the horn. Sullivan was turning on the Irish valley charm, and that took time, especially at the decibel level the old-timer required. It was not a process to be interrupted, so Green sat quietly while Sullivan shouted about fish and deer and the old logging days before finally steering the conversation to the missing duo.

"The older man's a Pettigrew from down the Rideau Valley. Someone was saying the Pettigrews used to own property

around here. Norm Pettigrew. You ever hear—"

"Not Norm, but his father, yeah. I knew his father going back...oh, must be sixty years? During the war. He started coming up here winters to do some logging, help keep the farm afloat. Yeah, he bought a little place back then, when there weren't no roads, no hydro most places outside the towns." Brady relaxed against the doorframe, almost garrulous. "We'd take a horse and sleigh in winter, boat in summer. We had some good times back then, when he used to bring Norm and his kids up for a spell. Haven't seen them in years, though. Place was sold."

"When?"

Brady squinted. "Maybe twenty-five years ago? When the old timer died? Like as not, Norm needed the money. Hah, don't we all?"

Unable to stand it any longer. Green climbed out and sauntered over, hoping his appearance would speed up the process without causing the old man to shut down. Behind Brady, an equally scruffy dog stared Green down with unblinking eyes.

"My partner, Mike Green," said Sullivan dismissively. "What's the name of the lake Norm's dad had the place on?"

"Black Lake. 'Course we called it Lost Lake back then. If you found it, you knew you took a wrong turn." Brady's chuckle revealed a few yellow teeth still clinging to their posts.

"And is there a road up there now?"

"Oh yeah, they got roads all over now, eh? Used to be an old logging road, opened up now. Matter of fact, the place is only a few miles from here through them woods, but the road takes the long route round."

"So someone could get there on foot?"

"Half day, easy. We used to do it all the time. The drive's the tricky part."

Green listened as Brady described the landmarks and turns

they should follow, none of which had any road signs or names that Brady was aware of. But Sullivan thanked him profusely, shook his hand and set off confidently towards the car.

"You fellas like a snack from the store?" Brady called after them, as if now reluctant to see them go. "There's some nice, home-baked brownies just going to waste."

Sullivan broke into a broad grin, signalled to Green and disappeared inside the man's home. The front windows lit and Green drummed his fingers impatiently as he waited. He hadn't eaten since his late lunch with Robbie, but the knot of apprehension in his stomach drove away all thought of food. A few minutes later, Sullivan reappeared with two grocery bags packed with food, which he loaded in the back.

"In case we find Tom and Kyle. They may be hungry."

"Can you still remember those directions?"

Sullivan settled behind the wheel and crammed a massive brownie into his mouth, nodding as he sucked chocolate icing off his fingers. Then he eased the car into gear and slowly began to make his way down the dark road. The sky was now a clear, brittle black sprinkled with a thousand stars but not even a sliver of moon to light the way.

Sullivan braked to eye a laneway dubiously. "First left, he said."

"That's a cow path, not a road."

"No, it'd be a road around here." Sullivan turned in, his headlights sweeping the bush that bordered the road. Two hundred yards further, the lane petered out.

"Okay, it's not a road." Sullivan reversed back up the narrow track he could barely see. Branches clawed at the side panels of the sparkling new cruiser, causing Green to wince. He wondered if Barbara Devine would prove as forgiving as Jules had been. Somehow, he doubted it.

"Okay, it must be the next one," Sullivan said once he'd backed out onto the road.

They missed the next left, which appeared as a fleeting gap in the bush as they passed. On reversing, they saw a small wooden arrow marked Duncan Lane tacked to a post.

"Oh, it has a name," Green remarked as Sullivan turned in.

"Probably not to Brady."

They negotiated Duncan Lane to its end and found themselves at the junction of a larger road. Still dirt, but at least with the potential to avoid a head-on collision.

Sullivan turned right. "Now we look for Jack Hensel's farmhouse."

"Oh, that's right. 'Big red one on the hill, can't miss it'?" Green recited as he looked out into the yawning blackness. "What hill? Who sees anything but the fucking bush at the edge of the road?"

They crawled down the road, which dipped and turned like an endless roller coaster. Finally up ahead, Green spotted a tiny lane with a dozen names on wooden arrows tacked to a tree. "Stop." Green peered out. "Do you see a farm house?"

To their left, a darker smudge stood out against the pallid wash of the surrounding field.

"This has to be it. I'm going to kill the lights," Sullivan said, swinging cautiously into the little lane. They bumped down the road, following the strip of pallor between the blackness on either side. They passed the first drive.

"Did Brady remember who owned the place now?" For some reason Green found himself whispering.

Sullivan shook his head. "Fuck, there's at least a dozen properties. Watch for a glimmer of light, or the smell of wood smoke."

They passed the second drive, then the third. The darkness

and the silence were absolute. Nothing but vast, yawning emptiness, Green reflected as he strained his city eyes to decipher the alien black. Suddenly, a flash of metal caught his eye.

"Stop!" he whispered. "Back up. More. There! It looks like a vehicle!"

Cautiously, they pulled the cruiser off the track under cover of some trees, eased open the doors and slipped out. The vehicle sat about twenty feet from the entrance to the drive, which was so overgrown it was barely discernible except for the flattened tire tracks. As they approached, Green saw it was an old silver Grand Am.

"False alarm," Sullivan muttered and turned back to the cruiser.

Something stirred in the back of Green's memory—a vehicle parked in the laneway to the rear of the real estate office in Ashford Landing. He laid his palm on the car's hood. Warm.

"This is it!" he whispered hoarsely. "Sandy switched cars! That's why the OPP never spotted him."

The two men peered down the grassy driveway and sifted the night air for sounds. "Looks like they came alone," Sullivan whispered. "There's no sign of Scott's Blazer."

"Sandy wouldn't want him along. Probably ditched his mother too."

Sullivan turned to the road. "I'll notify Riordan."

"They'll never find the fucking place, and if they do, they'll come screaming in here like a bunch of banshees."

"Give them some credit, Green," said Sullivan as he headed back towards the cruiser.

Green began to grope his way cautiously down the drive, fighting through grass and burrs that reached his thighs. The night was full of sounds he didn't recognize. Rustling leaves,

distant hoots, rhythmic chirps and howls that seemed to echo forever. Suddenly, an all-too-human scream sounded in the distance, followed by an angry volley of shouts. Men's voices carried on the wind. Green froze and glanced back at Sullivan, who was visible in the cruiser's cabin light, settled in as if for a long chat. Another shout, closer. Its raw rage sent a chill down Green's back.

He raced through the grass, rounded a corner, and confronted a steep, curved rise in the track. The shouts were coming from straight ahead, but he could see nothing. Not the cruiser behind him, not the danger ahead. Did Brian even realize he'd gone? Green cursed his own stupidity for setting off alone without even a goddamn flashlight, which was probably safely stowed in the cruiser. He really had been behind a desk too long. Groping for his holster, he flipped the tab off and pulled out his pistol.

God, he hated the thing. He'd never fired it off the range and probably couldn't hit anything if he tried, but tonight, with his blood pounding in his ears and his breath so deafening it blocked out all else, he was glad he had it. Its cold, heavy weight felt reassuring in his hand as he crept up the rise.

The shouts had died down, but Green could hear a man talking, his words punctuated with angry curses. The targets seemed to be moving and were now up ahead on his right. As he reached the top of the rise, he caught a brief glimmer of light through the trees. The cottage? The light danced, moved and played on the trees around it.

No, a flashlight! The light was coming his way, and as his eyes adjusted to the dark, he could make out movement. Legs, boots striding, the dull metal glint of a rifle barrel. Fuck, he thought, tightening his grip on the Glock. The men were coming straight up the lane toward him, closing the gap at a

rapid pace. The one at the rear had the flashlight and the rifle, whereas the one in front was stumbling in the darkness, his every move betraying his fear.

"Sandy, what the hell are you talking about!" exclaimed a rough voice Green immediately recognized as Tom's. "I didn't kill Derek!"

"Just shut the fuck up and walk!"

Green ducked off the track as they approached and crouched poised for attack. He could see the two men clearly in the dancing light, but there was no sign of Kyle. Green scanned the darkness behind them anxiously. Nothing.

"Lawrence killed Derek," Tom said. "I swear on my life—"

"Like that means anything. You hated Derek. You couldn't stand that he was smart and was going to make something of himself. You couldn't face that your whole moronic, loser life was your own fault—"

"But I wouldn't kill him, for Chrissake." Tom stopped in his tracks and turned to face Sandy. "Get hold of yourself and think about this!"

Sandy played the flashlight off Tom's face. At fifteen feet away, Green could see every quiver of fear in Tom's eyes. Slowly the rifle barrel rose, its muzzle point blank against his chest. "Who's going to know, huh Tom? You're a dangerous fugitive who kidnapped my brother. I'll be a hero."

Tom shook his head. "You'll know. You'll have to live with it for the rest of your life, and believe me, that's a hell of a lot harder than you think."

"And you should know. Right, you bastard?" The rifle clicked.

Green felt his fear in his bowels and in the slick gun barrel in his shaking hand. He gripped the Glock with both hands and raised it.

"Sandy," he called gently. "Police officer. Don't move."

The flashlight leaped wildly, swung in an arc and settled on Green. Blinded, Green kept his gun and his eyes trained on where he knew Sandy to be. He hoped his voice sounded calmer than he felt.

"Lower the weapon, Sandy."

"Inspector Green! What the hell are you doing? He killed his own brother, and he was going to kill mine!"

"Lower the rifle. Then we'll talk."

Sandy kept the flashlight trained on Green, and his voice took on a contemptuous tone. "You can't see a thing, I know you can't. I can shoot Tom, run away and you'll be so blind you won't be able to get a single decent shot off."

He was dead right; Green was absolutely powerless as long as Sandy had that damn flashlight. Green cast about for a way to throw him off balance, all the while wondering where the hell Sullivan was. Nothing for it but to use my wits, he thought. I walked into this mess like an idiot without any back-up, so I'm going to have to get myself out.

"Sandy, where's Kyle?" he asked.

"Kyle's fine. He's down in the cottage with my mother."

"Don't you think he's been through enough? Do you want to add to his trauma by shooting Tom?"

"That's why I brought Tom up here!" Sandy snapped. "Kyle won't even know."

"He's a good kid," Tom interjected. To Green's relief, he sounded calmer. "He knows more than you guys think. Take it from me, you can't run from these things."

"I don't give a damn! You've already ruined too many lives."

With the flashlight still blinding him, and the rifle barrel steadied once more on Tom's chest, Green scrambled for another tack. "What do you think, Sandy?" he said. "Will it

be easier the second time around? Killing a man, I mean."

"What?"

"You're the one who killed Derek. You knew he was going off without you, and you couldn't stand that."

"What?" It was Tom this time, astonished and disbelieving.

"Sandy was Derek's lover, Tom."

"That's ridiculous!" Sandy cried. "I was just a kid."

"You were seventeen," Green said. "Plenty old enough to be in love. But Derek decided—"

Tom found his voice. "That's bullshit! My brother wasn't a fag!"

"Shut up, you Neanderthal!" Sandy cried. "Just shut the fuck up!"

In his outrage, Sandy jerked the flashlight back toward Tom, and in that instant Green dropped to a crouch and aimed his gun. Sandy swung the rifle barrel in a wild panicked arc, searching for him. Green was fractions of a second from squeezing the trigger when a powerful light flooded the scene, and a voice boomed out of the darkness on the other side.

"Police! Freeze!"

Sandy swung his flashlight back and forth, catching first Green and then Sullivan in its beam. Sullivan stood rock solid, with his legs apart, his Glock in one hand and a flashlight held overhead in the other. Sandy's rifle barrel drooped, and in that instant Tom leaped forward to grab it.

"Tom!" Sullivan roared. "Don't fucking move!"

Tom froze, but Sandy seemed oblivious to him. The rifle now dangled harmlessly at his side as he stared at Green in disbelief.

"Put the weapon on the ground and back away, both of you!" Sullivan said.

As they did so, Green moved in to retrieve the rifle and

eject the cartridges from its barrel. All passion seemed to drain out of Sandy, who was barely able to stand.

"How can you think I'd kill Derek?" he said to Green. "I loved him."

"That's why," Green replied. "He was leaving without you, so you sent him a note to meet you in the shed—"

"No!"

"We have the note, remember! With your bloody fingerprint on it." Well, not exactly, but in a pinch, whatever works.

But Sandy just looked bewildered. "But that was the note from him I was waiting for. With the bus times and all. I never got it!"

"Yeah?" Sullivan snarled, unhooking his cuffs. "Tell that to the judge."

Green's mind was racing. Something was askew. If Sandy had killed Derek, why had he come up here in the middle of the night to kill Tom? Why was he accusing Tom of murdering Derek when he had absolutely nothing to gain from it? Unless he believed Tom was the murderer.

In which case, Sandy couldn't be. Something in his bewilderment about the note and in his desperate claims of love rang true. There had to be someone else. But even as Green thought it, Sandy voiced the exact same question.

"If Tom didn't do it, and Lawrence didn't, then who did kill Derek?"

In the distance, up towards the road, a car ignition turned over and caught. Sandy spun around in the direction of the sound.

"Oh, my God!" he gasped.

Twenty-Two

B y the time the four of them reached the top of the drive, the silver Grand Am was nowhere in sight, but an engine howled in the distance and a whiff of exhaust hung in the air. Sandy ran toward the police cruiser, shouting. Sullivan caught him in mid air and without hesitation threw him against the side of the car.

"You stay put! The OPP are on their way, and they'll intercept her, if you give us time to call them."

Green was already on his radio with mobile command, who said back-up was on the way. Green urged caution. No sirens, no weapons unless absolutely necessary, he said. There's a child involved.

Sandy thrashed against Sullivan's restraining bulk. "You don't understand! She won't stop! You don't know what she's like when she flips out."

"I think we have an idea," Green said grimly once he'd signed off.

"But she wouldn't hurt her own kid, would she?" Sullivan stared at Sandy. "Would she?"

"Kyle's not hers. He's Jeb's son, and Mom didn't know he was retarded when she married Jeb. She doesn't even pretend to love that poor kid when Jeb's not around. She just uses him. And when something stands in her way—" He broke off with

an anguished roar. "Oh, Derek!"

The shriek of an engine interrupted them, and they turned to see headlights bouncing along the trees from the direction of the main road. An instant later the silver Grand Am burst into sight and the four of them barely had time to jump out of its path before it hurtled on past them down the lane. A quick glance behind them revealed no pursuing headlights or tell-tale red flashes on the trees.

Where the hell are those guys, Green raged to himself as he turned on Tom. "Where does this lane lead?"

Tom shrugged desperately. "I ain't been here in over twenty years. It used to end in a boat launch down at the lake."

Green turned to Sandy. "Does she have a gun?"

Sandy sagged back against the car. "She asked me to leave her the shotgun. Because of bears."

Green and Sullivan exchanged rapid glances and Green saw the same "we're fucked" expression on his friend's face. With still no sign of the OPP, there was no need for words. They couldn't take two civilians on a high-speed chase, but they couldn't let either of them loose to their own devices either. Faced with a pair of impossible alternatives, there was nothing for it but to choose the less impossible. Green jabbed his finger at Tom.

"You ride up front with me. Sandy, get in back with Brian and the least sign of trouble, he handcuffs you to the door. And both of you, do exactly what we tell you!"

They piled into the car, which Green gunned ahead before he'd even closed his door. Rocks and potholes thudded the bottom of the car and branches raked its sides as they rocketed down the lane. The smaller, nimbler Grand Am was a pinpoint of red that vanished around curves and over hills in the distance.

"What the fuck is she doing!" Tom cried, hanging on to the dash. "She can't possibly escape!"

"Doesn't matter," Sandy snapped. "It's worth the risk. She knows Kyle can't swim, but she's a strong swimmer. I know her! She figures she has an outside chance, and if not..."

Fighting the wheel to keep the car in control, Green didn't dare take his eyes off the road. "If not, what?"

"She'll kill herself before she faces the humiliation!"

Green glanced at Tom. "And there's a boat launch up ahead?"

Tom nodded grimly. Green had a split second to make a decision. Either to stop the chase so they didn't drive her into the water, or to speed up so they could catch her before she did. Or at least before Kyle sank beneath the surface. Green held his breath, trying to think.

"Go faster, Mike," said Sullivan in his soft, calm voice. Gratitude flooded through Green at his intuitive good sense.

Green tromped on the gas pedal, ripping up grass and stones beneath the wheels as the cruiser surged ahead. The red lights flicked out of sight behind a curve just ahead. Seconds later, Green skidded around the curve, and suddenly a huge drop yawned before them as the road plunged down the hill to the glistening black expanse of the lake. In the nanosecond before he reacted, Green saw a massive splash as the Grand Am hit the water. Green slammed on the cruiser's brakes, hurtling it sideways down the hill. The big vehicle rocked and bucked as he fought to straighten it, but he was powerless. All around him, glass exploded and metal shrieked.

"It's going to roll!" someone shouted. Green hung on as they continued their downward descent, clipping rocks and trees but miraculously staying upright. The car finally shuddered to a stop against a tree at the bottom of the hill. Ahead in the oblique beam of the cruiser's headlights, they could see the roof of the Grand Am slipping out of sight.

Green flung himself against his door, but it wouldn't budge.

Tom was first out of the car, dragging himself headfirst through his broken window. Without a second thought, Green followed him, barely feeling the shards of glass that tore at his hands. He dashed to get the emergency equipment out of the trunk. Sullivan was already out of the car and heading to the water's edge when Tom dove headlong into the chilly water. Green pried open the trunk, grabbed a coil of rope and yelled to Sullivan.

"I'll make a noose and stay on shore to help you pull them out."

Barely pausing to nod, Sullivan kicked off his shoes, took two giant steps and plunged into the lake. Seconds ticked by as Green stared at the roiling surface. Tom and Sullivan surfaced about thirty feet from shore, gasping and shaking their heads. Sandy hobbled down from the car, nursing his knee. He watched them dive again, then peeled off his boots.

"You stay here," Green snapped.

"Make me!" Sandy shouted, wading out towards the driver's side of the sunken car. Soon Green was alone on shore, scanning the surface. Water splashed and churned, then Tom popped up again, sputtering and flaying about. "Help me! Take him!"

Green cursed his inner city inadequacy. He'd never taken swimming lessons and could count on one hand the number of times he'd been in a lake beyond his waist. Fuck it, the dog paddle will have to do, he thought as he plunged out into the water and tossed the rope to Tom, who was hauling something large and unwieldy. Tom wrestled the loop around Kyle's torso and together they dragged the unconscious boy to shore. Green checked his airways, then rolled him rapidly onto his stomach and pressed down on his back, forcing the water out of his lungs.

"I'll look for blankets," gasped Tom as he scrambled dripping and shivering up to the car.

Once Green was satisfied Kyle's lungs were clear, he rolled him onto his back and began CPR. Mechanically, methodically, he counted, dredging his memory for skills he'd never had to use beyond the classroom.

Sandy and Sullivan surfaced yet again, splashing and gasping. Sandy screamed to Tom for the rope.

"Forget it," Tom shouted from the car. "She's been down too long."

"Throw the fucking rope!" Sandy yelled.

Tom came back with a blanket and bent to cover Kyle before retrieving the rope and reluctantly helping the two others tow Edna's inert weight to shore. Once they'd tugged her half out of the water and splayed her body on the muddy ground, Sullivan sprinted up to the cruiser to radio for help. Green heard him asking for two ambulances and as many paramedics as they could muster.

After what seemed an eternity, he felt Kyle's chest heave beneath his hands as the boy spasmed in a cough. Green stopped CPR and rolled him on his side, watching through a film of grateful tears as Kyle coughed and retched weakly back to life.

Sandy was bent over his mother, frantically trying to do CPR. Green gestured to Tom. "Take care of Kyle for me while I help Sandy."

"Forget it!" Tom snapped as he cradled Kyle against him gingerly. "Let the bitch die!"

Sandy whirled on him, tears mingling with the water dripping down his face. "I'm not going to let her fucking die! She's going to pay!"

*　*　*

It was four in the morning before all the crises had been contained, the charges sorted out, and the proper paperwork completed. Green had refrained from demanding to know why the OPP had taken so long to arrive, and they in kind had not mentioned his multiple violations of procedure that had placed himself, a fellow officer and four civilians in serious jeopardy. The police cruiser was still lodged against the tree at the bottom of the hill, an expense and complication that would thrill Barbara Devine when she assumed her post Monday morning.

Still, from the brass's perspective, even though the methods weren't pretty, the end result would sound good on the morning news. No one had died, and the bad people had been arrested. Edna and Kyle McMartin had been taken to Belleville General Hospital, where Edna had regained consciousness and was already screaming police incompetence, suggesting that prolonged oxygen deprivation had not altered her brain one bit. The cold water was the saving grace, the doctors intoned, but Green suspected it was her stubborn refusal to admit defeat. She would need every ounce of that in the months ahead, if he had any say in the matter.

After a thorough check-up, a hot meal and a good night's sleep, Kyle was set to be discharged from hospital in the morning into the care of his grateful but very shaken father. Sandy had been checked over at the medical centre in Madoc and given a clean bill of health, and after some consideration, Green and Sullivan had declined to press charges. Under the circumstances, Sandy had paid dearly enough.

"I didn't even know that she knew I was gay," he said as he and the two detectives waited at the Madoc OPP station for Jeb

McMartin to arrive. Sandy paced the reception area, exhausted but too wound up to sit. "She must have found our notes."

"Or Derek's father told her," Green replied. "He wanted you two stopped as well."

"Derek was my first lover. Knowing Mom, she'd think it was all his fault. Her baby, corrupted by a depraved pervert." He gave a bitter laugh. "Poor mother. Two flawed failures for sons, like some kind of divine punishment. Over the years, she's kept pushing women on me. What did she think? That I could just switch it off if a good enough woman came along?"

"Probably."

"And Lawrence!" Sandy exclaimed, his emotions flooding out. "Poor innocent Lawrence comes home looking for a little home comfort—after all those years in the asylum for a crime she committed!—and what does he get? His worst nightmare! The witch from hell! You know, she actually showed the church that afternoon, because I was off duck hunting when the client came along. That's probably when she spotted him." He clenched his fists, paced faster. "I knew she was a hard woman, but I never believed her heartlessness ran so deep. I hope you can nail her!"

Green assured him they'd do their best, but privately, once Sandy had left, Sullivan shook his head doubtfully. The two of them slumped wearily over cups of coffee.

"We don't have much to nail her on," Sullivan said. "Even on the attempted murder of Kyle, it's going to be hard to get past reasonable doubt. She can just say some strange car chased her into the lake. You forgot to turn the goddamn siren on, you know. As for either of the Pettigrew murders, all we have are the confused reports of a couple of boys and one bloody fingerprint that we can't really link to Derek's death.

Unless forensics gets really lucky with the axe and we can get some usable blood from it to match to the blood on the fingerprint."

Axe! Green sat up as a memory leaped into his mind. All pain evaporated. Pulling out his cell phone, he dialled home. The phone rang and rang before Sharon's groggy voice came through. Belatedly he glanced at his watch. Four a.m.

"Sorry, honey," he said. He'd already given her a full report earlier in the night, and he suspected she might have only just managed to fall asleep. "Nothing's wrong," he added hastily. "I'm fine, but I have a question to ask Hannah."

To her credit, Sharon didn't protest or demand answers, but simply went to wake his daughter up. There was a long delay, during which Sullivan watched him curiously, before the phone picked up again.

"What?" came his daughter's surly voice.

"Hi, honey, I thought you might like to know Kyle is safe."

"I heard. Lucky for you."

He felt a flare of anger. No "how are you, Dad? I heard you were in an accident." How long was she going to make him pay? He glanced at Sullivan, whose children had been all over him when he called, clamouring to know about the chase. But now Sullivan was eyeing him, and his mystified look brought Green back to the issue at hand.

"I have a question about what Kyle told you in the barn."

"I already told you everything."

"But you said it was all jumbled up and hard to connect. Did he say anything about the bad person who was chasing the man who died? Did that person have anything in their hand?"

"What the hell?"

"Think, honey."

"No. He was talking about bells. He said something was too dangerous and he said bad boy and get in trouble and no wood, and fall—"

"No what?" Green scrambled to make the connections to what the boy might have seen.

"No wood. He said that several times."

Bingo, Green thought, his spirits soaring. In the mind of a child, what use was an axe with no wood? "Thanks a million, honey! I love you! Go back to bed."

He waited until seven o'clock before calling Cunningham, for he wanted the man wide awake. "I've got a challenge you're going to love, Cunny. I want you to make up a life size dummy of Lawrence Pettigrew—same height, same weight distribution—and I want you to take it to the church tower. There's a rusty old axe in the sanctuary I want you to test for prints. Then I want you to take this dummy up to the top and experiment with pushing it over the edge. Backward, forward, sit it on top, make it jump."

Cunningham was laughing. "You want a ring-side seat for this?"

"Absolutely. I want to see what makes it land on its stomach with its head towards the tower. I'm betting it's when the dummy's back is to the wall and someone else pushes its chest back and flips it over the wall."

When he'd hung up, Green turned to Sullivan triumphantly. "That's how we're going to nail her, Brian!"

"She's not strong enough to push him over."

"She didn't have to. She had the axe, and when she came at him, he backed up so far over the wall that he flipped over. Some kid in the square heard him screaming 'get away, get away'. He was terrified. To him, remembering the last time he'd seen her with an axe, she must have seemed like the devil incarnate."

Green could tell from Sullivan's expression that he didn't share Green's optimism, but it didn't matter. The evidence might be circumstantial, just one small piece in the theory they would lay in front of the jury, but it gave him something to work on. Some hope of exacting a small measure of justice for all the victims in this case.

Of all those victims, Green was most worried about Tom, whom they had to leave in the custody of the OPP after his clearance by the Medical Centre. Peters would be accompanying him back to Ottawa to face multiple charges, once proper transportation could be arranged. As the final act of his command, Jules seemed hellbent on making sure someone shouldered the blame for the crisis, and right now his sights were set on Tom. Whose shoulders were pretty frail already.

While Sullivan arranged the loan of an OPP vehicle to get himself and Green back to Ottawa, Green wandered back to the lock-up to give Tom a final word of encouragement. He had to wait five minutes in the interview room before the door opened and Tom shuffled in, his hands cuffed and a grey blanket draped around his shoulders. His eyes were bruised and puffy as if he'd been physically battered, and he barely acknowledged Green as he sank into a chair.

Green instructed the OPP officer to remove the cuffs and wait outside. Once they were alone, Green pulled out a pack of cigarettes from his pocket and laid one on the table.

"Thought you could use one of these."

Tom shrugged. "No smoking allowed."

"Take it."

Tom massaged his wrist, then picked up the cigarette and stuck it in his mouth. It trembled as Green extended a light.

"Thanks."

Green watched the ravaged man, who barely had the

energy for his nicotine fix. Green didn't know what to say or even why he had come. Just that someone had to come.

"I'm going to do everything I can, Tom."

Tom squinted through smoke. "To nail her?"

"That too. But I meant to help you."

Tom stared at the table a long time, not smoking, not moving. "How was I supposed to know?" he said finally. "I came home, found Lawrence in the shed holding Derek in his arms. Blood all over him, this great fucking axe at his side. I tried to get him away, but he kept saying he had to save Derek from the devil." He tried to raise his cigarette to his lips, but it dropped from his fingers. Green rescued it and held it while Tom fought a silent war with his pain. "I damn near killed him on the spot, but Mom and Dad came along. He wouldn't stop screaming. We locked him up, and he screamed the whole night. Mom and Dad fucking tied him up to drive him to Brockville, left Benji and me to clean up the mess."

Tom began to tremble all over, his eyes glassy with tears. He blew out a shaky breath and sucked in another. "Oo-h boy. Ain't never thought about this without a few stiff ones along for the ride. Benji and me were supposed to burn Derek up with the place, but we couldn't stand the idea. I mean, him curling up like a steak on a barbeque. We laid him out nice in the ground underneath before we burned the shed down."

Green struggled to find something rational to say. "Why didn't someone in the family call the police?"

"Dad said that wouldn't bring Derek back, only blow the whole thing up in the papers and all. Said Lawrence was sick and belonged in a hospital. I guess I should've fought the old man on that one, but he kept saying it must've been some kinda God's will. Derek's punishment. I never knew what the hell that meant, till now."

Green felt the horror like a physical blow to the stomach, and he fought to draw breath. "Jesus," was all he managed.

"Yeah. Jesus. He figured we'd get rid of it all. All the sins, all the ugly little secrets." Tom took the forgotten cigarette from Green's fingers and sucked the smoke deep into his lungs. "Benji never did get away from the nightmares. Till he took the only way out he could think of. And Lawrence... Fuck, look what we did to that poor kid. He could've had some kind of life, with the drugs there are now and us sticking by him."

Green regained his professional footing with an effort. "He didn't have a bad life in St. Lawrence, Tom. He did have a family of sorts."

Tom didn't seem to hear. He twirled the cigarette in his hand. "I was so mean to him when he was a kid. He was a nice little kid, kinda cute, you know? But he should've been protected, like Kyle. But you can't go back, eh? Even the old cottage ain't the same no more." He shrugged as if disappointment was second nature to him. "Me and Robbie figured we'd bury him out in the village in that little graveyard by the church. Can't think of much else I can do to make it up to him."

It was a nice idea, Green told him, to give him something to hold on to in the days ahead. After the OPP officer led Tom back to his cell, Green sat alone in the interview room for almost five minutes, gathering the courage to get up.

On the long drive back into the city, the two detectives picked over the case in a desultory fashion, trying to gain their own sense of equilibrium with the events of the past few days. But their hearts weren't in it, their bodies ached and their minds were too foggy for creative thought. Finally Green tilted his seat back and shut his eyes, profoundly weary. Even with two strong painkillers, every muscle in his body ached, and his bandaged hands throbbed.

"Jesus, what a night," he murmured. "I'm getting too soft for this kind of thing."

Sullivan glanced at him. "You violated just about every rule in the book, you know. Luckily, they'll never know the half of them."

Green opened his eyes. Smiled. There was a ring of the old warmth in Sullivan's tone, from the days when they were partners. "And luckily, you were right there to fix them, eh?"

Sullivan nodded. Flicked his signal casually and pulled out to pass a tractor. "I might have to stay in CID just to keep you from getting killed."

Green didn't reply. Didn't dare jinx it. He let the painkillers wash over him, and the next thing he knew, Sullivan had pulled into the driveway of his Highland Park home. Sharon folded him into her arms, led him straight upstairs and settled him in bed with a hot cup of tea.

"I see the house is still standing," he murmured as he sank into the pillows.

"Yes, but Bob's working on it." She chuckled as she closed the blinds against the midday sun. "Do you want to sleep?"

He reached his bandaged hand to hers. "Stay with me while I have the tea."

She snuggled in beside him and laid her head on his shoulder. "What an incredible story. Look at how many lives that woman ruined."

"Not just her. All the parents." Anger knotted his stomach. "There's no way to get back all those lost years or stolen lives. But at least we got her, and maybe that will help the survivors get their lives back on track."

"I keep thinking about Tom," she said. "In a crunch, he came through and saved Kyle's life. Maybe the first time he's ever done something right."

He nodded. "Probably surprised himself."

She traced her fingers down his arm. "I don't suppose there's any way you can persuade Jules not to press charges on all those violations he racked up."

"Officer's discretion?" He gave a wan smile. "I'll be working on it. But even with Jules or Devine's blessing, I won't have the power to make everything disappear. I can probably avoid a kidnapping charge, because it seems clear he didn't know Kyle was in the truck. Plus he took good care of him once he found him. We may even be able to drop the vehicular theft. I don't imagine Edna McMartin will be making much noise."

"And her husband is probably grateful Tom saved his son's life."

Green sighed. "But the media and Jacques Boisvert would crucify me if I tried to drop the assault on Isabelle. I mean, bashing nice ladies on the head is a no-no, no matter how you spin it. Besides, Tom has to learn that even though you don't get dealt a fair hand in life, you can always try to tip the balance in your favour by doing what's right."

"Maybe he's made his first small step in that direction." She snuggled closer and wrapped her arms around his waist. "I wonder if he'll move back up here when he gets out. I'd kind of like at least one happy ending to come out of this."

"Happy ending?"

"For him and Robbie. Maybe they'll buy back the farm from that obnoxious Boisvert guy and start over again. You never know."

Green remembered the care with which Tom kept Kyle warm on the beach, the crushing regret he'd finally faced up to at the Madoc jail. For the first time, Green felt a little hope. Well, you never know.

He set down his tea and slipped his bandaged arms around

her. Her skin felt soft against his and the warmth of her body sent a yearning through him that eclipsed pain and fatigue. He tilted her chin and kissed her.

"Where's Tony?" he whispered.

"Down the street at Jesse's. I asked if they could play."

"Clever woman." He kissed her again, revelling in her delicious taste and in the tingling softness of her tongue. Just as he was groping beneath the sheets for flesh, the door slammed and footsteps mounted the stairs. Hannah's head appeared in the doorway.

"Oh. You're back." Deadpan Hannah.

He disentangled himself and arranged a hasty smile on his face. "Hi, honey. Thanks for your help this morning. It might make the difference to our convicting her."

"Oh, gee," she said. "And that'll make up for twenty years of heartbreak in a flash."

"Nothing will. But—" He trailed off, for her head had disappeared and the only sound he heard was the soft closing of her door. He eyed the empty doorway with a pang of sadness. "Tough cookie, that one. She's making me pay."

"Well, you know, Green," Sharon replied. "Speaking of happy endings, teenage daughters don't come cheap."

Barbara Fradkin's work as a psychologist provides ample inspiration for her tales of murder. She has an affinity for the dark side, and her short stories haunt several anthologies and magazines, including Storyteller and the New Canadian Noir and Ladies' Killing Circle anthologies.

Fifth Son is the fourth in the Inspector Green series. The first, *Do or Die*, was published by RendezVous Press in 2000. The second, *Once Upon a Time* (2002), was shortlisted for an Arthur Ellis Award for Best Novel. A third, *Mist Walker*, followed in 2003.

Barbara lives in Ottawa and is an active participant in Canada' crime writing community. She is currently the president of Crime Writers of Canada.

More information on Barbara's activities can be found at www.barbarafradkin.com